Trap Bastard

Born to Die. Bred to Kill

Penned by:
Askari
AKA
The King of Philly Street-Lit

Lock Down Publications
Presents
Trap Bastard
A Novel by: *Askari*

Lock Down Publications
P.O. Box 944
Stockbridge, Ga 30281
www.lockdownpublications.com

Copyright 2021 by Askari
Trap Bastard

First Edition March 2021
Printed in the United States of America

Lock Down Publications
Like our page on Facebook: Lock Down Publications @
www.facebook.com/lockdownpublications.ldp
Cover design and layout by: **Dynasty Cover Me**
Book interior design by: **Shawn Walker**
Edited by: **Shawn Walker**

Stay Connected with Us!

Text LOCKDOWN to 22828 to stay up-to-date with new releases, sneak peaks, contests and more…

Thank you!

Submission Guideline.

Submit the first three chapters of your completed manuscript to ldpsubmissions@gmail.com, subject line: Your book's title. The manuscript must be in a .doc file and sent as an attachment. Document should be in Times New Roman, double spaced and in size 12 font. Also, provide your synopsis and full contact information. If sending multiple submissions, they must each be in a separate email.

Have a story but no way to send it electronically? You can still submit to LDP/Ca$h Presents. Send in the first three chapters, written or typed, of your completed manuscript to:

LDP: Submissions Dept
P.O. Box 944
Stockbridge, Ga 30281

DO NOT send original manuscript. Must be a duplicate.

Provide your synopsis and a cover letter containing your full contact information.

Thanks for considering LDP and Ca$h Presents.

DEDICATION

This book is dedicated to the *TRAP*. I know you like the back of my hand, so why not write about you? Many authors have tried, but the stories they write rarely do you any justice. That's because MOST authors really don't know you. They don't know how deep and dark you can get, or how vicious and savage you become whenever turned on by a real nigga. They don't know about the graveyard shift, or hugging the block for a week straight, surviving off of rice and gravy. They don't know about the pistol on the tire, the work stashed in the lot, and them early morning testers to get the fiend on they job. Nah, these half-assed niggas wit' they watered down stories don't know you. At least not as intimate as me and mine do. My only regret is that we know ya ass all too well.

ACKNOWLEDGMENTS

First and foremost, shout outs to my two sons, Spanky and Qua; my two beautiful daughters, Keyonti and Diamond; my two precious granddaughters, Angelisa and Aria; their wonderful mother, Jazmin; my nephews, Kanyè and Powerful; and my niece Sahala. I love every one of y'all, and I miss y'all like crazy. Insha Allah, I'll be home soon.

Shout outs to my bros on lock: TALI DA DON (I love and miss you, Brozay. Hold ya head and remain firm, we up next. Big Bizness!!!); BABY JAMES (In broaaaaaaad muthafuckin' daylight!); KENT "HARLEM" OWENS (Good looking for the love and support, my nigga. Hold ya head.); shout outs to every Esu and all the RealRights—east to the west!!! Mad love to all the bros on lock, all around the country, who salute and show love when they hit me. I salute back, real shit. Y'all brothas hold y'all heads. Keep rumbling, and DON'T STOP! #FreeAGee

Shout out to the best editor in the world, *my editor*, the Queen, Shawn Walker. You are absolutely amazing! There's no way to thank you enough for all of your assistance, words of wisdom and insight. But most of all for helping me change my life. You believed in me since day one, and I'm forever grateful. I salute you, Queen. Peace.

And shout outs to the strongest team in Street Lit: *THE ALMIGHTY LOCK DOWN PUBLICATIONS*. Aye, yo, CA$H, you got this shit jumpin' like a mah'fucka! When you first touched down in 2018, that shit was like LeBron coming off the bench. We were already up by 30, then the big dawg came home and ran the score up 50. Every magazine and catalog coming through the jails, all you see in them mah'fukas is LDP; not to mention the paperbacks. These other street lit crews couldn't touch us if they wanted to. This shit is a marathon, they started off fast and now they wheezing in the back.

And me being me, a fair nigga wit' firm principles, I said to myself: *"Askari, gawn and fall back for a year and give these other street lit crews a chance to catch up."* But then *TJ EDWARDS* came through...bombed 'em! *TRANAY ADAMS* came through...bombed 'em! *GHOST* came through...bombed 'em! *MARCELLUS ALLEN* came through...bombed 'em! *JAMAICA* came through...bombed 'em! *ARYANNA* came through...bombed 'em! *DESTINY SKAI* came through...bombed 'em! *MEESHA TURNER* came through...bombed 'em! *JELISSA, MIMI, NICOLE GOODSBY, RASHIA WILSON, AND EVERY HITTER FROM LDP THAT'S HOLDING DOWN THIS ALMIGHTY EMPIRE*...came through and bombed 'em!

Aye, yo, *CAAAAA$$$$$$HHHHHHH,* this shit ain't even fair no more!!!! *IT'S A BLOWOUT*!!!! *HOWEVER THEY WANT IT, THEY CAN GET IT*!!!! *LDP, WE OFFICIAL OVER HERE*!!!! *THIS IS URBAN AND STREET LIT AT ITS BEST*!!!!

And now I'm back, baby. *THE KING OF PHILLY STREET LIT* is back! *THE PRINCE OF LDP* is back! I'm on my Anthony Davis shit, ready to cut they mah'fuckin' lights out. I'm done playing games wit' these weak-ass suckas and they wack-ass books. So, now I gotta separate myself from the pack and leave *NO DOUBTS* about who's the *BEST MALE AUTHOR* of this *NEW GENERA-TION.* And just for the record...*REAL BOSSES* don't need validation from others about who they are and what they represent. *REAL BOSSES VALIDATE THEMSELVES*!!!!

And shout out to my FIRST and ONLY wife, who I don't know and never met. I'm looking for you, Ma, where you at? Come get'cha King. I've got sum'n for you...

#BloodOfABossSeries
#ShadowsOfTheGame
#TrapBastardSeries

PROLOGUE
July 14th, 1996

The project's night scene was dark and grim, scarcely illuminated by the Philadelphia skyline that towered over from a few blocks down. On the east side of 11th Street, between Poplar and Cambridge, where a young murder suspect had just fled, was the recently condemned, high-rise building that accounted for one half of the Cambridge Homes. The twelve-story, mortar brick structure was filthy and unlivable—graffiti covered its walls and blue tarps with dingy gray plastic covered its windows. The hollowed-out building was desolate and quiet, nothing close to the three-story buildings that were lined along the opposite side of the street.

There, the shot-out streetlights, the blaring loud music, and the shadowy figures that moved about from one building to the next, was enough to make a young Steven Lorenzo think twice. Yet and still, he knew the importance of catching his man. He needed to prove to his fellow officers back at the precinct that he, the new kid on the block, was fit for the task of working the projects.

Lorenzo approached the building cautiously. His Glock .9mm was clutched in his right hand, while his flashlight was gripped in his left. Arms overlapped with his flashlight leading the way, he pushed open the rusty front door with the tip of his shoe.

"Philadelphia Police Department!" his booming voice echoed throughout the abandoned lobby. "I know you done ran up in this mah'fucka, 'cause I seen you!" The dialect of his voice changed, sounding more like a gangsta's than it did a police officer's. "Real shit, dawg, this ya last mah'fuckin' warning. If you make me come up in this mah'fucka looking for you, the same place I find you gon' be the same place I leave you. I done told you project niggas, but clearly y'all ain't understanding my mah'fuckin' message. It's a new day and time, and I ain't playing wit'chu niggas. Ain't *shit* going down 'round this mah'fucka unless *I* say so!"

Still standing at the doorway, he listened for a reply. But the only sounds he heard were the eerie squeals of large vermin being chased down and devoured by the larger alley cats who now occupied the building.

"The irony," Lorenzo stated with a chuckle, amused by the double entendre. Because just like the alley cats who were feasting on the vermin, he, too, was on a mission to hunt down and devour every hustler in the projects, from the pack-boys to the brick-layers.

Lorenzo stepped one foot inside the building, then he stepped back out. Looking over his shoulder, he saw the red and blue lights *of* an unmarked police car. The gray sedan was cruising down the street in the wrong direction.

"Well, goddamn, it's about time," he mumbled under his breath, as the unmarked unit rolled to a stop. The driver's side door swung open, and Detective Adam Smith, a ten-year veteran on the force, climbed out slow. He was dressed in a dark pair of slacks, with a bulletproof vest strapped over his powder-blue dress shirt. His silver Detective badge glimmered in the dark, his nickel-plated .357 did the same.

""So, how many ran inside?" asked Detective Smith. "Was it both suspects, or just one?"

"It was only one. The other bastard got away," Lorenzo answered, then he stepped aside so Detective Smith could take charge and lead the way.

"These little bastards. They usually run to either one or two places—the pussy they came out of, or the pussy they're cumming in. But running inside of an abandoned building? Where nobody can hear him screaming? *Really?*" The white cop chuckled, then he pulled out his .357 Magnum. "Well, damnit, I'd have to say he's the dumbest sonofabitch in the whole wide frickin' world."

Instead of replying, Lorenzo just nodded his head and smiled. Because after all, Detective Smith was the dirty cop who turned him bad in the first place.

TWO DAYS EARLIER...

Askari

CHAPTER ONE
June 12th, 1996

It was the summer of '96, and after two years of being locked down in Juvie, I was happier than a mah'fucka to finally be free. The second I stepped outside, the air was more crisp and fresher than I remembered. The distinct aroma of newly cut grass invaded my nostrils, reminding me of the ten pounds of smoke that my sister, Daphney, had set aside for me.

Speaking of Daphney, she was standing outside in the parking lot waiting for me. It was her, my boo-boo, Erica, and my right-hand-man, Uzi. They were all standing in front of Uzi's new Pathfinder, smiling at me and waving.

Daphney was my half-sister on my pops' side. Not to be judging my own folks, but sis was one of them chocolatah, Foxy Brown, Ill Na Na type of bitches. She had a dark-brown complexion with silky black hair, and had the prettiest light-brown eyes. Just like me, she bore a striking resemblance to my pops. The only difference in our features was that Daphney's were softer and more feminine than mines. Other than that, we could have easily passed for twins, and that's exactly what we called one another: *Twin.*

At the age of nineteen, Daphney was older than me by three years, but those three years might as well been ten. Her lust for the gravy was way stronger than mines, which was something she learned from being around my pops 24/7. Their relationship was tighter than the bond that he and I shared, even though I was the one who inherited his name: *Alvin Rines, Jr.* And I ain't saying I was beefing with my pops or no shit like that. It was just that Daphney's mom was the woman he married, and my moms was the down-ass bitch that he groomed for the game.

So, being as though he and Daphney lived under the same roof, she was the one he catered to and spent the majority of his time with. Me, on the other hand, I was the one he jokingly referred to as his *Trap Bastard.* But even then, he still made it known that he was there for me.

I remember when I was just a shorty, around eight or nine, Pops would come through and bring me new clothes and toys. At other times he would drop off large stacks of money and take me shopping with him at the Gucci store in Atlantic City. Sometimes he'd even take me to see the Eagles or the Sixers playing. But majority of the time that nigga was running the streets, chasing paper. My pops was, still is, and will forever be a bossed-up nigga, even though six years earlier he was given a life sentence for Racketeering and Murder. He and his crew, the *YBM*, aka the *Young Black Mafia*, were legends on the streets of Philly. The money they made and the work they put in, making niggas get down or lay down, came second to none. My sole mission upon my release was to further that legacy.

"Aye, yo, *Sheffield?*" I barked up at the corrections officer who was working the tower, wondering why the barbed wire fence that stood between me and my destiny wasn't already open. "Pussy, I know you see me standing here. Why the *fuck* you ain't popped open this mah'fuckin' fence?"

"Excuse me?" Officer Sheffield shot back, scowling at me with his arms folded across his chest. Sheffield was one of them red-necked, peckerwood mah'fuckas. He was always pressing a nigga, praying they would fuck him up so he could get some time off on paid leave. There was more than one occasion where he tempted me to take him up on his offer, but catching another Two-to-Four on a jailhouse case wasn't happening. I had a whole city waiting on a nigga to come home and takeover. So, fuck Sheffield, my mind was on the money.

"Aye, yo, Sheffield, fa'real, though. You know it's my release date. If it wasn't, I would'a never made it this close to the front gate. Now, stop playing and let me up out this mah'fucka. I served my time."

Moving slower than molasses dripping off a turtle's ass, this nigga stepped back inside the tower. He reappeared a few minutes later, looking at me and shaking his head. Sucking his teeth like a bitch, he said, "You'll be back, Rines. Two months, tops. And I'll be right here waiting for ya."

"Yeah, whatever, nigga. Smoke a dick and choke."

I was walking up out that bitch, and there was nothing that Sheffield could do to stop me. I started to grind his ass to dust, but the cranking sound of the fence being opened had me hyped up something vicious.

Zzzzzzzzzzzzzzzz. Click!

It was game time.

I slung my nap sack full of letters and pictures over my shoulder, then I stepped out the belly of the beast. The weather was a warm 88° and the sun was beaming down, causing my jailhouse glow to shine even brighter. I was dipped in a fresh white Polo Tee, blue and yellow Polo trunks, and a crispy pair of white-on-white Nike Air Forces. Each item was dropped off by Daphney and Erica the day before when they came to visit me. According to them, that was the new style for the '96 summer.

Erica was looking sexier than a mah'fucka standing there. Her beautiful brown face, mango-sized titties and juicy phat ass was the shit I'd been dreaming about since the day I got booked. I didn't even make it two steps before she ran over and bum-rushed me.

"Baby! Baby! Baby! Oh, my God! I can't believe they finally let you out of there! That shit felt like forever!" she stated with excitement, kissing my neck when she said it. She wrapped her arms around me and held me tight. Her soft, curvy frame melted against me, and my dick stiffened.

"Damn, boo, it's like that?" Erica looked up at me with lust-filled eyes, smiling because she felt my wood pressed against her stomach. She reached down and gripped it with both hands. "Them two years did ya body good, huh? This big ol' thing. A bitch know just what to do wit' it, too."

She damn sure wasn't lying about me getting my grown man on. Not only did my dick get bigger, I packed on about twenty-five pounds of nothing but muscle. I was tall and lanky when I first went in. But after two years of push-ups, pull-ups and dips, I was huskier than a mah'fucka—6 feet 3 inches tall, and weighing in at a dangerous 240 pounds of rock-solid gangsta.

The streets were in trouble.

"Oh, yeah?" I replied to Erica's comment, looking at her accusingly. I had just popped her cherry a few days before I went to the bing. So, hearing shorty talk so freely about my dick and what she could do with it, had my mind on some other shit. I couldn't help but wonder if she was fucking other niggas while I was gone. I started to ask, but I knew better than to ask questions that could lead to answers I wasn't ready to hear, so I left it alone. Besides, when it came to holding me down where it counted the most, baby girl did her thing. In addition to keeping money on my books and sending me pictures every week, she accepted every collect call and came for visitation at least once a month. But the shit that touched me the most, was how she helped my moms out with my three little brothers, Jahlil, Jabril, and Jacobi. So, assuming she *did* give the pussy away, I gave her a pass so long as she cut that shit short. And if she didn't, then the bitch could get her brain busted, too. Anybody could get it, and I meant that shit.

"Damn, Erica, let the nigga breathe," Uzi said with a chuckle, as he strolled over towards us. I was glad that he said it when he did, because Erica let go and I finally caught my breath. I was so backed up and sexually depraved, that I damn near busted in my draws from the feeling of her tender body pressed against me. Them two years had me horny as shit.

"Uzi, you'sa fucking hater." Erica gave him the finger, then she wrapped her arms back around my waist. "Always got some hating shit flying out'cha mouth. Ol' fake-ass, LL Cool J looking ass nigga."

"Yeah, whatever," Uzi said, then he leaned forward and gave me some dap. "Welcome home, my nigga. I hope you got'cha mind right this time. 'Cause nowadays niggas is on some real-live get money shit. All that stick-up shit is for the birds now. Nah mean?"

The nerve of this nigga, I thought to myself, as I cracked a smile. If there was one thing I learned from the many letters that I received from my pops, it was to never express my true feelings. He said that by disguising my true feelings, any and all who opposed me would be kept off balance, never having the advantage of predicting my next moves based off my perceived emotions. This was something that I'd taken to heart, knowing the streets would surely come for my top when they started seeing all the moves that I planned on making.

I hated to admit it, but that included Uzi, as well; my right-hand-mans or not. Because even though we came up from the mud together, who's to say the day would never come when either he or myself would be responsible for sticking the other in a pine box covered in rocks? It was a fucked-up way to be thinking about my man, but Pops' letters had me on some other shit—some straight ride or die, Nino Brown and G-Money, gotta *smoke a nigga on the roof* type of shit. I was playing for keeps, and I trusted no one.

"*The game's dangerous, and nobody's safe,*" I could hear Pops' voice in the back of my mind. His words were so clear that goosebumps covered my arms. "*The closest ones to you are usually the ones who stab you in the back, just look at Julius Caesar.*"

Still looking at Uzi, I thought of all the stories that I'd heard about him while I was locked down—how he stepped his game up on the streets and how he and his brother, Zion, were serving niggas mad weight in Uptown Philly. But to actually see my nigga, live and in living color, dipped down in Moschino and twirling around his fingers the keys to a cocaine-white Nissan Pathfinder, I was like, *Damn, this nigga really out here doing his thing.* It didn't surprise me, because Uzi was a hustling-ass nigga always on the hunt for his next dollar.

Uzi and me came off the steps together in '94, just snot-nosed young buls juggling our first 8-ball. Unfortunately, the old heads around the way weren't having it; this old head nigga named Mook, in particular. According to Mook, who back in the day was one of my pops' street lieutenants, Uzi and me were too young to be out there hustling. So, naturally, our next best form of a steady payment was robbing niggas. We ran down on damn near everything moving, and made a little name for ourselves in the process. Shit was going good for a minute, but then I got knocked.

I remember that shit like it was yesterday. It was somewhere around one in the morning, and I had just finished fucking my young jawn, Kia, from Southwest Philly. Me and Kia were lying in bed, when Uzi hit me on my Motorola pager. I knew from the 911 code that he left after his number, he needed me to go on a jammy mission with him.

That was the thug rule between us: any time we went on a *jammy* mission, we had to ride out together, so that way we could always be there to watch one another's back. I couldn't explain why, but that particular night I wasn't feeling it.

Kia was bitching about me fucking her and leaving, but aside from me having to bolt, my stomach had a vicious case of the bubble guts. The last thing I felt like doing was stealing a car and driving all the way back to North Philly, but I did it anyway. I was obligated to be there for my nigga.

I met Uzi on the corner of 10th and Poplar, right outside of Kim's Deli. It was late as a mah'fucka, so the hood was basically a ghost town. The only mah'fuckas who were still outside were the late-night hypes and the niggas in the 'jects that fucked with us. The Papi stores in the Bad Landz were already closed, so the only thing left for us to rob were them niggas across town. The way we saw it, them niggas were strait laced pussy. Even if they knew Uzi and me were the ones who robbed them, we knew they would never come across Broad Street looking for us. The projects we came from, the almighty Richard Allen, was a no-fly zone, and them bitch-niggas knew it. They knew better than to come around fucking with us real niggas.

We drove around their neighborhood for close to an hour looking for a vic, and eventually ran into this nigga on 16th and Brown. He was dressed in a black, one-piece Dickies suit, a scuffed pair of Timbs, and had a gold chain with a Jesus piece hanging out the top of his zipper. We assumed the nigga was out there hustling, but we couldn't have been more wrong.

I hopped out of the car and caught the nigga with a vicious right hook, and Uzi shot his pockets the second he hit the ground. We jacked him for his money and drugs, and kindly relieved him of his bullshit chain. We thought we came up on a nice lick. But, then as soon as we hopped back in the car and got ready to pull off, the cops swooped in on us out of nowhere. We would have never guessed it, but the nigga we robbed was actually an undercover narc working on a sting operation. Them mah'fuckas locked us up faster than two bunnies fucking.

Uzi got away with only six months of probation, which was basically a slap on the wrist. But me on the other hand, being who I am, *Alvin Rines, Jr.*, the so-called *"Prince of the YBM"*, that black-ass, Sambo judge hit me with a two-year sentence. At first, I was sick, because the longest bit I had ever done was a 90-day stint at the Youth Study Center. I wasn't even home a whole two months before I caught my last case, all thanks to Uzi. And now this nigga was talking about he hope I had my mind right.

This nigga must'a bumped his fuckin' head!

"Welcome home, Twin," Daphney said with a smile, as she walked over and gave me a hug.

"Thanks, Twin. It's about time, huh?"

"Nigga, hell yeah, it's about time." She playfully punched me on the arm. "And I was talking to Daddy on the way over here. He wants us to come visit him tomorrow. He said that he needs to speak to you in person."

"No doubt." I nodded my head. "He sent me the same message in his last letter."

"Look, boo, check us out," Erica said as she stood beside Daphney. "We look like Lil' Kim and Foxy, don't we?" I knew they had grown close over the two years I was down, but the way they were dressed was a little over the top. Not only did they have matching hairstyles, they were pretty much rocking the same outfit—a Chanel overalls short-set with the letters C-H-A-N-E-L printed down the straps. Beneath the overalls, they each wore a white, linen, Chanel dress shirt, and had oversized Chanel sunglasses propped up on their foreheads. The black, crocodile sandals they wore had gold Chanel C's buckled on the front, and the black Chanel handbags they sported had the same exact scheme. The only difference in their outfits was that Daphney's was hot-pink, and Erica's was soft-yellow.

I looked back and forth between them, and cracked up laughing. Uzi caught on, and laughed along with me. "Lil' Kim and Foxy?" I clowned them. "Y'all look more like Beavis and Butthead."

"Fuck outta here, boo, you hating." Erica pouted. She folded her arms across her chest, fronting like I hurt her feelings.

"Nah, I can't even hate, y'all killing em' right now. I'm just try'na figure out how y'all walking around looking like Chanel models, and I'm standing here in some goddamned swimming trunks. Fuck is up with that?"

"I done told you, boo, that's the style right now," Erica said as she stood on her tippy toes and gave me a kiss. "That's what the guys be wearing now, designer swimming trunks—Tommy trunks, Nautica trunks, Polo trunks, and white Tees. Sometimes they even be wearing the matching designer hats. So, you good, boo. You look cute."

I looked at Uzi, whose Moschino fit had to cost him every bit of $1,000, and he shrugged his shoulders. Talking like the young boss he was quickly becoming, he said, "To each his own, ya heard? Moschino's my shit, all the way down to my boxers and socks. I'd even wear Moschino condoms if they made them shits. Playa shit, fam. What'chu want me to do?"

"Here, Twin, this is for you," Daphney said as she handed me the stack of money she pulled from her Chanel bag. "And this, too." She reached back inside of her bag and pulled out a gray Motorola flip phone. "It's already doing about $500 a day from my weed clientele. They're mostly a bunch of Temple students looking for smoke. They're too scary to be going around the hood to get it, so they be calling me. They asses be smoking like chimneys, too. So, with all the money they be spending, you'll be buying all the new fly shit you want," she cut her eyes at Uzi, "clothes *and* cars."

"Is that right," I slowly replied, doing my best to sound appreciative. $500 a day was chump change, nothing close to the paper that I planned on making. I was thinking more like *$50,000* a day, and why not? My pops had the whole Philly on smash, so it was only right that I picked up where he left off.

"That's what's up, Twin. Good looking," I said, then I stuffed the phone she gave me inside of my pocket. I began counting the money she passed off, but I stopped at $400 when I saw the way Uzi was looking at me. *Ol' hungry eyes mah'fucka.* Once again, I was thinking about Pops. His words of wisdom were manifesting right before my very eyes.

No matter if he's friend or foe, the next nigga should never know how much paper you got, he explained in the last letter he sent me. His words were on point like a mah'fucka. I wasn't even two steps away from the jail, and was already seeing the evil side of the game through my newly trained eyes.

"Come on, y'all, let's get up outta here," I said as I grabbed Erica's hand and led the way back to Uzi's Pathfinder. "I'm try'na get back to the city, so I can hit up the 'jects. Then, after that, I gotta shoot past my moms' crib, so I can check out my lil' brothers. I miss my lil' niggas like a mah'fucka."

Askari

CHAPTER TWO

The ride back to the city was shorter than I'd thought it would be. We were listening to the 2Pac's new album, *All Eyes on Me*, and getting dumb high from passing around two blunts of this bomb-ass weed they were calling *Hydro*.

I had only hit the mah'fucka three times, and was already zoned out with the craziest shit running through my mind. Out of all things, I was thinking about the so-called beef between Bad Boy and Death Row Records. I was somewhat out the loop, being as though I'd been locked up for most of the shit. But supposedly, Biggie had something to do with 2Pac getting shot up and robbed, and according to 2Pac, he fucked Biggie's bitch. The whole shit was goofy as fuck, because real beef was settled in blood not lyrics. But if I had to choose a side, I was Team Pac all day.

Exhaling a thick cloud of smoke, I nodded my head to the music and rapped along with 2Pac's lyrics.

"Mama, I'm still thuggin', the world is a war zone. My homies is inmates, and most of 'em dead wrong. Full grown, finally a man. Still scheming on ways to put some green inside the palms of my empty hands. Just picture me rolling."

No bullshit, this nigga had me in my fucking bag; his music was way harder than Biggie's. And speaking of hard, Erica had my dick harder than a mah'fucka. Uzi and Daphney were seated up front, while me and Erica were seated in the back. She was leaned against me, kissing my neck and talking all this freaky shit in my ear. Her right hand was slowly jerking my dick through my Polo trunks. On my mama, that shit felt good! But instead of finger-fucking her pussy like she wanted me to, I just continued hitting the blunt and stared out the window as we cruised up Girard Avenue.

The everyday hustle and bustle of the city was something that I'd forgotten about, as everything seemed to be moving way too fast. And because I'd been stagnated for the past two years while the rest of the world was still moving forward, I paid super close attention to everything around me. I zeroed in on every car that we drove past, and made a mental assessment of every street corner where I saw niggas hustling. In due time, I would step to every one of them niggas to see if they were friend or foe, customer or competition. Either way, they would soon bow down to my gangsta.

"Now, that's what the fuck I'm talking 'bout, home sweet home," I mumbled under my breath, as we cruised under the 9th Street bridge. We were approaching the Cambridge Homes, the projects where I was born and raised.

The twelve-story-high, double towers were an unofficial extension of the Richard Allen projects. The first tower was situated on 10th Street, between Cambridge and Poplar. The second tower was one block away on 11th Street. Each tower had its own basketball court, but 11th Street was where all the rough, rugged and raw niggas played. And I'm not talking about no mah'fuckin' basketball, neither. I'm talking about crack dealing and cap peeling. Straight like that. It was there, on 11th Street, that I witnessed my first murder and had seen more tragedies than I could count.

The worst tragedy was when my cousin, Rell, stabbed my other cousin, Leon, in his head over a cheese steak. I thank Allah that Leon didn't die. But I'll never forget the way that nigga was running around the basketball court bitching and screaming with that big-ass steak knife sticking out of his forehead. And to make matters worse, Rell and Leon were half-brothers. But that's the Trap for you, the streets will turn mama's little baby into a savage nigga quick. Especially the streets of North Philly.

"So, this is how they look now?" I asked Uzi, as we cruised out from underneath the bridge, approaching the corner of 10th and Girard. I was referring to the twin towers. Both buildings had been shut down by the city a few weeks earlier, and that was my first time seeing them since they'd been deserted. The parking lot was completely empty, and the same could be said for the basketball courts, notwithstanding the dozen or so homeless people who had turned them into tent cities. The lobby door on the 10th Street building was boarded up, and the windows were covered with blue tarps and gray plastic. The 11th Street building was too far away to see, but I was sure they looked the same way.

"Yeah, that's how they look now," Uzi said as he looked back at me, whipping the ride with one hand. "This shit is crazy, right? Niggas don't know what to do wit' they'self now that the towers is down. Mah'fuckas had to move away and shit, scattered all around the city. Most of 'em done migrated to Southwest, in the Bartram Village projects. And you know how the Allen do, niggas done went down there and took over they mah'fuckin' projects. Got them shits looking like a miniature Richard Allen. Word."

"Yeah, I heard that," I replied, while shaking my head. I had recently read in the newspaper that the murder rate in Southwest Philly had increased by 50%, so everything that Uzi said was right on point. I had plans for Bartram Village, as well.

"But, I'm saying, though," I locked eyes with Uzi through the rearview mirror, "what's the real reason they shut down the towers?"

"Boo, I done already told you," Erica said as she kissed my earlobe, and pulled her hand out from in between my legs. "The tenants were complaining about a foul smell coming from the heating vents. Nobody knew what it was, but it was happening all winter. Then lo and behold, back in December when the Housing Authority came out to do an inspection, they found all these dead bodies stuffed inside the heating units. That was the foul smell the tenants were complaining about. These crazy-ass niggas were killing people and stashing the bodies on the goddamned roof. They even found Ms. Lorraine, Tee-Tee and nem's grandmom, stuffed inside one of the units. Big Mama damn near had a heart attack when she found out. You know her and Ms. Lorraine used to be real close back in the day. I'm telling you, boo, that shit was crazy as hell."

"Yeah, I remember you telling me that. But I never saw it on the news, or read about it in the papers. I just figured it was all a rumor."

"A rumor, my ass," Daphney interjected. "The city just covered it up, try'na act like it never happened. No disrespect, Twin, but that's the reason I hate coming down here. Y'all Richard Allen niggas ain't wrapped too tight, just as crazy as all outdoors. Don't make no damn sense."

I disregarded Daphney's comment, and returned my attention to Uzi, who had just turned left on 10th Street. "So, what's up wit' Big Jabby now that the towers are down? He had them jawns doing about ten stacks a day."

Big Jabby, just like Mook, was one of my pops' street lieutenants before he went to prison. The YBM pie was cut numerous ways after the indictment, with each faction being obligated to kick up 20% of all proceeds to the soldiers who were serving Life upstate. In regards to Richard Allen, my pops appointed Big Jabby and Mook as the two overseers. The twin towers were given to Big Jabby, and the low-rise, three-story buildings were given to Mook. Those buildings included: Reno Place, Ogden Place, Hutchinson Place, and The Village. Each housing unit was good for $2,500 a day.

"Who you thought I was talking about when I said niggas ain't know what to do wit' they'self? No disrespect, E, 'cause I know Big Jabby's ya folks and all dat. But duke gon' fuck around and start a war," Uzi said as he looked at Erica through the rearview mirror, then he brought his gaze back to me. "Right now, he's try'na finagle his way into the low-rises. But we all know Mook ain't going for that."

"Excuse me, but can we please change the subject?" Daphney said as she rolled her eyes at Uzi. She seemed to have taken what he said personal, and I didn't know why.

"Yes, please do?" Erica backed her up, catching an attitude as well. Her sister, Ebony, and Big Jabby had been going together for years, and we all knew that Erica saw him as an older brother.

"Don't get mad at me, I'm just saying," Uzi defended himself, as we cruised down 10th Street.

Erica turned her head to see my reaction, but I shrugged my shoulders and looked away. As far as I was concerned, there was no advantage to be gained without conflict. Big Jabby and Mook going at one another was exactly what I needed. The inner strife between them left me with two options: step in and play the role of a mediator, or create more chaos that would further their divide. Either way, I would surely gain control in the process.

The projects were jumping like a mah'fucka when we pulled up on 10th and Poplar. DJ Cosmic Kev, the deejay from *Power 99*, had his turntables set up outside of Kim's Deli. He was doing his thing on the wheels of steel, mixing and scratching, while RAM SQUAD'S new hit single and neighborhood anthem, *Fortunate*, was thumping from the speakers.

Some fortunate, some less fortunate. Some get it, some get acquitted. Some having it, some straight flabbing it. Drug deals, fly girls on the pill. Richard Allen, how we do? How we do? Richard Allen! Richard Allen!

"Yo, hold the fuck up. You mah'fuckas knew the hood was having a block party, and ain't none of y'all tell me?" I blurted out loud. I looked around the Pathfinder waiting for an answer, but nobody said a word. "That's crazy, yo. Y'all niggas outta pocket," I continued, as they all remained silent.

"Calm down, Twin." Daphney looked back at me and smiled. "It's not just a block party, it's a *Welcome Home* party—for you. Daddy put it together"

"So, why the fuck ain't none of y'all tell me?"

"Uuuuuhhhhhh, because it's a surprise party," Erica said, then she playfully doinked me on the head. "Duh."

I looked out of the window, and it seemed as though the entire hood was there. They were all smoking and drinking, dancing and having a good time, all on the strength of me. If their intentions were pure and their love for me was real, then half of my battle was already won.

Looking around the intersection, from one corner to the next, I inventoried every familiar face; especially the faces of the niggas on my team. The first face that stood out was Lil' Man, a young wild nigga from the 10th Street tower. He was standing on the Cambridge Homes side of the street, directly across from us.

Lil' Man was five years older than me, and next to Uzi, he was my closest friend. His entire family were all midgets. But even at 4 feet, 7 inches tall, Lil' Man was just as deadly as they came. Standing beside Lil' Man was my nigga, Black Mooch, who was also the son of a fallen YBM kingpin. His pop, Moochie Love, was my pops' second-in-command. His territory was the entire North Philly, but Richard Allen was his headquarters. Black Mooch was blacker than a mah'fucka, just like his pops. He was also just as deadly and ruthless. He was born and raised in the 11th Street tower, but was now living on Brown Street with his baby mama, Reiny.

A few more of my niggas, Top Cat, Beetle, J-Dawg and Blizzard, who were all from Reno Place, were standing on the Richard Allen side of the street. And just like Erica said, they were all wearing fresh white Tees, designer swimming trunks, and had on a fresh pair of white-on-white Nike Air Forces.

Big Jabby and Mook were also on the scene.

Big Jabby's money-green Chevy Suburban was parked on the Cambridge Homes side of the street, where Lil' Man and Black Mooch were standing. He was seated behind the steering wheel, smoking a blunt and talking to his right-hand-man, Dev, who was seated on the passenger's side with the door wide open. Big Jabby was a big, 6 foot 9, Suge Knight looking nigga. He had a light-brown complexion with a shiny bald head, and had a thick bushy beard that was lined up to perfection. Dev was a skinny, brown skinned nigga who resembled Chris Tucker. He was short and scrawny, but was known for making his heater clap.

Mook was a tall, black, gorilla-looking nigga, but his paper was mad long and everybody knew it. He was standing on the Richard Allen side of Poplar, leaned against the driver side door of his cranberry GS 300 Lexus. An agitated expression was written across his face, as he stood there talking on his Motorola flip phone. Top Cat, Beetle, J-Dawg and Blizzard were standing on both sides of Mook's Lexus. The small bulges sticking out the sides of their T-shirts was a clear indicator they were all strapped.

"See what I'm saying?" Uzi pointed out the tension between the two groups. "That's the reason I moved up Germantown with Zion. Ain't nobody got time for this shit. We all used to be squad, but now these niggas on some other shit. Then to make matters worse, Big

Jabby and Mook is the only mah'fuckas getting money. The rest of them niggas scrambling for crumbs."

Instead of replying, I just continued looking out the window, sizing up the entire situation. The animosity between the two groups couldn't have been more apparent. A line had been drawn in the sand, and niggas had already taken sides. My niggas from the low-rises were soldiering for Mook, while my niggas from the towers were rocking out for Big Jabby.

Clearly, I had my work cut out. I was the youngest on the team, and seemed to be stuck somewhere in the middle. I needed to find a way to convince my niggas to not only believe in me, but to also believe in my vision of taking over the streets, while at the same time establishing myself as the Top Dawg and undisputed leader of the pack. I knew the task would be daunting, but I also knew that I was mentally strong enough to make it happen. This was yet again, another lesson that I learned from my pops.

Never fight a battle if you can't foresee winning the war. It's useless. You'd be better off chasing air.

My plan to conquer was solid. The first order of business was taking the images of Big Jabby and Mook, which I knew my niggas idolized, and tarnish them mah'fuckas at any and all cost. Secondly, I would bless my niggas with opportunities and gifts they would not have otherwise received fucking with Big Jabby and Mook. Then finally I would deliver a blow so devastating to each one of their empires, that my niggas would have no other choice but to ride my wave once the smoke cleared. And if they proved themselves to be loyal and true, I would make them all millionaires by the age of twenty-five. This strategy was more than plausible; my pops did the same exact thing.

"Yo, you heard me, AJ?" Uzi raised his voice, snapping me out my trance. "I said look behind the seat, next to the speaker box. I've got sum'n for you."

I reached back behind the seat and moved my hand around until I felt the strap of a book bag. I grabbed the book bag and pulled it over the seat. There was a large, hard object at the bottom of the bag, and based on the shape I could tell it was a gun. There was also a second item inside of the bag that was lumpy and hard, and seemed to be about the size of a miniature basketball.

"Fuck you got in this mah'fucka?" I asked Uzi, as I sat the book bag down on my lap.

"Nigga, just open the bag." Uzi smiled at me.

Daphney and Erica were both looking, waiting for me to open the book bag so they could see what Uzi had stashed inside for me. I would have rather waited until nobody was around before I opened it, but my curiosity got the best of me.

Fuck it.

I pulled the zipper down and carefully opened the bag. The first thing I saw was a Ziplock bag with a big ball of crack inside of it. I picked up the Ziplock bag and examined it closely. Instead of being one large mound of crack, it was actually five or six boulders pressed together. I didn't even know how much it was worth, because prior to then, the most crack I had ever touched was a quarter-ounce that I shared with Uzi.

For a brief second, I began to doubt myself, but then I shook that shit off. I was the son of a boss, born to die and bred to kill. This hustling shit was my fucking destiny.

"That's nine ounces right there, a quarter-brick," Uzi said, still smiling at me. "It's already rocked up, so all you gotta do is move it. Whatever you make, that's you. But if you wanna keep pushin', you gotta bring me back $5,500 for another one. That's the best I can do for you. Niggas Uptown is paying $6,200 all day, $24,000 for a whole bird."

My eyelids became two dark slits.

"Nah, I'm good." I placed the crack back inside of the book bag, and then pulled out the Smith & Wessin .40 that was stashed at the bottom. "I'ma roll wit' this, though."

I held up the gun and ejected the clip. A copperhead, cop-killer was sticking out the top, and nine more were stuffed down inside of it. I loaded the clip back in the gun, and then chambered a live round.

Click! Clack!

"Look y'all, here they come," Erica blurted out, as she pointed across the street where Lil' Man and Black Mooch were walking toward us.

I popped open the back door and climbed out slowly. I placed the .40 on the small of my back, and then moved around the front of the Pathfinder to greet my niggas.

Askari

CHAPTER THREE

"Goddamn, AJ! Ya ass got big as shit!" Lil' Man shouted in his raspy voice, reminding me of Bushwick Bill from The Geto Boys. The only thing he was missing was a prosthetic and some nappy-ass dreads. But aside from that, he could have passed for Bushwick Bill any day of the week.

"My fuckin' boy." I smiled at Lil' Man, then I reached down and gave him some dap.

"A to the mah'fuckin' J," Black Mooch said as he embraced me with a brotherly hug. "Well, damn nigga, it's about time they kicked ya ass off the plantation. What the fuck you was doing up that jawn? Lifting the whole jail? Bul, you done swelled up sum'n crazy."

"I was grinding, man. Lifting weights and doing calisthenics all day."

"Well, it's good to have you back, my nigga. We missed you out here," Black Mooch said with a smile, then he looked inside of the Pathfinder. "Yo, what took y'all so long? Niggas been out here since early this morning waiting for y'all to bring this nigga home. Ol' super slow mah'fuckas."

"Boy, shut up," Daphney said as she reached her hand out the window and popped Black Mooch on the back of his head. She looked down at Lil' Man, who was cracking a blunt down the middle, and called his name mad aggressive.

"*Lil' Man*? Where Meesha at?"

"She's over there," Lil' Man replied, then he pointed down the block at his baby mama.

Meesha was 6 feet tall and fat as shit, the exact opposite of Lil' Man. They'd been going together for as long as I could remember, and had two sons Mykah and Mookah. Mykah was the normal size for a five-year-old, but Mookah, who had just turned four, was already diagnosed as a midget. Both boys were bad as shit, and had steamy hot tempers just like Lil' Man.

"Why, what's up?" Lil' Man looked at Daphney with a creased brow. "What'chu need her for sum'n?"

"You damn right, I need her for sum'n. A bitch try'na get her fade on, and Meesha's ass is the one with the liquor."

"A'ight, well like I said, she's over there wit' the kids," Lil' Man replied, then he squinted his eyes. He was looking down the block at Meesha, being over protective as usual. Lil' Man was crazy as hell when it came to Meesha. "So, you and Meesha are still going strong, I see." I playfully punched him on the shoulder, knowing it would piss him off.

"Yo, AJ, man, what the fuck is wrong wit'chu?" he shot me the look of death, then he cracked a smile, showing off his gold teeth. "You know I 'on't go for none of that play fighting shit. The wrong nigga see you playing, try his hand, and get blammed on, fa 'real. You know what I'm talking 'bout?" He lifted up the front of his T-shirt, showing me the nickel-plated .38 that was tucked underneath. "I got a speed-loader for this mah'fucka, too. I'll bust a nigga's ass out this bitch—quick, fast, and in a fuckin' hurry. Ain't shit changed wit' Lil' Man. I'm still the same ol' G."

I looked at my nigga, and couldn't stop smiling. I missed my niggas like a mah'fucka; especially him. His Napoleon complex was the worst, and that's the reason we called him *Lil' Man*.

"Come on, E, let's go over there and see what's up with Meesha," Daphney's said as she climbed out of the Pathfinder and motioned for Erica to do the same.

"You hungry, boo?" Erica said, as she climbed out the back seat and closed the door behind her. "Big Mama hooked up some barbecued ribs, and Ms. Val made her world-famous potato salad. Ebony's pregnant ass fried all the chicken, and Ms. Nann fried the fish. You want me to fix you a plate?"

"Yeah, ma, go 'head and do that for me." I rubbed my stomach and inhaled deeply, taking in the savory aroma of the barbecue that was cooking. "You already know I 'on't fuck wit' no pork. Beef ribs only. And tell Big Mama I'll be over there to see her in a minute."

Erica kissed me on the lips, then her and Daphney walked across the street where everybody was dancing to 112's new hit single, *Only You*.

Girrrl, I waaaant to, beeee with yoooouuuu. Noooo one eeeelse. Onnnnly yoooouuuu. Whyyyy can't we just, maaaake it haaaappen? Baaaaby, I needed yoooouuuu in my liiiife. It was only a matter of time before everybody realized that I was there, and then came over to see me. So, while I still had a few minutes left, I figured that I'd set a few things straight with my niggas. I was just about to check their temperatures to see how loyal they were to Big Jabby, but then something hit me. Out of all the people who came out to celebrate my first day home, I didn't see my young jawn, Kia. She was mad cool with Lil' Man and Black Mooch, so I assumed she knew about the party, and if she did, then chances were she was already there. The problem with that was her and Erica couldn't stand one another, and would surely come to blows if they ever crossed paths. I wanted to make sure that didn't happen.

"Aye, yo, Black, you seen Keys out here? I'm looking around, but I don't see her."

"Nah, AJ, I ain't seen her," Black Mooch said. "And I've been out here since early this morning. Matter of fact, I ain't seen Keys in a while. You think she might'a came?"

"I 'on't know. I hope not. Lil' Man, you seen her?"

"Not at all," Lil' Man replied. "But I know what I *did* see, this new gank that I got out here on the block. This that Oscar The Grouch right here," he held up the blunt he just sparked, "this that *super* sticky icky. I even got these lil' trash cans that I sell it in. Check out this fly shit right chere." He reached inside of his pocket and pulled out a tiny plastic container that resembled a trash can. "This the best shit in the city, AJ. Huhn." He held the blunt out for me to smoke, but I shook my head *no*.

"Gawn and chief somma this fiyah. Don't leave ya nigga hangin'."

"Nah, Lil' Man, I'm good. Go 'head wit' that shit."

I was still looking around for Kia, and ended up locking eyes with Top Cat. He and Beetle were standing across the street talking to Mook, but pointing at me. J-Dawg and Blizzard were also standing there looking at me. It seemed as though they wanted to come over and holla at me, but instead they just stood there looking stupid.

"Yo, what's up wit' these niggas?" I looked down at Lil' Man and scrunched my face. "What, they need Mook's permission to come over here and bark at us? Fuck is going on 'round this mah'fucka?"

"Shit ain't the same no more," Lil' Man replied, puffing on his blunt. "The squad ain't the same no more," he spoke in between tokes, "and the love between us *definitely* ain't the same. I hate to say it, but shit done changed. You 'on't feel it," he exhaled a thick cloud of smoke, "all this mah'fuckin' tension in the air?"

"I do." I nodded my head and flexed my jaw muscles, becoming more agitated by the second. I looked at Uzi, who was leaning back in his driver's seat and talking on his flip phone. He met my gaze, then he disconnected the call and climbed out of the truck. He dapped it up with Lil' Man and Black Mooch, and then checked the time on his diamond bezeled Movado.

"Look at these niggas." Uzi guided our attention to Top Cat and Beetle, who were walking toward us. "I know one thing—they better not come over here wit' none of that weirdo shit."

"AJ, what's up, nigga?" Top Cat and Beetle greeted me at the same time. They showed love to Uzi, but ignored Lil' Man and Black Mooch.

"See what I'm saying, AJ? This is the sucka, nut shit I'm talking 'bout," Lil' Man scoffed, then he stepped off, ice-grilling Top Cat and Beetle.

"Hit me up later, A," Black Mooch said as he followed behind Lil' Man. My number's still the same," he said to me, but was scowling at Top Cat. "I'm still the same nigga, you heard? Ain't shit changed wit' me."

"Fuck outta here, nigga. Ya ass just mad," Top Cat said with a smile, then he looked back at me. "Them niggas had they chance to run wit' the winners, but they chose not to. That's on them."

"*The winners?*" I looked at him like he was crazy. "Who's winning? Y'all or him?" I pointed across the street at Mook. "Matter of fact, fuck all this beating around the bush shit. I'm addressing this nigga, head on."

"Yo, AJ, man, what the fuck is you doing?" Beetle said, then he reached out and grabbed my arm when I stormed off in Mook's direction.

"Nigga, you ever touch me again, I'll rip ya fuckin' head off." I spun around and stepped in his grill.

"Nah, fam, no disrespect. I didn't even mean it like that," Beetle started bitching. "I'm just saying, nah mean? Niggas got a good thing going wit' Mook. He sent us over to talk to you. He said he's got a spot for you on the team. But don't fuck it up like Lil' Man and Black Mooch did? This shit is a one-time deal."

Instead of replying, I scowled at him until he looked away, then I looked at Uzi, whose right hand was tucked under his shirt, gripping his steel. No words between us were needed. I continued walking in Mook's direction, and Uzi followed. I could see Lil' Man and Black Mooch out the corner of my eye. They were trailing us from behind, sizing up Top Cat and Beetle. The second them niggas tried some shit, I knew Lil' Man and Black Mooch would start blasting. That's how niggas from the towers got down for one another.

Mook saw me coming his way, and he cracked a smile. It wasn't a scared smile, it was more like he knew something that I didn't, and for that reason he had the upper hand. The closer I got to this nigga, the more I could hear Pops' voice in the back of my mind.

"Always remember, Trap, you're not the only student of war. There's always the possibility your enemy is just as sharp as you are, and could be maintaining his power the same way that you maintain yours. So, never be too confident when engaging in battle. The perfect enemy is capable of defeating you, never forget that."

It felt like the earth stopped spinning when I stepped to Mook. The music turned low, then everybody looked at me and pointed. It must have been the look on my face. I was bricking this nigga hard as shit.

"What's up, lil' nigga? Welcome home," Mook greeted me. He extended his right hand, but I smacked that shit away.

"Oooooohhhhhh!" the crowd gasped, boxing us in like spectators at a schoolyard brawl. The niggas from the low-rises were standing behind Mook, and the niggas from the towers were standing behind me. One wrong move, and bullets would start flying from both sides.

"Damn, lil' homie, it's like that?" Mook pulled his hand back, confused by my hostile approach.

"You mah'fuckin' right, it's like that." My ice-grill was official. "Ain't this the way you want it? The towers and the low-rises beefin' over who's gonna control the 'jects?"

"Yo, lemme stop you right there," he spoke calm and cool. "Before you step out of line more than you already have, you need to go holla at'cha pops. There's mad shit going ya way right now, but clearly, you're not aware of it. So, again, before you—"

"Ahn-ahn! No! *Fuck no!*" Daphney's voice rang out, cutting this nigga off mid-sentence. She barged her way through the crowd and stepped in between us. "Twin, what the hell is wrong with you? What are you doing?"

I pushed Daphney out the way and threw a two-piece at Mook, trying to knock his fucking head off. The entire hood was watching, so I figured it was the best time to catch him slipping and humiliate his image beyond repair. But unfortunately, what I failed to consider was that Mook had a mean box game. He side-stepped my jab, leaned away from my hook, and then pivoted to an angle that I couldn't defend. He had a clean shot at my face and ribs, but he didn't take it.

"Nigga, this the last time I'ma tell ya," he cautioned with a fiery look in his eyes. "Go holla at'cha fuckin' pops, and then report back to me. *Young bul.*"

Now, why the fuck he had to say that? It was bad enough that he easily thwarted my advance, but that was the third time he spoke condescendingly when addressing me. First it was *"lil' man"*, and then it was *"lil' homie"*. That *"young bul"* remark was the last fuckin' straw.

Fuck outta here, nigga. I got'cha young bul.

I reached for the burner that Uzi gave me, but before I could pull it, Erica's grandmother, Big Mama, stepped forward and grabbed my arm.

"Chil', you better stop that foolishness. *Right now,*" she demanded in her motherly tone, causing me to regret my actions almost immediately.

Erica was standing beside her grandmother, crying. She dropped the plate of food she prepared for me, and then took off running towards her grandmother's building.

"Damn, nigga, you was gon' bang me?" Mook looked at me with his nostrils flaring. "You right." He backed away, shaking his head. "You 'posed to be my youngin', but I guess not. You right."

"Pussy, you know where I'm at. I ain't going nowhere." I grilled his ass back, certain that I'd made my point. "Twin?" Daphney looked at me with tears in her eyes.

"Come on, Daph, we out," Mook said, still walking backwards with his soldiers from the low-rises flanking him. Every last one of them niggas had their hammas out, but so did my niggas from the towers. Whatever they wanted, we had it.

"And what the fuck is this?" I scowled at Daphney when she followed after Mook. "You're taking this nigga's side over mines?"

Surprisingly, she offered no reply; she couldn't even look me in the eyes. She just lowered her head and continued following Mook, reminding me of a scared little girl who'd been chastised by her father. It fucked me up, seeing that shit. There was clearly something going on between them, and I was determined to find out what.

I continued watching, as Daphney and Mook climbed inside of his Lexus. His soldiers from the low-rises climbed inside of two Ford Excursions. Both trucks were jet-black, sitting on dubs, and had dark tinted windows. The first truck was parked in front of Mook's Lexus. The second truck was parked across the street, slightly behind it. The first Excursion pulled away from the curb and stopped in the middle of 10th Street, followed by Mook's Lexus. The second Excursion pulled out last, securing Mook's Lexus from the rear. Beetle, who was seated on the back-passenger's side of the second Excursion, rolled down the window and stuck his head out. He looked right at me.

"*AJ, what the fuck is you thinking?*" he mouthed the words, as the three vehicles pulled off slowly. "*Just chill out. I'ma do what I can to fix it.*"

I didn't say a word. I just stood there looking at him with a million scenarios running through my mind. The outcome wasn't exactly how I planned, but I definitely set the tone. Even better, I grabbed Big Jabby's attention. He didn't know it, but I was watching him out the corner of my eye, as he and Dev stood beside his Suburban watching me. It was only a matter of time before he stepped to me, and offered a high-ranking position on his team. If he did, then I was well on my way to winning my first battle.

"Chil', you ought'a be ashamed of ya'self," Big Mama scolded, reminding me that her and everyone else from the party were still standing there. "All of these people came out to welcome you home and encourage you to do something good with your life, and *this* is how you repay 'em? By acting a damned fool? Boy, you done lost your everlasting mind?"

My breathing intensified, as I anxiously bit down on my bottom lip. Had Big Mama been anyone else, I would have smacked the shit out of her for disrespecting me in front of all those people. But she wasn't anyone else, she was a second mother to me; and not just to me, but to every little kid who grew up in Richard Allen with a drug addicted mother and an absentee father. So, because I loved her too much to ever disrespect her, I remained quiet.

"Yo, who the fuck is that?" Lil' Man broke the silence. He was pointing down the block, directing our attention to three mah'fuckas who were creeping up the street.

"I 'on't know. I can't really tell wit' them sunglasses they wearing," Black Mooch said as he tucked his hamma behind his leg. "It fuck around and be the cops, somebody might'a called 'em."

"The cops?" I looked at Black Mooch, then I shifted my gaze from Lil' Man to Uzi. "Three black mah'fuckas wearing sunglasses and trench coats in the middle of the summer? And got latex gloves on they mah'fuckin' hands? That shit don't sound like the cops to me."

I looked back down the street at the three niggas creeping, and realized who they were. The second it hit me, I heard Big Jabby's booming, deep voice. He was yelling at us from across the street.

"Somebody grab Big Mama! It's a hit!"

Askari

CHAPTER FOUR

No sooner than Big Jabby said it, the drama was on. The three niggas walking toward us got busy without warning, spraying up the block with the M-16s they pulled out from underneath their trench coats.

Bdddddddddddddddddoc!
Bdddddddddddddddddoc!
Bdddddddddddddddddoc!

"Big Mama, get down!" I shouted as I tackled her to the ground. She lifted her head, but I pushed it back down, ducking my own when the zipping sound of a high-caliber bullet whizzed right past me.

Bdddddddddddddddddoc! Bdddddddddddddddddoc!
Boc! Boc! Bdddddddddddddddddoc!

"Agh, shit!" I shouted, shaking off the burning shell casings that rained down, courtesy of the hammas that my niggas were using to bust back.

Boom! Boom! Blakka! Blakka! Boom! Boom! Boca! Boca!
Boom! Boom! Boca!

Peeking over my shoulder, I locked eyes with Meesha. She was laying on the ground about three feet away, trembling and crying, and holding onto Mykah and Mookah for dear life. I attempted to get up, but the weight of a dead body slammed down hard on the back of my neck.

Blam!

The unexpected pain left me dizzy and shook, but seeing that the body was Black Mooch hurt even worse. His bloody, gray brains were dripping down his face like a cracked melon's pulp, and the left side of his dome, from his cheekbone back, was completely missing.

Shaking away the image, I grabbed my gun with my right hand and tugged on Black Mooch with my left. I pulled him in close, and then draped his body over Big Mama's.

"Don't move, Big Mama, stay down!"

I can't say for sure, but it sounded like Big Mama was calling on Jesus. Well, it just so happened that Jesus had a new name, *Smith & Wessin .40,* and by the power invested in me, that ten-shot mah'fucka was about to start baptizing shit.

Blakka! Blakka! Blakka! Blakka!

After busting off a few quick rounds, I ran towards the street and dipped behind the fender of an old school Cadillac. I reached my .40 around the taillight and continued busting at the trench coats.

Blakka! Blakka! Blakka!

The intersection of 10th and Poplar was covered in smoke, as gunfire exploded from every direction. The trench coats were giving it up nonstop, showing no signs of retreat. My niggas did the same.

Boc! Boc! Bddddddddddddddddddoc! Bddddddddddddddddddoc! Boc! Boc! Bddddddddddddddddddoc!

Boom! Boom! Boca! Boca! Boom! Boom! Blakka! Blakka! Boom! Boom! Boca!

Our small caliber pistols were like candles in the sun compared to those M-16s. But all of that changed when Big Jabby ran towards the back of his Suburban, popped open the back doors and pulled out his AR-15.

Bddddddddddddddddddoom!
Bddddddddddddddddddoom!
Boom! Boom! Bddddddddddddddddddoom!

"Flank right! Flank right!" Big Jabby shouted over the gangsta music, commanding his troops from the towers to move in from the right, while he and Dev moved in from the left.

Lil' Man, Uzi, and a few more niggas that I knew from the towers did exactly as Big Jabby commanded. My ammunition was nearly depleted, so I kept my black ass behind the Caddy.

Bddddddddddddddddddoom! Bddddddddddddddddddoom! Boca! Boca! Boom! Boom! Boca!

The trench coats were backing away, but their M-16s were still spraying, tearing up the parked cars that were lined up and down the street. I could feel the Caddy rock each time it was hit, but it provided great cover. The only thing that touched me was a downpour of broken glass from the back window being shattered.

Bddddddddddddddddoc!
Bddddddddddddddddoc! Bddddddddddddddddoc!
It had only been a matter of minutes since the shooting began, but it felt like an hour. Then suddenly, a pair of headlights sliced through the smoke as a black utilities van that was built like a war machine came speeding down the street. The entire van was fortified with steel beams, and had two AK-47 barrels sticking out of both sides. The choppa fire sprayed the block, as the van continued speeding. Two of the trench coats jumped out the way. But the third trench coat, some big, fat, beanbag looking nigga, got his fat ass splattered. He flew into the air with his gun spraying wildly, and then came down hard with a devastating thud.

Wham!
The war van's side door swung open, and another shooter hopped out. He was dressed in all-black, with a black ski mask covering his face. His automatic shotgun thundered like a cannon.

Boom! Boom! Boom! Boom! Boom! Boom!
My niggas shot back, but the brief exchange was only a diversion, giving the two trench coats the time they needed to make an escape. They climbed inside of the van, then the shooter who hopped out, hopped in behind them.

Scurrrrrrrrrrrrrrrr!
The war van murked out, leaving behind the one trench coat who'd been run over. We ran out into the middle of the street and let loose on the van, but our bullets were useless. The only damage done were the fiery sparks that leaped off the van's exterior.

"Where the fuck is this nigga at?" I shouted like a madman. I was looking around the smokey intersection for the one trench coat who'd been left behind.

"He's over here, AJ! I got his ass right here!" Lil' Man shouted back.

The smoke began to clear, as I walked over to Lil' Man, who was standing over the trench coat. The punk mah'fucka had his legs all twisted, but was using his arms to pull himself forward. I kicked him in his ass and he lurched forward, landing on his stomach.

"Urgghh," he released a loud groan, still struggling to pull himself forward. He stretched his arms out reaching for the M-16 he dropped during his fall, but I knelt down and grabbed the mah'fucka before he could reach it.

"Pussy, turn ya ass over." I kicked him in his ass once more, and then flipped him over with the tip of my Nike. Looking at me with fear in his eyes, he started to say something, but I never gave him the chance. I shoved the gun in his mouth and did his ass the same way they did Black Mooch.

Boca!

His limp body bounced off the ground, as his warm blood splashed me in the face. I didn't even wipe it away. If anything, the feeling of his blood on my face excited me. Nostrils flaring and chest heaving, I jammed the barrel through his left eye and continued shooting until his head turned to mush.

Bdddddddddddddddddoc!

"Bitch-ass nigga. That's for Black Mooch. Tfft!" I spat on his dead body.

CHAPTER FIVE
Later That Night

I was laying low in Uptown Philly with Lil' Man and Uzi, smoking blunts and pouring out liquor for my nigga, Black Mooch. It was never my intention for Black Mooch to get his shit pushed back, but I charged it to the game as a casualty of war. The destruction that I left in my wake was for the cops and coroners to sort out, and I couldn't have cared less about either one. I wasn't even worried about a witness coming forward, because I knew my projects would never turn on me; especially over some fuck niggas who tried to come through flexing. My only concern was my pops.

The second Pops learned that I stepped to Mook and set off a chain of events that led to his best friend's son being murdered, I knew he would flip out on me; or at the very least take back his promise to put me on my feet when I came home from Juvie. Even then, I held no regrets, because I did what I had to.

Stepping to Mook was a calculated risk, and the outcome was still in my favor. In regards to my pops, I knew he would be more upset with Mook than he was with me, and when it came to Big Jabby and my niggas from the towers, they each had a chance to see that my gangsta was official and that my generalship was worthy of being followed. The only thing left for me to do was smooth things over with Pops, convincing him to cut off Mook *and* Big Jabby, and making me the sole link between the streets and his connect. I needed to be in a position to feed my troops and keep them secured. Because once I established that, then every drug crew in the city would have two options: either bow down to the new king, or lay on the swords of their own denial.

"Yo, I'm mad as *fuck* right now," Lil' Man said as he exhaled a cloud of smoke. He was high as a kite and halfway drunk from the pint of Henny he was sipping. "Them niggas violated. They killed my man, and now they *all* gotta die!"

"You mah'fuckin' right, them niggas gon' die," I supported his stance. I was mean-mugging on the outside, but smiling on the inside. I looked at Uzi, who hadn't said a word since we arrived at his crib, and gritted my teeth. "And what's ya whole thing? Me and Lil' Man been sitting here talking about avenging Black Mooch, and ya ass ain't said a word. Mah'fucka, is you thuggin' or not?"

Uzi released a long sigh, then reclined back on his leather sectional. He wasn't really known for busting his gun, but I needed to know if his interests were aligned with mine. Because if they weren't, then my only option was to kill him. Again, this was something that I learned from my pops.

If his true ambitions are not sympathetic to yours, then dispose of him immediately. If he can't be trusted among your troops, then he certainly can't be trusted among your enemies, and if you keep him in your presence, he could very well rush to the other side and reveal your plans when it is least expected. You can never afford to take such a chance.

I was still looking at Uzi, waiting for his reply. Surprisingly, he sat up and said that he was down for the cause.

"Black Mooch was my mah'fuckin' heart, AJ, and you know that shit. I wasn't gon' say nuffin', but I already got in touch wit' Zion. I told him what happened, and he reached out to our two cousins, Rahman and Jihad. Both of them niggas is fit for war. In fact, they're already en route looking for Mook's Lexus. The second they see him, it's on."

Aw, fuck! Daphney!

"Nizzaw, homie, that's a no go." I waved him off. "The last time I saw Mook, he was riding in the car wit' Daphney. You gotta call them niggas and tell 'em to stand down. At least for the time being."

"Daaaaaamn, that's right," Uzi was on some animated shit. "She *did* leave the party wit' them niggas. And right before they killed Black Mooch."

The sarcastic tone of his voice, had me hot. He must have felt my energy, because he fixed that shit with the quickness.

"Don't even sweat it, bro. I'ma handle that shit right now," Uzi spoke more sensibly. He leaned forward and grabbed his Nokia cell phone from the coffee table. He thumbed in seven digits, then he placed the phone to his ear.

"Yizzo this lil' cuz. I need y'all to fall back on that situation."
He paused for a second and carefully listened to whatever his cousin
was telling him. "Most def, but it's only temporary. I forgot that my
man's sister was riding in the car wit' this nigga. So, that's a no go.
We gotta do it another time." He nodded his head, then he looked
back and forth between Lil' Man and me. "You damn right, my niggas are official. My one man, AJ, you prob'bly know his pops, Alvin Rines. Yup, you already know. Fa' sho. I'ma see you when you
get here. Peace."

Uzi disconnected the call, then he sat his phone back down.
Looking at me, he said, "That's a done deal. But check it, though,
my cousin Rahman, he said he's coming through to holla at'chu."

"Holla at me about what?" I shot him a strange look, and then
looked down on the coffee table where my gun was lying beside the
ashtray. "That's ya peoples, not mines. Fuck he wanna holla at me
for?"

"I 'on't know. He said he used to roll wit'cha pops back in the
day. So, I'm assuming it has sum'n to do wit' that."

I hit the blunt I was smoking super hard, and then exhaled the
smoke from my nose. My pops was thoroughly respected in Philly,
but he was also very much hated. He and his crew had mad enemies
when they left the streets, so there was no telling whether Rahman
was friend or foe. I looked back down at my gun, and figured that
I'd let my nigga, Jesus, decide.

"Fuck it, I'll holla at the nigga. He said he used to run wit' my
pops, so I'll give him an audience. But just so you know, I'm going
up the jail to visit my pops first thing in the morning. I'ma ask him
about ya cousin. If he's not who he says he is," I looked down at
Jesus, then I looked back at Uzi, "you already know."

Uzi's jaw muscles pulsated.

"If he said he was down wit'cha pops, then that's what it is. My
cousin ain't no mah'fuckin' fraud."

"We'll see." I gave him a stern look, and then plucked the ash
from my blunt into the 40oz bottle that I just finished drinking. "So,
Lil' Man, I see you ready for war, huh?"

"You mah'fuckin' right, I'm ready for war," Lil' Man professed, then he took a swig from his Henny bottle. "My mah'fuckin' girl and my kids were out there when them niggas came through bustin'. And Black Mooch," he lowered his head, shaking it slowly, "you seen the way they did my nigga. Had his brains all leaking the fuck out. I ain't letting that shit ride, AJ. Not the fuck at all."

"So, what about when the smoke clears? What'chu plan on doing then?"

"What'chu mean, what I plan on doing then?" he raised his voice and then pulled out his .38 revolver. "I'm Richard Allen Mafia 'til the day they smoke me! Nigga, I'm *mobbin'*!"

I bit into my bottom lip, satisfied with Lil' Man's answer.

"And what about you?" I looked at Uzi.

"Nigga, you know my steez, I'm 'bout dem dollaz. I'm try'na get rich out this mah'fucka."

I was satisfied with Uzi's answer as well.

"So, how y'all feel about Big Jabby?" I looked at Uzi, then I looked at Lil' Man, studying their overall demeanors.

"Oh, that's the big fella," Lil' Man slurred, then he knocked down the rest of his Henny. "You know the big fella gon' ride. You seen the way he was bustin' that AR. Him and Dev gon' always make sure we straight."

I was just about to dig a little deeper to see how loyal he was to Big Jabby and Dev, but the ringing from the flip phone that Daphney gave me grabbed my attention.

Ring! Ring! Ring!

I grabbed the phone from my pocket and flipped it open. I was hoping the caller was Daphney, so I could ask about her relationship with Mook. But when I pressed the phone to my ear, the caller was Beetle.

"Beetle, what the fuck you want?" I deliberately said his name, so Lil' Man and Uzi would know who I was talking to.

"Yo, dawg. I just got'cha number from Daphney. Y'all niggas good?"

"Are we good? Fuck you mean, are we good? You bitch-ass niggas shot up my fuckin' party."

"Wait, wait, hol' up. You thought that was *us*?"

"You mah'fuckin' right, that was y'all. Who else could have done it?"

"Nah, fam, you buggin' right now. That shit wasn't us. That was them Bartram Village niggas who came through and did that."

"Them niggas from Bartram Village?" I was taken aback. "Who told you that?"

"Nigga, turn on the news. That's the only thing they talking 'bout. They said the nigga that got smoked was some young bul from Bartram Village. You know them niggas is beefin' wit' Big Jabby about taking over they projects. I guess they thought it was sweet, came through and tried to catch niggas slippin'."

The fact that the nigga I killed was from Bartram Village threw me for a loop. It was something that I didn't see coming.

"But, yeah, though," Beetle continued, "that's the reason I'm calling. I heard about what happened to Black Mooch, and niggas ain't feeling that shit. I know the low-rises and the towers ain't seeing eye to eye right now, but at the end of the day, we all from Richard Allen. So, whenever it's outside beef, then we all riding. Nah mean? I already talked to Mook, and he told me that he set up a meeting wit' Big Jabby for next week, when he returns from his Cali trip. He said he's gonna bring us all together as one, so we can go at these Bartram Village niggas wit' everything we got. Nah mean? This is Richard Allen we talking 'bout, we got a mah'fuckin' rep to protect. The second we let some outside niggas get away wit' sum'n like this, the whole city gon' try they hand. We gotta shut these niggas down."

"That's a fact." I nodded my head in agreement. "But dig, right, I'm kinda in the middle of sum'n. So, I'ma get back wit'chu and see what's up wit' this meeting."

"A'ight, my nigga, do ya thing. And tell Uzi and Lil' Man I said to get wit' me. I wanna make sure we all on the same page."

"I got'chu. Peace out, my nigga."

"Peace."

Click!

"Fuck was this bitch-ass nigga talking 'bout?" Lil' Man slurred. He was so drunk that he passed out right after he said it.

"So, what he say about them niggas from Bartram Village?" Uzi asked me.

"He said it was them who came through and did that. They was going at Big Jabby for taking over they projects."

"And you believe that shit?" Uzi gave me an incredulous look.

"Man, I 'on't know what to believe. All I know is that Black Mooch is dead, and somebody gotta pay for that shit."

"That's word right there," Uzi nodded his head, then he leaned back and closed his eyes. He appeared to be in deep thought.

"But dig, right, lemme hold the Pathfinder for the night. I gotta shoot out Southwest to go see Kia. I was supposed to had slid up on her a few hours ago, but the bullshit happened."

"But what about Rahman? He said he was coming through to holla at'chu."

"Yeah, I know. But tell him to catch me tomorrow. I'ma slide through when I come back from seeing my pops."

"A'ight, I'ma tell him," Uzi said as he pulled out his car keys and handed them to me. "But don't take the Pathfinder, take my other car. It's the rimmed-out Honda Accord wagon at the top of the block."

"Damn, nigga, you out here doing it like dat?" I smiled at him. "You got *two* cars?"

"Yeah, man. I told you niggas was out here getting money. Hopefully, when all of this is over, we can get back to it. 'Cause we damn sure can't do both. That shit don't mix."

I figured he was indirectly talking about me, being as though I had just come home and we were already going to war. But instead of replying, I just brushed it off.

"And, AJ?" he called out, as I grabbed Jesus from the coffee table and headed towards the door.

"Yeah, fam, what's up?" I looked back over my shoulder.

"Be on point out there."

"I'm good, bro. Believe dat."

When I stepped outside and closed the door behind me, I pulled my phone back out and star-sixty-nined Beetle. He didn't know it, but his stupid-ass was my inside track in Mook's operation. The second he stuck his head out the window and said that he would advocate for me, I knew I had him right where I needed him. My first objective was to squeeze out of him everything he knew about Mook's operation. This would give me the advantage I needed to fully destroy Mook, and at the same time establish an empire of my own, whose foundation originated from his. My final objective was to flip Beetle completely over to my side. This final feat would be easy, especially when considering that Mook barely fed his troops. The only thing I needed to do was keep Beetle's belly full. His unyielding loyalty would soon follow, right along with the rest of Mook's soldiers.

Ring! Ring! Ring!

"Who dis?" Beetle's voice came through the phone.

"It's AJ. Yo, where you at right now?"

"I'm back in the 'jects. It was hot as shit out here for a minute, wit' them boys being out. But they gone now, so niggas is right back to clocking. Why, what's up?"

"Nuffin' too heavy. I just wanted to hit back and see if we could link up. I need to holla at'chu about sum'n." "Holla at me about what?"

"I just wanna touch base, nah mean? See what we can do about bringing the young buls together, and stop all this beef between us. The meeting between Big Jabby and Mook is for the ol' heads. The young niggas still gotta do our part, nah mean?"

"Most def."

"Plus, I'm going up the jail to visit my pops in the morning. He's supposed to be hitting me off wit' a nice amount of work, and since you and the crew is already doing y'all thing, I figured y'all could help me move it. I got a spot out Kensington that's already doing the pussy. This papi nigga I was locked up wit' put me on. I just need my crew behind me, nah mean? So that way if them niggas around there start hatin', we can take it straight to 'em. That Kensington money on a whole 'nother level, nah mean? I'm try'na take over they whole shit, YBM style. You down?"

"Nigga, hell yeah, I'm down!" I could hear the hunger in his voice.

"My man. So, tomorrow night, around eleven o'clock. I'ma be down the way. Just meet me at the old hangout."

"The old hangout? But how? The towers is shut down."

"Yeah, I know. But meet me there, anyway."

"You want me to bring the crew wit' me?"

"Nah, just come by ya'self. I wanna make sure we got our game tight, nah mean? Before we bring it to everybody else."

"Say no more. I'ma see you tomorrow night."

"That's a bet. Peace out, my nigga."

"Peace."

Click!

CHAPTER SIX

I was headed out Southwest to check in with Kia, but a phone call from Erica made me turn back around. She told me she was at my moms' crib waiting for me, and asked if I could stop by McDonald's to pick up some food for her and my brothers.

So, without a second thought, there I was, at the McDonald's drive-thru on Broad and Diamond, leaned back in the driver's seat smoking a big fat blunt. The sound system was bumping Nas' new album, *It Was Written,* and the bass was so strong that it felt like somebody was kicking my back.

I never brag, how real I keep it. 'Cause it's the best secret. I rock a vest, prestigious. Cuban link, flooded Jesus. In the Lex watching Kathy Lee and Regis. My actions are one with the season. A Tec squeezing, executioner. Winter time, I rock a fur. Mega popular...

The parking lot was packed with a bunch of young niggas, who were more than likely looking for a late-night vic. A few of them were nodding their heads to the music, and a few others were pointing at Uzi's deep-dished, three-star rims. I ice-grilled every last one of them niggas, daring them to try something. I had Jesus clutched in my right hand, ready to clap. The first nigga that moved was catching it.

Still watching them niggas, I turned down the music and cruised up to the intercom box.

"Welcome to McDonald's, how can I help you?" a soft, feminine voice eased through the speaker.

"Yeah, though. Lemme get three Happy Meals, two orders of large fries, and two orders of chicken nuggets. Twenty piece," I placed my order, never taking my eyes off the rearview mirror.

"Would you like anything to drink with that, sir?"

"Yizzeah. Two medium Cokes, and three Sprites for the Happy Meals."

"Okay, sir. That'll be $16.95. Please pull around to the window."

Still watching them niggas through the rearview mirror, I pulled around the bend that led to the pick-up window. It fucked me up when I saw the face of the soft, feminine voice. It was this brown skinned chick named Monica, who I knew from the last school I attended. She hopped right on my dick the second she saw me.

"Damn, boy, I ain't seen ya ass in forever." Monica smiled, looking more beautiful and sexier than I remembered. Her real name was Kori, but everybody called her *Monica*, because she looked just like the R&B singer.

"I know, right? I was locked up. I just came home today."

"Well, damn, nigga, I see you ain't waste no time getting that money."

"Ain't shit." I flashed her a smile. I pulled out the thick knot of money that Daphney had given me, and then peeled off the first hundred to pay for my order.

"See what I'm saying?" Monica smiled, as she accepted the small-face Benji. We shot the shit for a few more minutes, then she gave me her phone number.

"And you better call me, AJ," she said as she pushed the bag of food through the window.

"I got'chu."

"I'm not playing wit'chu, AJ, fa' real. You better call me." She handed me the tray of drinks.

"Oh, yeah? And if I don't?"

"If you don't?" She seductively bit down on her bottom lip. "Then I guess you won't be getting none of this bomb-ass pussy."

"Damn, shorty, it's like dat?"

"Humph. You ain't know?" She pursed her lips and folded her arms across her chest. "This that good-good right here."

"Say no more."

I cranked the music back up, and then pulled off with a stiff dick. I needed some pussy bad as shit, and was hoping that Erica would give me some, even though I knew she was still mad at me. But just in case she didn't, I spent the next few minutes memorizing Monica's phone number. And if Monica was all talk and no action,

I was shooting out Southwest to kick it with Kia. Either way, I needed to get that two-year monkey off my nuts.

★★★★★

It was a quarter past ten when I pulled up in front of my moms' new house on Franklin Street, between Susquehanna and Diamond. I already knew the address from the many letters that I sent my brothers during the last three months of my bit, so the house wasn't hard to find.

It was an old, three-story row house that was owned by the city, but funded through Section 8. When the city shut down the towers, the residents were displaced all throughout the city, some were even housed as far away as Montgomery County. But luckily for me, my moms got a spot just a stone's throw away from our projects.

I grabbed the food and drinks from the passenger's seat, and then climbed out the car and locked the doors. I headed up the steps that led to my moms front porch, then I knocked on the door.

Knock! Knock! Knock!

As I stood there waiting for somebody to open the door, I looked back over my shoulder and inventoried the block. It was dirtier than a mah'fucka on Franklin Street, but still not as dirty as the projects. I looked down the street and saw a bunch of niggas standing on the corner in front of a Chinese store. They appeared to be out there hustling. I already knew a few niggas who lived around there, so I was straight when it came to the typical new kid on the block shit. And if I wasn't, then one phone call would turn Diamond Street into another Richard Allen. Them niggas didn't want that smoke.

Knock! Knock! Knock!

I knocked on the door some more, wondering why nobody opened it from the first few times that I knocked. I listened closely, and could hear a dog barking from the other side. The barking grew louder, then it simmered to a whimper, eventually becoming a mixture of both. I could also hear the grinding sound of a dog scratching his claws against the door. I knew exactly who it was, so I cracked a smile. It was Lucifer, my all white, red-nosed pit bull. I knew it was him, because he always did the same exact shit when we lived back in the towers. I would run the streets for days at a time, and when I finally came home, Lucifer's crazy ass would be standing at the front door waiting for me. He'd be barking and whining, scratching and going crazy like he hadn't seen me in years. This time, he was right.

The door opened, and my moms was standing on the other side. Lucifer darted out from behind her, jumped on his hind legs and tried to lick my face. His large head was like a white milk crate with a tongue sticking out. His muscular body was brolic and stout from the boiled chicken and rice he'd been eating since a pup.

"Goddamn, Lucifer, calm down." I moved my head, so he couldn't lick me.

"Hey, Poe?" Moms smiled, calling me the nickname she gave me as a child. She pushed Lucifer out the way, then she stepped forward and gave me a hug. I wanted to ask her why she didn't attend my welcome home party, or at least send my brothers, but doing so would have only been a waste of time.

My moms was funny like that. I knew she loved me, she just had a weird way of showing it. She never wrote a letter or came for visitation my entire bit. She never even sent me any pictures. The only contact I had with brothers the entire two years I was down, were the letters and pictures that Erica sent me.

"Well, come on inside," Moms said as she gestured for me to come in the house. "Erica's here."

I looked in the dining room and saw Erica emerging from the kitchen, smoking a cigarette. I could tell from the look on her face that she was still mad at me for the drama I caused at the party. She walked over and pecked me on the lips, and then sat down on my moms' sofa.

"So, where my brothers at?" I looked at Moms, then I held up the bag of food and the carton of soft drinks. "I brought 'em some Mickey D's."

Moms looked at the food and scoffed.

"Them lil' bastards is downstairs in the basement, on punishment *as* usual."

My moms was a mah'fucka, always in the middle of some ghettofied drama. I'd always known her to be a go-getta, even though she started smoking crack about six years earlier, right around the time my pops went to prison. I guess him going to jail for Life was too much for her to handle, and smoking crack was the only thing that helped her cope. I never judged her for getting high, nor did I ever try to convince her to stop. It was a fucked up position to take, being as though she was my moms and shit. But dissatisfaction brings about change. So, I figured if she wanted better, she would do better. The choice was hers. My only gripe was that her crack addiction affected my three little brothers.

Jahlil, Jabril, and Jacobi, my three little brothers, were six-year-old triplets, all born addicted to crack. Their pops was an old head smokah bul named Easy, who the streets say used to be a boss. Yeah right. The Easy I knew was a fucking bum. He'd been dealing with my moms, on and off, for the past seven years, even though she claimed that my brothers weren't his sons. She swore up and down that my pops got her pregnant before he went to the bing, but that was bullshit. All three of my brothers looked just like Easy. The only notable difference between them and Easy, were their natural born eyes. Easy's eyes were a hazel, light-brown, and my brothers' eyes were an icy blue. I never understood how two black parents could have children with blue eyes, but all three of my brothers had them. I guess it had something to do with all the crack Moms was smoking during her pregnancy.

"So, what they on punishment for?" I asked Moms, as I stepped past her and looked around the living room, seeing that her shit was still on point despite her addiction. Her entire living room had a black and gold, Egyptian theme. Her coffee table and lamp stands were black pyramids, topped off with gold-lined glass squares; her entertainment system was all black, except for the gold trimmings; and her sofa and love seat were two different shades of black leather and suede. Even the picture frames that hung on the walls were black and gold. That was one thing about my moms that she never lost: her sense of appearance. She smoked crack like a chimney, but based on the way she dressed and how she kept her house clean, a person on the outside looking in, would have never known. Especially since she was a master booster, capable of stealing the socks off a nigga's feet while he was still wearing them.

"So, what'chu got 'em on punishment for?" I asked again when she hesitated to answer. I saw how timid she was, and began thinking the worst. "Damn, Ma, it was *that* bad? Fuck them niggas do?"

Moms looked at me, then she looked at Erica.

"Baby, can you excuse us for a minute?"

"Umm-hmm." Erica nodded her head. "I'll just go upstairs to AJ's room." She grabbed her food from the McDonald's bag and gave me a look that said, *"We seriously need to talk."*

I watched Erica's phat ass jiggle up the stairs, then I looked back at Moms. She sat down on the edge of her sofa, then she leaned forward and grabbed her pack of Newport's from the coffee table. She pulled one cigarette from the pack, and then sat the pack back down.

"Sum'n ain't right wit' them brothers of yours," she said as she placed the cigarette between her fingers. "The shit they be doing ain't normal."

"The shit they be doing, like what?"

She leaned forward to grab her matches from the table, then she struck one and lit the tip of her cigarette.

"That damn Jahlil is the ring-leader. Jabril and Jacobi do whatever he say."

"Come on, Ma, you're talking in circles right now. Just tell me what they did."

She sucked in a drag from her Newport and inhaled deeply. Speaking through a cloud of smoke, she said, "Miss Johnson, the old lady who lives across the street, she came over here to talk to me this morning."

"She came over here to talk about what?" I sat down the food and beverages.

"Them bad-ass kids." She sucked in another drag from her Newport. "She said she went outside this morning to feed the alley cats, and them sadistic muthafuckas was in the goddamned alley torturing the damned things."

"*Torturing the alley cats?*" I gave her an incredulous look.

"Umm-hmm." She exhaled the smoke. "And this was first thing in the damned morning. I'm thinking they lil' asses is down here watching cartoons and shit, but *noooooooooo*. The lil' bastards done snuck out the house and went across the goddamned street."

"A'ight. But how you know the bitch ain't lying?" I defended my brothers. "Anybody can say anything. That doesn't make it the truth. For all I know, my brothers ain't did shit."

"Ahn-ahn, Poe, don't even try it." She waved me off. "That sweet, old lady wasn't lying. She had even had some of the dead cats wit' her when she came over here. They wasn't nothing but some itty bitty, little kittens. She said she couldn't tell the boys apart, because they look just alike. But one of 'em had a pillowcase wit' a bunch of kittens trapped inside. He was banging the damned pillowcase against the wall until it turned red from all the blood that was soaked inside of it. And the other two, wit' they *big bad assess*, they done set the old lady's trashcan on fire, and was throwing the rest of the kittens inside the muthafucka. She said the goddamned kittens was squealing and crying and shit, scratching and clawing, try'na jump out the fire. But one of the boys had a stick he was hitting 'em wit', so they couldn't escape. About five of 'em got burned alive, and six more got bashed to death inside the pillowcase. The goddamned lady was crying and shit when she told me. You see, that's how they start." She took another drag from her Newport and inhaled deeply.

"That's how who starts?"

"Them goddamned serial killers." She exhaled the smoke. "They start off torturing animals, then they graduate to killing people. I'm telling you, Poe, them lil' brothers of yours ain't right. They're crazy, and that damn Jahlil is the main one."

"Where's the basement?" I asked her, then I looked around, not knowing where to go. I was a project nigga, born and raised, so the concept of having a basement was foreign to me. Not to mention, it was my first time being there.

"It's back there in the kitchen. As soon as you step inside, it's the only door on your left."

I took off in that direction, with Lucifer trailing right behind me.

"And you better go down there and knock some bones out they asses. 'Cause I'm telling you now, Poe, if they keep it the fuck up, I'm giving they asses to the state," she called out behind me. "I refuse to be afraid in my own damned house, looking over *my* muthafuckin' shoulder. Them damned kids is demonic."

I looked back and scowled at her, but continued walking. If she was right about my brothers having mental health issues, then clearly her crack-smoking ass was the one responsible. My brothers never asked to be born, and they damn sure never asked to be crack babies.

Stupid-ass bitch.

CHAPTER SEVEN

The first thing I noticed when I opened the basement door, was how dark it was inside. It was so dark, that I could barely see the top stair in front of me. I moved my hand along the wall feeling for a light switch, and when I finally found it, the shit didn't work. "Jahlil? Jabril? Jacobi?" I called my brothers' names, as I descended the stairs. There was no direct reply, but I could hear them whispering.

"*Dizzamn, it's like a dungeon down here,*" I mumbled under my breath when I reached the bottom of the stairs. The windows were boarded, and the only sliver of light was a blinking lightbulb that dangled from the ceiling. The gray, stone walls were molded and damp, and the rank odor of wet dog penetrated my nostrils.

I looked in the corner of the basement where Lucifer had run to, and I spotted my three little brothers. My heartbeat seized when I saw the condition that Moms had left them in. They were each standing side-by-side, facing the wall, and the only clothes they had on were boxers and socks. Their hands were strapped behind their backs, bound together with shoe laces, and black scarves were tied around their heads as a blindfold. I could easily tell which brother was which, even though they were facing the wall. Jahlil, the toughest of the three, was standing on the right with his chest out and his chin up like a G. The one in the middle was Jabril. He was just as hard as Jahlil, but he wasn't as strong. I knew it was him, because he stood there in total silence with his forehead pressed against the wall. Jacobi, the weakest of the three, was standing on the left. He was the only crying, so that's how I knew it was him.

"AJ, that's you?" Jahlil spoke without fear.

"That ain't AJ," Jabril said, then he nudged Jahlil with his elbow. "That's Mr. Easy. Mommy prob'bly sent him down here to feed us."

"I miss AJ," Jacobi whined. "I hope he take us away from here when he come home. I hate it here."

"Jacobi, stop crying like a punk," Jahlil commanded.

"Leave him alone, Jahlil. You know he's scared of the dark," Jabril defended our brother like I taught him.

"Yeah, Jahlil, leave me alone," Jacobi sniffled, but was still crying. "Before I tell Mr. Easy on you."

Damn, I thought to myself, as I shook my head and held back my tears. I could tell from the way they were talking they were accustomed to being in this condition. It was then, that I understood what my moms meant when she said they were always on punishment. The crazy bitch had been leaving them tied up in the basement. She used to do the same shit to me when I was younger; only instead of a basement, she would tie me up and locked me in the closet for hours on end.

"AJ, tell 'em that's you," Jahlil spoke assuredly.

I smiled at my little brother's confidence and strength. He was only six, but I realized then, that years later he'd be a force to reckon with on the streets.

"Front and center!" I drilled my little brothers, military style, which was something I'd been doing ever since they were old enough to walk.

On a dime, their three little bodies spun around with their chests puffed out. Jahlil and Jabril stood stoic and quiet, but Jacobi had a big goofy smile on his face.

"Jahlil, who are you?" I continued in a tone that was all business, no nonsense.

"I'm powerful," Jahlil spoke with conviction.

"Jabril, who are you?"

"I'm powerful," he replied with the same energy as Jahlil.

"Jacobi, who are you?"

"I'm powerful," he answered quick, still smiling from ear-to-ear.

"Jahlil, *what* are you?"

"I'm powerful."

"Jabril, what are you?"

"I'm powerful."

"Jacobi, what are you?"

"I'm powerful."

"And together, what are we?"

"*Powerful!*" we all replied in unison, then I scooped them in my arms, squeezing them tight until they each tried to break free.

"Damn, I missed y'all lil' niggas."

I kissed each one of their foreheads, then I sat them down and removed their blindfolds and restraints. Had it not been for my pops and the way he taught me to always respect my moms, I would have tied the bitch up and left her stupid-ass in the basement.

"Dang, AJ, you look like Superman!" Jacobi smiled, reaching his hand out to feel my biceps. I leaned forward and flexed for him.

"Look y'all! These big ol' muscles feel like rocks!"

"Yo, how long y'all been down here?" I asked them.

"I 'on't know," they replied in unison, shrugging their shoulders at the same time and in the same exact manner.

"Mommy be putting us down here all the time, ever since we moved away from the old house," Jahlil answered for all of them.

"Oh, yeah?" My jaw muscles pulsated.

"Umm-hmm." Jacobi nodded his head. "She be making us come down here whenever she gets mad. But Mr. Easy, he 'on't like it when we come down here. He be making us go back upstairs. I like Mr. Easy."

"So, what's this I'm hearing about y'all killing some cats across the street? What's that about?"

Jabril and Jacobi looked at Jahlil, indirectly telling me it was all his idea. I looked at Jahlil.

"So, Jah, what happened?"

"Man, they the ones that started it," Jahlil replied, confusing the fuck out of me.

"They, who? Who started what?"

"Them stupid ol' cats," Jabril spoke on our brother's behalf. "Mr. Easy bought us some hoagies when he came over here yesterday. We was sitting outside on the steps eating our hoagies, and them stupid cats stole 'em."

"Yup, AJ, that's what they do," Jacobi interjected. "My hoagie was the one they took. It's this big fat mommy cat that lives over there. It was her the one that took it. She ran up, jumped up on me, stole my hoagie, and then took off running across the street. She had my hoagie right inside of her big ol' mouth. Right, Jahlil? Right?" I looked at Jahlil.

"Yeah, that's what happened." Jahlil nodded his head. "So early this morning we snuck across the street, so we could kill the mommy cat."

"But the mommy cat wasn't there," Jabril chimed in, becoming more excited by the second. It seemed as though he enjoyed the thrill of a nice hunt.

"So, that's when we killed the baby cats," Jacobi stated, then he looked at Jahlil. "Right, Jahlil? Right?"

"And that's what happened," Jahlil finished the story, showing no signs of remorse.

I understood exactly where they were coming from, even though killing a bunch of kittens was a bit extreme. I looked at all three of them, and they looked back at me, waiting for my approval. Because after all, I was the one who taught them to always stick together, and that when one of us had beef, we all had beef.

"A'ight, man, I get where y'all coming from, but y'all can't be doing shit like that no more. Especially, if you know you might get caught. Y'all got that?"

"Umm-hmm," they replied in unison, nodding their heads at the same time and in the same exact manner. "Now, how much money y'all got?"

They looked at me and laughed.

"So, I guess y'all ain't got no money, huh?"

"Nope." Jacobi smiled, then he stuck his hand out. "You gon' give us some? Mr. Easy be giving us money sometimes. Right, Jahlil? Right?"

Jahlil looked at me, and shook his head.

I fell out laughing.

After giving my brothers $100 apiece, I told them to get dressed, then we sat down and ate our McDonald's food together. I also had a stern talk with my moms. I told her that if she couldn't get her shit together and be the mother that my brothers needed, I would take them away and raise them myself. It wasn't something that I planned on doing prior to my release, but I loved my brothers. I would have gladly given my life for them, so there was no way I could stand by and allow my moms to fuck up their mental more than she already had. So, if push came to shove, my little niggas were coming with me.

CHAPTER EIGHT

I headed up the second flight of stairs, following the music that I knew had to be coming from my bedroom. It was weird as fuck living in a three-story house, but it was also a nice change of pace. Especially for a nigga who had just spent the past twenty-four months living inside of a jail cell. The entire house had a total of five bedrooms—three on the second floor, and two on the third floor. I reached the top of the stairs where the first bedroom was located, and continued walking down the hallway. The smooth sounds of 702's new hit single, *Get It Together,* was coming from the second bedroom, so that's where I went.

The loud aroma of Hydro weed filled the hallway, so I knew Erica was in there getting her chief on. I saw that she left the door cracked, so I stopped at the threshold and peeked inside.

The entire room was decorated in blue, red and white Polo Sport everything. Polo was my shit, so Erica splurged on my room in a manner that she knew I'd appreciate. There were Polo Sport curtains, Polo Sport bed sheets and pillowcases, and a Polo Sport rug. She even hooked me up with an oversized Polo Sport teddy bear. He was seated on the Polo Sport blow-up chair in the far-right corner of the room. The shit was dope. She even bought me a big boy, 62" television. It was placed against the wall adjacent to the bed. A brand-new Sony stereo system was placed on top of the television, and its four-foot-tall speakers were positioned on both sides. My babygirl did her thing.

After looking around the room and nodding my approval, I looked back at Erica. My baby was looking good as shit, all natural with no makeup. The only thing she was wearing was a white T-shirt and a silk headscarf. She was seated on the bed, Indian style, smoking a blunt and singing with her eyes closed.

"I don't really wanna staaaay. I don't really wanna goooo. But I really need to know, can we get it togetherrrr? Get it togetherrrr?"

As I stood there listening to Erica sing, it was clear to me why she chose that particular song.

Growing up in the projects was hard, and some of the main things that helped us survive were the love, support, care and concern that we always had for one another.

Both of our fathers had gone to prison for Life. My pops' situation hurt the fuck out of me, but Erica's situation hurt even worse. Her father received a Life sentence for killing the man who raped and murdered her mother. So, the pain between us ran deep.

We'd been going together since the age of twelve, but had known one another our entire lives. And during that time, Erica had seen me go from bad to worse when it came to the streets. There were many conversations between us during the course of my bit, where Erica made it known that she wasn't feeling my thugged-out lifestyle. She even went as far as to say that I was killing her softly, and that her biggest fear was that I'd lose my life to the streets, whether it be a jail cell or a coffin.

She told me that her patience in our relationship was wearing thin, and that she didn't know how much longer she could hold on to someone who was pushing her away. My last bit was the longest time I had been away from her, but it wasn't my first. She wanted me to make a promise that I'd never go back, and if I did go back, then she was free to walk away, leaving behind no hard feelings or regrets.

I loved shorty to death, but I couldn't make her that promise. My mind was already made. I would get rich on the streets, or die trying.

Erica must have felt my energy. She stopped singing, opened her eyes and then looked straight at me. She sat the blunt she was smoking into the ashtray on the nightstand, and then grabbed the remote control to the stereo. She turned the music down, but I told her to turn it back up. She met me halfway. She turned the music back up, and then switched the song to *I Can Love You* by Mary J. Blige.

I can love yoooou. I can love yoooou. I can love you beeeetter thaaaan she caaaan. I can love yoooou. I can love yoooou. I can love you beeeetter thaaaan she caaaan.

At the time, I assumed Erica was indirectly calling me out for creeping with Kia. But in hindsight, the *her* she was actually referring to was my first love—the streets.

I looked Erica straight in the eyes and slowly removed my T-shirt, revealing my muscular chest and six pack abs. Erica's eyes left mines, then meticulously studied each and every chisel on my chest and torso. I moved over to the bed, kissed Erica's forehead, and then grabbed the remote control from her hand. I switched the stereo function from *CD* to *RADIO*, and turned on Power 99's late-night show, *The Quiet Storm*. As usual, Golden Girl, the show's host, was playing nothing but the hottest R&B. The smooth sounds of H-Town's, *Emotions*, came easing through the speakers.

Emotions make you cry sometimes. Babaaaayyyy. Emotions make sad sometimes. Sugar, sugar darling. Emotions make you glad sometimes. So glad, babaaaayyyy. But most of aaaallll, maaaake yoooou faaaallll in loooove.

Saying nothing at all, but still locking eyes with my baby, I reached down and grabbed her hips, and then pulled her towards the edge of the bed. She traced my abs with the tip of her nose, and then softly placed kisses on each one. Returning her gaze to mines, she slowly untied the drawstring on the Moschino sweat shorts that I borrowed from Uzi. She pulled down the sweat shorts and my big dick shot up like a flagpole, harder than steel.

Erica was more than impressed. In the two years I was away, my dick grew another three inches, adding to the six I was already packing. Erica rubbed her face up, down, and all around my shaft, never breaking eye contact with me. She licked my helmet, kissed the tip, and then slowly made it disappear inside of her mouth. I could feel the vibrations of her hungered moans, as she sucked my dick nice and slow.

"Ummmmm!" Erica moaned some more, as she pulled me out of her mouth. We were still locking eyes when she spat on my dick and jerked me with both hands. It felt so good, that I leaned my head back and stared up at the ceiling.

"Ahn-ahn." Erica squeezed me. "Look at me. I want you to pay attention and watch. I want you to see what's at stake. I'm dead-ass serious, boo. You gotta make a choice. It's either her or me."

Before I had a chance to respond, she stuffed me back inside of her mouth and twirled her tongue around my pulsating bulb. She pleased me with her tongue and tonsils for the next few minutes, then she scooted back on the bed. She spread her legs wide open for me, showing me the softest place on earth. Her juicy, fat pussy was completely shaved, reminding me of a strawberry that had been sliced down the middle. Her clitoris was thick and erect, and her pussy lips were glistening wet.

The beast inside of me began to emerge. My nostrils flared and my jaw muscles pulsated. My balls tingled and my big dick throbbed. I'd been waiting on this moment for two whole years. So, if shorty didn't know how much I missed her, she was damn sure about to find out.

Erica pulled off her T-shirt, exposing her voluptuous titties. She stuck her index and middle fingers inside of her mouth and began sucking them the same way she had just finished sucking me. After making her fingers nice and wet, she pulled them from her mouth and then used them to spread her pussy lips open. Her center was juicy and pink. She massaged her clit, and then buried her fingers deep inside of her pinkness.

"Uuuugggggghhhhhnnnnnnn!" Erica cried out, as she arched her back and continued finger-fucking herself. Her fingers became more and more creamy with each and every dip. "You wanna taste me, boo? You wanna see how good I taste?" She pulled her fingers from her pussy, showing me how creamy they were. She closed her eyes and placed her fingers back inside of her mouth, mesmerized by her own savory taste.

"*Ummmmm!*"

It was a wrap after that. I simply couldn't take it anymore. Growling like a hungry pit bull locked inside of a cage, I grabbed Erica's legs and pulled her back towards me. I lifted her body in one swift motion and brought her pussy straight to my mouth.

"Uuugggnnn! Goddamn, daddy, shit! Lick that pussy, boo! Lick that shit! Eeewwwwww!"

My word, that pussy tasted so good. It was warm and sweet, and had a pure fragrance like distilled water. Her inner thighs rested against my biceps, as I carried her around the room. I was sopping that box like my life depended on it. I flicked my tongue against her clit, then I dipped it back inside of her hole, pulling it back out so I could get right back to the clit. I wrapped my lips around it, sucked on it softly and caressed it with the tip of my tongue.

"Oh, shit. Oh, shit. Oh, shit," Erica panted, raking her fingernails across the back of my shoulders. "Yeah, daddy, like that. Eat this pussy. Just like that. Eat this—*ooooooooooohhhhhhhhhhh!*" Her body began to tremble. "*Ummmmmmmmm, shit! Uuuuggggghhhhhhnnnnnn!*"

Maneuvering Erica's body with ease, I moved her pussy away from my mouth and then guided it down on my pulsating thickness. That pussy felt like heaven when it swallowed me whole. I hit the bottom, and Erica damn near jumped out of my arms.

"Fuck is you going?" I growled at her. "Ya ass gon' take this dick."

Clap! Clap! Clap! Clap! Clap!

"Oh, my fuckin' God!" Erica yelped. She was rolling her hips and doing her best to adjust to my size. "Shit! Shit! Shit! Fuck! Fuck! Fuck! Uuuuggggghhhhhnnnnnnn, *shit!* God—damn you working this pussy! *Fuck!*" *Clap! Clap! Clap! Clap! Clap!*

I was knocking the lining out that mah'fucka, lifting Erica's body and slamming it back down on nothing but dick. They could have locked me up and charged me with First Degree Murder, the way I was killing that pussy. I would have copped out and pled guilty.

Clap! Clap! Clap! Clap! Clap!

"A—J! God—damn! *Uuuuggggghhhhhnnnnnnn!*" Erica screamed, as her entire body seized. She wrapped her arms around the back of my neck, and held on for dear life. Her legs began to tremble and shake, and the intense vibrations sent shockwaves through my dick and balls.

"Hummmm," I growled some more, as my ab muscles tightened. My legs began to shake and my teeth began to chatter. I fought like hell to keep strong, but it was no use. The pussy was way too good. So, before I knew it, I was gripping Erica's body tightly and filling her pussy with my juicy, warm seeds. My knees buckled and we toppled over on the bed.

"Goddamned, babe," I said in between breaths. "I remember the pussy being good and all dat. But *goddamn!*" I looked at her and shook my head. "You gon' fuck around and have a nigga sprung out this mah'fucka. Shit."

Erica giggled, as she fought to catch her breath. That big dick action was a mah'fucka, had shorty looking like she'd seen a ghost. After taking a few more breaths, she fanned herself down.

"Ahn-ahn! Boo, look at him." Erica said as she lifted her head and pointed across the room.

I looked back to see what she was pointing at, and laid eyes on Lucifer's freaky ass. He was hunched over the Polo Sport teddy bear, humping away. I forgot to shut the door when I came in the room, so Lucifer must have crept in while Erica and me were doing our thing.

"Lucifer!" I shouted his name. "Shamooyah!" I gave him the command word to stop, but he didn't. He just looked back at me and continued humping with his tongue hanging out. I was still wearing my Nikes, so I pulled one off and threw it at him, clonking him on his big-ass head.

Uuuurrrrrrrrrrrrnnnnnnnn!

Lucifer yelped, then he jumped off the bear and ran towards the door. His pink rocket drug across the rug, leaving behind a gray trail of doggy cum.

Erica and me cracked up laughing.

Lil' nasty bastard!

An Hour Later

Erica and me were lying in bed, smoking a blunt from the stash of Hydro that Daphney had left in my closet. It was a total of ten pounds, and each one was shrink wrapped with the air extracted. According to Erica, who apparently had no issues with me selling bud, Hydro was more expensive than regular smoke. A gram of regular was worth $5, but a gram of Hydro was worth $20. I did the math in my head, so if I sold each pound by the gram, I would bring back $89,600. But that was before I paid my runners. And besides that, I still needed a trap spot to move it. I was scheduled to meet my papi homeboy, Raphael, in the next few days to see about this block he had for me out Kensington. But most important, I needed to make sure that everything was still good with Pops. Because once he hit me off with the work he promised, the rest was history.

"So, dig, right, me and Daph are going up the jail tomorrow to visit Pops. Are you coming wit' us to go see yours?"

"I haven't decided yet. I mean, I want to, you know what I'm saying? I just hate leaving him there. I wish that I could stick him in my pocket and walk right out the door wit' him. So, I 'on't know, boo. It's mad stressful going up there. I hate seeing my daddy all stressed out and depressed like that. It's the worst feeling ever."

I thought about what Erica said, but I couldn't relate. My pops took his time like a G. I couldn't think of one time where he complained about being there.

"As far as I'm concerned, I'm winning right now," Pops said to me years earlier when I asked him how it felt to be locked down for Life. *"I'd rather be tried by twelve than carried by six. My enemies are dead, but I'm still breathing. So, it's all about the get-back, Trap. As long as I'm still alive, I still have my health, and my morals are still intact, I'll make it home eventually. And when I do, I'ma tear the city a new asshole. You mark my words."*

I hit the blunt and inhaled deeply, then I passed it to Erica.

"So, lemme ask you sum'n." I exhaled the smoke. "When you said that about ya pops, how you feel a certain way at the end of every visit. Have you ever felt that way when you came to visit me?"

"Nah, not really. I knew ya situation was temporary, so it was only a matter of time before you came home. It's different wit' Daddy. Them people said he's *never* coming home. He's gonna die in there."

"Lemme ask you sum'n else. Have you ever been downstairs in the basement?"

"Ahn-ahn." She shook her head *no*. "Why?"

"Nah, I was just asking. My moms be sending my brothers down there on some punishment shit. I just wanted to know if you had ever been down there. That's all."

"Nah, boo, I ain't never been down there." She hit the blunt super hard, and then passed it back to me. "Lemme ask you one more question."

"Go 'head." She exhaled a cloud of smoke.

"Well, actually two more questions." I sat up and rested my back against the headboard. "Would you die for me?"

"I mean, like, yeah. If I had to save your life or sum'n like that. So, yeah," she nodded her head, "I would die for you. I love you."

I looked her dead in the eyes, searching for any signs of disloy-alty.

"Would you kill for me?"

"Would I kill for you? Boy, you must be crazy asking me sum'n like that. I'm not a killer. I wouldn't take a life for anybody. If anything, I would *make* a life for you, give you some babies. But *killing* somebody? That's a bit much, don't you think?"

I didn't reply. I just stubbed the blunt in the ashtray, then rolled over and went to sleep.

CHAPTER NINE

The Following Morning

Beep! Beep! Beep!

I looked out of my bedroom window and saw Mook's Lexus parked outside. The sound system was bumping *Ain't No Nigga* by Jay-Z and Foxy Brown, and I could see Daphney through the sunroof window. She was seated behind the steering wheel, nodding her head to the music and checking her reflection in the sun visor's mirror.

Seeing that she was driving Mook's whip made my blood boil. I was so hot that my nostrils began to flare, and my left eye twitched. I had trained myself to hate that nigga, so that way I wouldn't hesitate when it was time to kill him. Because truth be told, Mook was a solid nigga. He was loyal to my pops and had been there for me whenever I needed him.

I remember when he stepped to me a few years earlier when he heard that I was hustling. He practically begged me to leave the streets alone and go back to school. He promised that if I graduated, he would pay my full college tuition, and if I didn't want to go to college and preferred to run the streets, he vowed that he'd make me his Number Two.

Mook's love for me was real, and I could see it in his eyes. But what he failed to consider was that my street dreams were bigger than him, so being his second-in-command was simply out the question. Fuck being his top lieutenant, my aspirations were to he his *boss* and make him my top lieutenant. But this was something that I knew Mook would never accept. So, therefore, my only option was to knock him out of position, whether it be persuasion or force.

The last year of my bit, my hatred for Mook became firmly rooted. And now that I was home and suspected he was fucking my sister, that shit was just more fuel to the fire. My pops trusted Mook to hold down his family in his absence, not fuck his daughter. So, yeah, I was coming for that nigga's crown without a doubt.

I was already showered and dressed, so I left my bedroom and headed down the stairs. When I stepped down into the living room, Jahlil, Jabril, and Jacobi were seated on the floor eating cereal and watching cartoons. The old head, Easy, was seated on the sofa reading a *Final Call Newspaper*. We looked at one another and nodded our heads, but no words were exchanged. It wasn't because we disliked one another, it was just the way we did things. I gave Easy his space, and he gave me mines. Whatever he and my moms had going on, that shit was between them. I already had a pops, so that steppop shit was out the fucking window.

"AJ, where you going?" Jacobi spoke first, looking at me like he wanted to tag along. The bond he and I shared was the tightest among our brothers. Jacobi would follow me to hell and back.

"I'll be back, lil' soldier. I gotta go see about sum'n."

"You promise, you coming back?"

"Yeah, bro, I promise." I reached down and rubbed Jacobi's head, then I reached over and did the same to Jahlil and Jabril. "And don't be going across the street no more. Y'all hear me?"

"Umm-hmm," they replied in unison, nodding their heads at the same time and in the same exact manner.

I looked into the dining room where my moms and Erica were seated at the table. They were eating scrambled eggs and turkey bacon, and talking about a bunch of nothing. Erica looked at me and pointed at the plate of food beside her.

"Boo, you hungry? I made us some breakfast."

I was still feeling some type of way about the shit she said the night before. So instead of replying, I just stared at her and gritted my teeth. She was always telling me how much she loved me. But how could she love me, and not be willing to kill for me? So basically, if a nigga had a gun to my head ready to smoke me, she would rather that he blow my brains out than bust a hamma to get him up off me? What type of fake-ass, fuck shit was that? I needed me a ride or die, love without a limit, Mary J. Blige type of bitch. A down-ass shorty who would ride for me the same way I was down to ride for her. Anything less than that, was a waste of time.

Erica had already told me that she wasn't riding with us to go see her pops. That shit was fine by me. I was pissed off to the point that I didn't want her fake-ass around me. And besides that, I needed some time alone with Daphney. I needed to find out exactly what her and Mook had going on between them.

"Poe, you heard what Erica said to you?" Moms asked me, talking with a mouthful of food. "She said that she made some breakfast for you."

"Nah, I'm good." I finally spoke to Erica. "I'ma get sum'n to eat on the way there."

"Alright," she softly replied. She got up from the table, came over and gave me a kiss. "Have a good visit wit'cha dad, and tell him that I said hi."

"Yup." I nodded my head, then I turned around and headed towards the door.

Stepping outside on the front porch, I adjusted Jesus on the small of my back. Daphney must have peeped the gesture, because she rolled down the passenger's side window and told me that I couldn't bring him. "Nah, Twin, you can't take that. The prison guards be doing random searches, and sometimes they search the cars."

The griminess in me had me thinking some crazy shit about my own damn sister, wondering if she was lining me up for Mook. I hesitated, but quickly dismissed the thought.

Nah, Twin wouldn't do me like that.

"A'ight," I slowly replied, and then strolled over to Uzi's Honda Accord wagon. I deactivated the alarm, pulled open the driver's side door and then stashed Jesus under the seat. No sooner than I closed the door and locked it, the old lady, Miss Johnson, from across the street stuck her snitching-ass head out the screen door. I ice-grilled the old bitch and spat on the ground. She mumbled something under her breath and then slipped back inside of her house.

"Yo, turn the music down," I told Daphney, as I climbed down inside of the Lex. I closed the door and looked straight at her.

"I wanted to talk to you as well," Daphney said as she turned the music down and pulled away from the curb. "What's wrong wit'chu? Why did you step to Mook like that? Do you even know everything that he has in motion for you right now? You were outta pocket for that, Twin. Straight up. And then the shit that happened after we left? You better hope don't none of them project muthafuckas tell on you. I heard you shot that boy in his face, and in broad fucking daylight. What the fuck is wrong wit'chu?"

"Man, fuck all dat," I sharply replied, somewhat annoyed because she put me on blast about what happened at the party. Somebody was running they fucking mouth.

"Nah, Twin, this is real shit I'm kicking to you," Daphney continued. "You wasn't even home a whole day and you killed somebody, right in front of the whole fucking projects. This shit ain't no fucking movie. This shit ain't *New Jack City*. This shit is real muthafuckin' life. And the last time I checked, there's no statute of limitations for a fucking murder."

Daphney shut me all the way down with that shit. Not once did I ever think, or even suspect that my actions could one day come back and bite me on the ass. But fuck that. I side stepped the thought and got right back to my issue with her and Mook.

"So, what the fuck you and Mook got going on? You pushing this nigga's car and shit. And then yesterday, you took his side over mines. So, clearly y'all got sum'n going on. I wanna know what the fuck it is."

Completely ignoring me, she leaned back in the seat and whipped the Lex with one hand.

"Yo, I know ya ass ain't just igg me." My eyelids became two dark slits. "Answer my fuckin' question, Twin. What the fuck you got going on wit' this nigga? 'Cause it damn sure ain't no regular friendship. You fuckin' this nigga, ain't you?"

Daphney's jaw muscles pulsated.

"*Twin*?" My energy intensified. "Either tell me what's up, or I'ma tell Pops what's up. See what the fuck he gotta say about this shit."

"*Don't*," Daphney shot back at me. "Nah, Twin, you can't do that. You can't tell Daddy."

"And why the fuck not?" My forehead creased. "This nigga ain't got no business fuckin' the boss's daughter. That's like an un-written rule or some shit. Pops put this nigga in position, he practically handed Mook his whole shit. Not even Big Jabby got situated the way Pops did Mook. So how the *fuck* he gon' cross Pops like that? That's a flat-out violation, Twin. Word."

"Lemme ask you a question," Daphney said, as we stopped at a red light. "You and Erica, would you call that love?"

"Yeah, that's love. Erica's my bitch. She ain't queen status yet, because I still need to groom her. But of course, I love her. That's my bitch."

"And nobody can tell you different, right?"

"Hell nawl, can't nobody tell me different. Shorty's my heart. She done rode out three bits wit' me."

"Well, that's how I feel about Mook. He's my world, Twin. My life."

"Nah, yo. I ain't feeling that shit."

"It's not about whether you feel it or not. It's about how much I love this nigga. He's my world, Twin—my everything. In some ways, it's almost like having Daddy back in my life full time. It's like, everything Mook does reminds me of Daddy. The way he han-dles his business, the way he splurges on me and satisfies my every desire. He even counts his money the same way Daddy did. I just love him, Twin, and I don't wanna stop. Nah, *fuck that*, I couldn't stop if I wanted to. That's how much I love him."

The traffic light turned green, and I turned my head to look out of the window. My feelings were conflicted, so I wasn't sure how to respond. On one hand, I was happy that my sister was happy. But on the other hand, I was steaming inside, jealous as fuck. The way she spoke about Mook and how he reminded her so much of Pops had me pissed off to the max. That nigga's name was Michael Brooks, not Alvin Rines Junior. I was the only son and namesake, the one who should have rightfully inherited Pops legacy and em-pire, *not Mook*. My word, I hated that nigga.

"You gotta promise me, Twin." Daphney looked at me when we stopped at another red light. "Promise that you won't tell Daddy about Mook and me."

I gritted my teeth and continued staring out of the window.

"*Twin?*" Daphney reached over the leather console and gently grabbed my chin. She turned my head to face her. "Promise me."

"A'ight, Twin, I promise," I gave my word that I wouldn't tell Pops she was creeping with Mook. But had she known any better, she would have told me to promise I wouldn't kill that nigga.

The first chance I get, I'm murking his ass, I thought to myself as I leaned back in the seat and continued looking out the window. I needed to recalibrate my thoughts and settle my emotions.

Weak emotions were like blood in the water, and Pops was a great white shark. He could smell that shit a mile away.

CHAPTER TEN

After stopping at IHOP to get something to eat, Daphney and me finally arrived at the Graterford state prison. The old prison was dark and gloomy like a medieval castle, surrounded by a forty-foot-high stone wall. A large surveillance tower peaked over the wall, and I could see the two-armed guards who were posted inside. The entire scene reminded me of the movie, *Shawshank Redemption.*

We climbed out the Lex and headed across the parking lot, entering the prison through the front lobby's door. It was a Saturday morning, so the lobby was packed to capacity, standing room only. There were baby mamas, bad-ass kids, old ladies and men, all packed together in one small area. We stood in line for the next twenty minutes, and then stepped to the front desk to register our visit.

"We're here to see Alvin Rines," I told the fat, white man who was working the officer's station. He checked our identification cards, and then flipped through his blotter.

"*Alvin Rines. Alvin Rines,*" he mumbled under his breath, as he searched for Pop's visitor's list. He verified that Daphney and me were listed, then he told us to go through double doors that led to the visiting house.

When we walked through the double doors, we were patted down by two female officers. I recognized one of them from my last visit before I went to the bing. Shorty batted her eyes and smiled at me. "Y'all have a good visit, and tell Alvin I'll be seeing him later," she told us with a sly look on her face. Daphney scoffed at her, but I shook my head and smiled. It was clear to both us that shorty was one of the c/o bitches that Pops was up there fucking. The word on the street was that he made two babies while being on lock. I figured it was only a rumor, but fucking with Pops, one never knew. He was just a boss like that.

We stepped into the crowded visiting room and looked around, searching for Pops. I spotted him in the back row of chairs, right across from the vending machines. His bodyguard, Bruno, was seated two chairs down from him. They were each dressed in cocoa-brown jumpsuits and had fresh haircuts. Pops looked exactly like me—tall, dark and handsome with a muscular physique. Bruno was bigger than both of us put together. He was 6 foot, 5 inches tall, thick and beefy. He had a light-brown complexion with a thin mustache and no beard. Bloody-red teardrops were tatted under both of his eyes. According to the streets, Bruno had a whole fucking graveyard. He was alleged to have committed over thirty murders, all at my pops' behest. The YBM was vicious like a mah'fucka.

Pops and Bruno were talking to one another, and didn't see Daphney and me until we reached the back row. Pops looked at me and flexed his jaw muscles. He then stood to his feet and embraced Daphney with a warm, fatherly hug.

"Hey, Daddy!" Daphney smiled with the side of her face pressed against Pops' muscular chest. "Look at what the cat drug in." She pointed at me, as Pops released his hold on her.

"What's up, Pops?" I shook his hand and gave him a hug. I shook Bruno's hand and then looked back at Pops, who had yet to say a word to me. He was a master at disguising his feelings, so it was hard to tell whether or not he was mad at me.

Daphney peeped the tension, and asked Pops if he wanted something from the vending machines.

"Yeah, babygirl. Grab me two chicken sandwiches, a bag of Doritos, and a Birch Beer," Pops placed his order, then he looked at Bruno. "You want sum'n?"

"Nah, A, I'm good," Bruno replied in his deep, husky voice. His beady black eyes were scouring the room when he said it.

"Twin, you want sum'n?" Daphney looked at me.

"Nah, Twin, I'm good."

As Daphney walked over to the vending machines, Pops gestured for me to take a seat.

"Listen, Trap, I've never been the type to beat around the bush, especially with the people I love and respect. So I'ma get right to it. That shit you did yesterday, stepping to Mook like that was the wrong move."

"I know, Pop. But—"

"Shut up and listen," he cut me off mid-sentence. "Had you done like I told you, reported to Mook and gave him the chance to bring you up to speed, you wouldn't be in this position."

"And what position is that?"

"You said you wanted to be your own man and stomp with the big dawgs, right?"

"That's a fact."

"So, how do you expect that to happen if you're out there bumping heads with Mook?"

"I mean, I'm saying, though. You're the one pulling the strings, and Mook ain't nothing but a puppet. So, the way I see it, as long as *you* say I'm good, then I'm good. Fuck Mook. It's all about you and how you feel. Right or wrong?"

Pops inhaled deeply and released a long sigh.

"Yes, you're right. But that's only to an extent. I'm *here*. Mook's out there. So, yeah, I call the shots as the owner of the team. But Mook is my general. He's the one in field leading the troops. So however he chooses to handle his business and keep the team afloat, that's solely up to him. For me to undermine my own general from afar, this would lead to nothing less than a mutinous result. I taught you this already."

"You most definitely did. But this is what I'm saying, Pop, *I'm* try'na be the general. *Fuck Mook.* As far as I'm concerned, he's just an obstacle standing in the way of me furthering your legacy. I'm built for this shit, Pop. I'm ready to takeover. The only thing I need you to do is link me up wit' the plug. I can take it from there."

Pops looked at Bruno, and they both started laughing at me.

"See, Trap, that's your problem. That's *always* been your problem. You wanna run before you learn how to walk."

Daphney returned and handed Pops his Birch Beer and Doritos.

"I still need to heat up these sandwiches for you. I'll bring them over as soon as I'm finished," she said to Pops, and then looked at me. Her facial expression said it all. *"Don't forget about the promise you made."*

I nodded my head, assuring Daphney that her secret was safe.

"So, Trap, lemme ask you sum'n," Pops said when Daphney walked away. "I'm a millionaire, twenty times over. I could have easily had you and your mother living in a mansion. But instead, I deliberately chose for you to grow up in Philadelphia's most notorious housing project. Why is that?"

"I 'on't know." I shrugged my shoulders. "I just figured that was the way you wanted it. It wasn't like you left me for dead, or never did shit for me. I had everything I wanted growing up."

"Nah, Trap, you're missing the whole point. It would have been *nothing*—at all—to give you the same life that I gave Daphney. The only reason that I chose for you to grow up in the projects was because of the struggle. I needed you to know the streets firsthand, so that the pulse of the ghetto would become your second nature. I needed you to feel the hardship and pain of growing up in the trap. So that way when it was time for you to take over and get'cha weight up, you would understand the magnitude of everything that's at stake. It's hard for a man to fully appreciate being at the top if he never experienced being at the bottom."

"I mean, I guess I can dig that," I slowly replied, already knowing there was more to Pops' motivation than what he was kicking to me.

"And that brings me to Mook. The reason I told you to come home and get with him from the rip, was because I wanted him to take you under his wing, the same way that I took him under mines. But now, after the shit you pulled, who's to say he's gonna wanna deal with you?"

"But that's my whole thing," I shot back. "Why you can't just give me a situation of my own? Why I gotta go through him? You already taught me everything that I need to know. So, why would I need Mook?"

Again, Pops sucked in a deep breath. He closed his eyes and slowly massaged his temples.

"Goddamnit, boy." He opened his eyes and shook his head. "You're just like my brother, Rayon, more brute than brain. I'ma give it to you like this, the most I can do is talk to him. But I can't make the man do something that he doesn't wanna do. I just sent him on a Cali trip to handle sum'n for me, and when he returns, he's gonna come up here to see me. I'll talk to him then. That's the best I can do for you. And that brings me to another thing. I know how close you were to Lil' Moochie. But the shit that's going on with Big Jabby and them niggas from Bartram Village, that's not your beef. So, you keep your ass from down them projects. You got that?"

"Yeah, Pops, I got'chu."

"Good. Because I need you to stay focused. You gotta keep your mind on the money. Everything else is secondary."

"But how can I focus on the money, when you're not even sure if Mook's gonna deal wit' me?"

"If things don't work out with Mook, just give me some time to explore other options. And that reminds me, when you go back to your mother's house, there's gonna be a gift waiting for you. It's just a small taste of what I have planned for you, so keep that in mind. But I'm telling you, Trap, from here on out, you need to do exactly as I tell you."

"Say no more, Pops. I got'chu."

Daphney returned with Pops sandwiches. She sat down in the empty chair between us, and then handed Pops his food.

"Here, Daddy. I brought you some more Doritos."

"Thanks, babygirl," Pops said as he bit into his first sandwich.

"Hey, yo, Pops, you know some niggas named Rahman and Jihad from Uptown?"

"Umm-hmm." Pops nodded his head. "I know them niggas. Why, what's up?"

"Nah, I'm just asking. I was talking to my man, Uzi, and Rahman and Jihad are his cousins. They were saying they knew you. That's all."

"Yeah, them niggas know me. They know me real well. We used to run together back in the day, back when I first got my start. Ain't that right, Bruno?"

"Yeah, AJ, them niggas is solid," Bruno replied, still watching everything around us that moved. "Whenever mah'fuckas ain't wanna *get down*, Rahman and Jihad was two of the niggas ya pops sent to make them niggas *lay down.* Them two niggas right there, they as rough and tough as they come. I can vouch for that."

Instead of replying, I sat back in my seat and cracked my knuckles one at a time. I heard what Pops said about laying low and staying focused, but I was already formulating my next move. Fuck sitting around waiting on Mook, I was determined to show Pops how serious I was about taking over his empire. I was done playing games. It was time to take matters into my own hands.

CHAPTER ELEVEN

It was a quarter past five when Daphney and me pulled up in front of my moms' crib. Surprisingly, Big Jabby, Dev, and another nigga I knew from the towers named, Kyle, were standing beside a money-green Infinity Q45. The rimmed-out sedan was parked across the street from my moms' crib, and right behind it was a platinum-colored Yukon Denali. The large truck had tinted windows, a chromed-out grill on the front, chrome light-protectors on the back, and was sitting on 22" chrome rims.

Big Jabby and his crew were talking shit and laughing, but the second they saw Mook's Lexus pull up, they each took a step back. Big Jabby squinted his eyes, then he softened his stance when he saw that it was Daphney and me. Dev and Kyle did the same.

"*Look at these clown-ass niggas,*" Daphney mumbled under her breath as she brought the Lexus to a complete stop. "Don't be letting these niggas have you out here on that dumb shit. And by the way," she looked at me and smiled, "gawn and have fun wit'cha new truck. It's a welcome home gift from Daddy."

"Oh, *yeeeaaaaah*?" I cracked a smile and began rubbing my hands together. "So, this is the gift he was telling me about?"

"Umm-hmm." Daphney nodded her head. "But I'm out, Twin. I've got a few runs that I need to make. Speaking of which, did you get those ten pounds that I left in your closet?"

"Yeah, I got 'em, Twin. Good lookin'," I said, then I leaned over the console and kissed her on the cheek. "And don't forget what I told you," Daphney said, as I climbed out the car. "Don't be out here acting all crazy. Especially with these—with these—*bozos.*"

I laughed at her. "Yo, stop drawin'. I'm good, Twin. Believe that."

"I'm serious, Twin," she shot right back. "I love you, and tell your mom and your brothers that I send my love."

"I got'chu."

I closed the door and watched Daphney as she pulled off with the system bumping.

"There he go right there, my mah'fuckin' nigga," Big Jabby said as he walked over and gave me some dap. "You know this is yours, right?" He pointed at the truck with a big-ass smile on his face, being way too friendly. We were both from the towers, and his girl was my girl's sister, but him and me ain't never really kicked it like that. This nigga was acting Joe as shit.

"Yeah, I know. My sister just told me," I said, as he handed me the keys. "What's up wit' y'all niggas?" I spoke to Dev and Kyle.

"Ain't shit, A. We was out here waiting on you," Dev replied, walking over with a blunt in his mouth. He gave me some dap, then Kyle came over and did the same.

"Yo, A, lemme holla at'chu real quick," Big Jabby said, then he gestured for me to walk with him towards his Infinity.

"Yeah, fam, what's up?"

"I appreciate the way you held it down yesterday. That shit was gangsta."

"No doubt." I nodded my head. "You know how the Allen get down."

"Fa' sho." Big Jabby nodded back.

"But'chu know that wasn't Mook and dem who did that, it was them Bartram Village niggas. We've been beefin' wit' them niggas for a lil' while now."

"Yeah, I heard about that. But all that coming through the 'jects try'na ride on niggas, I ain't feeling that shit. And to make matters worse, they killed Black Mooch. Them niggas gotta die for that shit."

"I already know," Big Jabby agreed. "I spoke to the nigga, Mook, and we 'posed to be coming together on this shit. So next week after Black Mooch's funeral, we all gon' get together and have us a lil' pow-wow. We wanna make sure everybody's on the same page."

"But I thought you and Mook was beefin' over the low-rises?"

I figured that I'd test the waters to see if I had room to infiltrate, especially since I noticed the way his demeanor changed when he saw Mook's Lexus pulling up. If shit was so good between them like he said it was, then why the fuck was him and his crew so tense? He exposed his hand, but he didn't even dig it.

"Nah, we ain't beefin', not exactly. You know the towers were my thing, and the low-rises were his. But once the city shut down the towers, that shit threw a monkey wrench in my game. The majority of my flow runs through the 'jects, so I couldn't just walk away from it. There was mad tension between us at first, but we agreed that I can do my thing out of Hutchinson Place. I'm good wit' that, at least for the time being. But dig, though, back to these Bartram Village niggas. I'm try'na strike back. You down?"

"I mean, I ain't got no problem riding, especially on the strength of Black Mooch. But at the same time, I ain't one of these crash dummy niggas." I looked at Dev and Kyle, who were still standing across the street. "Anything I do, there has to be a purpose behind it. Nah mean? I need sum'n to gain."

"Sum'n to gain like what?"

"I need a spot on ya team." I looked him dead in his eyes.

"Oh, fa' sho. I got a shift on the block for you."

"A shift on the block?" I looked at him like he was crazy. "Nah, yo, you buggin'," I said with a chuckle. "I mean a spot like right next to you. I'm try'na be ya Number Two."

"My *second-in-command*?" He looked at me like I said something wrong. "I already have one of those." He pointed at Dev.

"Yeah, I *hear* you. But that's my stance."

"Oh, that's ya stance, huh?"

"Without a doubt. And that's a courtesy, fa' real."

"A *courtesy*? And what the fuck is that supposed to mean?"

"It means that pretty soon my pops is gonna plug me in wit' his connect, and everything's gonna be running through me," I lied with a straight face, knowing damn well that Pops laughed at me when I asked him about it. "So, the way I see it, if you make me ya Number Two *now*, I'll make you my partner later. Fifty-fifty split."

Big Jabby squinted his eyes, staring directly into mines. I could tell from the look on his face that the wheels in his brain were spinning nonstop. That devil named *Greed* was a mah'fucka. So, I knew I had him hook, line, and sinker.

"Between you and me, Pops ain't really feeling Mook like that no more," I laid it on thick, "especially since he found out that Mook was fuckin' my sister. He said it's time for me to take my rightful spot at the head of the family and resurrect the YBM. He's talking about hitting me off wit' a hunnid bricks a month."

"Oh, yeah?" Big Jabby rubbed his hands together. "And where would that leave Mook?"

"It'll leave his ass in one or two places—under us, or under the fuckin' dirt. I really don't care which one. All I know is that I'm destined to be the next king."

"Well, I'll tell you what, if everything you're saying is true, I'm all in."

"As you should be." I cracked a smile. "Now, how you wanna handle these Bartram Village niggas?"

★★★★★

An Hour Later

I was still in front of my moms' crib, checking out my brand-new truck. Pops laced me like mah'fucka. In addition to the chromed-out grill, the chromed-out 22's, and the tinted windows, there were a total of five TVs, a portable VCR, and a JBL sound system with a 1500-watt amplifier. The VCR was screwed into the dash, directly under the glove compartment; the television screens were fitted in the headrests and sun visors, and the largest screen, a 7" Sony, was a feature the radio. When I hit the radio's TV button, the screen slid out like a CD tray and then flipped back. The shit was dope. I couldn't front if I wanted to.

"Damn, Trap, you really 'bout to have this shit jumping," I said to myself, loving the feeling of being home and doing my thing. I was leaned back in the passenger's seat with the door wide open, smoking a blunt and nodding my head to Foxy Brown's new shit, *The Promise.*

My mind is the drama, that got me looking back constant. Some don shit, Foxy, get ready to bomb shit. Blink an eye, miss a comet. The comment, is not a threat, it's a promise.

The Hydro I was chiefing on had me zoned out, thinking about the last twenty-four hours. In a day's time, the plan I'd been working on for the past two years was almost complete. The stunt that I pulled at the party left Mook on his heels, not knowing how to take me, and the shit I kicked to Big Jabby had him walking away with dollar signs in his eyes. Even better, Rahman and Jihad were on their way to come see me. I had called Uzi a few minutes earlier to see if he still had those nine ounces of crack for me. He told me that he did, but because he was too busy to bring them to me, he sent Rahman and Jihad instead. I was cool with that, because based on the way Pops and Bruno was talking about them, I knew the two hitters would be essential to my new plan moving forward.

I thought about bringing Uzi up to speed, but decided not to. For some reason, I had it in my mind that Uzi saw me as a fuck-up, just another young nigga with a thirst for money, but not disciplined enough to go get it. So, because of that, I figured it was best to bring him on board once I had shit rolling. In the meantime, I decided to make Lil' Man my Number Two. Lil' Man was just as hungry as I was, and if shit ever hit the fan, I knew he wouldn't fold on me.

So, after talking to Uzi, I called Lil' Man and told him to come through and see me as well. My next move was reaching out to Kia. I knew she was mad at me because I stood her up the night before, but I figured that I'd call her anyway. I grabbed my Motorola flip phone from the leather console, dialed Kia's number, and then turned the music down to zero.

Ring! Ring! Ring!

"Who is this?" Kia's voice eased through the phone.

"It's AJ. What's good?"

"Humph. I 'on't know, you tell me," I could hear the stank attitude in her voice. I also heard a bunch of mah'fuckas talking shit in the background.

"Yo, who the fuck is that? Them niggas loud as shit. They don't see you talking on the phone?"

"Nah, they good. They my peeps. We all out here chilling on the block."

"Chilling on the block? So, that's how we do it now? You just the typical around the way bitch, huh?"

"Fuck you, AJ," she sharply replied.

"Bitch, that's what you *wanna* do," I shot right back.

"Well, if you came to see me last night like you promised, I would have. But instead of coming straight home to me, you went chasing after that fucking Erica. Miss Queen All Fuckin' Mighty."

"Chill, shorty, we ain't doin' that."

"And why the fuck not?" Kia challenged. "What'chu mad 'cause I pulled ya card? Just keep it real. You don't rock wit' me the same way you rock wit' her."

I laughed. "And what makes you say that?"

"Because it's the truth and you know it. But that's a'ight, though," her voice trailed off. "I know my role, and I play it well. You ain't never met a bitch like me."

"That's a fact," I agreed without the slightest hint of hesitation.

Kia was the epitome of a ride or die bitch. Erica was my boo-boo, no doubt. But Kia was my mah'fuckin' hammer, the bitch I could count on when shit got thick. It was similar to how my pops had my moms. He married Daphney's mom, but my moms was his down-ass bitch and number one hitter.

"So, when is you coming to see me? I need this pussy ate."

"Damn, it's like that?"

"It's just like that."

"But I thought you already had somebody for that?"

"Nah, pa. She don't eat *my* pussy, I eat *hers*."

"Oh, *yeeeaaah*?" I could feel my dick slinking down my leg. "Well since it's like that, I'ma swing through tonight."

"Why you can't come now?"

"Why you asking me all these fuckin' question?"

"Whatever, AJ."

"Nah, fa' real, though." I started laughing. "I'ma swing through tonight."

"I'm not playing wit'chu, AJ. You better bring ya ass over here."

Click!

Shaking my head, I placed the blunt back to my lips, but the cherry had burnt out. I was just about to press the lighter button in the ashtray, but a quick movement out the corner of my eye made me look over my shoulder.

"*AJ?*" Jahlil said my name aggressive as shit. He was standing there with Jabril and Jacobi, and a few other young buls who I assumed must have lived on the block. "Tell 'em this ya new truck."

"Yeah, this my new truck. I just got it today."

"*Dooooooooyyyyyyyyyy!*" The four little boys started smiling and stomping their feet. They were holding their fists in front of their faces like they were talking into a microphone.

I laughed at them.

"Yo, Jah, introduce me to ya boys," I told my little brother.

"This is Meat." He pointed towards the chubby, dark skinned boy who was standing to his left. "This is Pee-Head." He pointed at the skinny light skinned boy who was standing beside Jabril and Jacobi. "Pee-Head and Meat is brothers. And that's Horse, and that's Boo-Boo." He pointed at the other two, who appeared to be half Black, half Puerto Rican. "Horse and Boo-Boo are brothers, too. This is my crew right here. Anybody mess wit' us, we beat 'em down."

"Is that right?" I looked at Jahlil, then I looked into the eyes of the four young buls. "So, y'all squad, huh?" "Yup." Jacobi nodded his head, then he looked at Jahlil. "Right, Jahlil? Right?"

I looked at Jahlil, and he nodded his head. The fire that burned in his eyes was way too intense for a boy so young.

"Y'all lil' niggas got some money?" I asked the four young buls.

"Yup," they replied in unison.

Each boy reached inside of his pocket and pulled out one half of a hundred-dollar-bill. Jabril and Jacobi did the same, and I realized their hundred-dollar-bills were also ripped in half. It dawned on me the hundred-dollar-bills were the same bills that I gave them the day before when we were downstairs in the basement. They had ripped the bills in half and shared them with their friends. The only one who still had his hundred-dollar-bill in one piece was Jahlil.

"Whatever we got, we share it wit' our crew," said Jabril.

"And that's gangsta," I told him, looking at my three little brothers with a new level of respect. "Now the six of y'all gimme those bills, and take these," I said as I reached inside of my pocket and pulled out my knot of money. I peeled away the first seven hundred-dollar-bills and gave each boy a bill of his own. Jahlil was the obvious leader of the crew, so he ended up with $200 while the rest of his crew had $100.

"See, I told y'all my brother was all that," Jacobi bragged to his friends, then he looked at Jahlil. "Right, Jahlil? Right?"

CHAPTER TWELVE
Later That Night

I was trained by my pops to always look a man in his eyes, because the eyes never lied. They would show his fears and concerns, his joys and pains, but most important his true aspirations and intentions. Equipped with this knowledge, it had taken me less than an hour to fully confirm everything that Pops and Bruno told me about Rahman and Jihad. I had no reason, whatsoever, to doubt what they told me. But seeing firsthand how the two hitters moved, I was more than confident that my ranks had been elevated to a new level of intensity. I was also confident they felt the same way about me. Real niggas just clicked that way.

They pulled up on my moms' block a few hours earlier in a black minivan with dark tinted windows. Lil' Man and me were already posted outside, and it fucked our heads up when we first laid eyes on them. They were each dressed in a black Muslim garment that hung down below their knees, and had assault rifles bulging out the sides from underneath.

Rahman was 6 foot, 2 inches tall and weighed somewhere north of 250 pounds. He had a shiny black complexion, a lazy right eye, a bald head, and a thick bushy beard.

Jihad was an inch or two taller than me, and weighed about 270 pounds. He was light skinned with short, wavy hair, and had a long curly beard. Both men were twenty years older than me, but the respect they had for my pops ran so deep that it naturally trickled down to me.

Our first hour kicking it, they went on and on about my pops, and how I looked just like him. They told me how my pops got his start as a stick-up kid back in the eighties; and even more intriguing was the love and respect they gave Easy when he came through to check out my moms and brothers.

I had already heard the rumors about Easy being a gangsta and one of North Philly's top hustlas back in the day. But to actually see niggas who were known for getting busy, bow down to the old head's gangsta and show him the utmost respect, I began seeing

Easy in a whole new light. Rahman even went as far as calling Easy a *Trap Legend*. He also suggested that I kick it with him and pick his brain about the pinnacles and pitfalls of the game. It was definitely something that I planned on doing, but for the time being, I wanted to get down to business.

We chilled outside of my moms' crib until the sun went down, then we took it inside and held court at my moms' dining room table. I was standing at the head of the table, and Lil' Man was seated across from me at the other end. Rahman was seated to my left, and Jihad was seated to my right. My three little brothers were eavesdropping from the bottom of the stairs, and Lucifer was standing at attention, watching us by the front door. He already knew Lil' Man from when we lived down in the towers, but Rahman and Jihad were strangers to him. I knew my dog like the back of my hand. So, as he stood there watching me, I knew he was waiting on my command to attack.

"So, this the thing," I began my spiel, looking around the table at the faces of my men, "the sooner we dispose of Mook, the sooner my pops is gonna plug me in wit' his connect. For the past few years, Mook had the line and was doing his thing. But that's over now. According to Pops, this nigga violated and must be dealt wit' accordingly. That's the price tag. The sooner we cash in on this nigga, the sooner we get paid."

"Yeah, I'm feeling that. I'm feeling that shit like a mah'fucka," Rahman spoke through a thick cloud of smoke. He puffed his blunt a few more times, then he passed it to Lil' Man.

"AJ, I'm wit'chu, dawg. You already know," Lil' Man stated, then he hit the blunt and inhaled deeply. "But'chu know Mook just as well as I do. So, you already know this shit you kicking is easier said than done. Mook is like a mah'fuckin' ghost on the street. If he 'on't wanna be seen, then we ain't gon' see him, let alone reach out and touch him. But on the other hand, he can reach out and touch us whenever he feels like it. So, how the fuck we 'posed to go to war wit' sum'n like dat?" He hit the blunt a few more times, and then blew the smoke from his nose. "Not to mention, he's got an army from here to New York, and then all the way back to Cali. You know he be on that Block Boy shit."

"On some Block Boy shit?" Jihad said, as Lil' Man handed him the blunt. "Where the fuck he think he at *Compton*? You know Philly niggas ain't down wit' none of that goof ball shit. At least, not when it comes to colors. That's weirdo shit."

"I hear you, but that's the way the nigga get down," Lil' Man replied, then he pointed at me. "AJ know."

"Yeah, he's a Block Boy. That's the reason my pops put him in position in the first place. He knew Mook had an international reach. But that's beside the point. I figure if we hit him in his pockets, attack his ass from every angle, we won't need to go looking for him, he'll come looking for us. We gotta smoke him out. His power is his money, not his troops. He's barely feeding them niggas, so their loyalty can only go so far. They're surviving off of bread-crumbs. So, imagine what they'd do if we gave 'em a bread truck."

"Goddamnit, bul, you sound *just* like Alvin!" Rahman laughed. "You got me feeling like it's '89 all over again. Let's do this shit!"

"Oh, we gon' do it a'ight." I nodded my head, then I looked at Lil' Man. "I feel where you're coming from, trust me. But paper tigers cease to exist. They burn up and disappear from the first flick of a flame," I quoted one of Pops' quotable quotes.

"Paper, *what*?" Lil' Man's forehead creased.

"Paper tigers are only paper, so they don't exist. The ferocious-ness they represent is only an illusion. They burn up and disappear at the first sign of adversity. This same concept allies to Mook. The power he appears to possess is only an illusion, it's not real. The *true* power belongs to my pops, and soon he's gonna pass it down to me."

"Goddamnit, AJ, talk that *shit*!" Rahman banged his hand on the table, causing Lucifer to take a step forward.

Uggggrrrrrr!

"Shamooyah!" I raised my voice, commanding Lucifer to calm down. He stepped back and squatted down, but was still watching Rahman. "Shamooyah. *Rah*!" I commanded him to lay down, and he did.

The nine ounces of crack that Uzi blessed me with were clutched in my right hand, and sprawled out across the table were six of the ten Hydro pounds that Daphney gave me. I had already given each man two pounds apiece as an appetizer, so the next step was telling them what I planned to do with the nine ounces.

"This nigga, Beetle," I looked down at Lil' Man, who was the only one familiar with the name. "We're gonna use these nine ounces to get out of him everything he knows about Mook's operation. The locations of his money and trap houses, the blocks he controls, all the way down to the pillow his fat fuckin' head sleeps on. I wanna know *everything*."

"And you really think he's gonna risk his life for nine ounces of crack?" Lil' Man shot back, looking at me like didn't believe it could happen.

"What other choice does he have? Either he tells us what we need to know, or get his stupid-ass smoked. Simple as that."

"Well, shit, I like them odds," said Jihad, then he passed me the blunt.

"You and me, both." I hit the blunt and inhaled deeply. "You and me, both."

★★★★★

Beetle was a low-level meatball nigga, so the second he saw those nine ounces he told us everything he knew about Mook's operation. I already knew about the low-rises and the few blocks that he had down the way. But what I didn't know was his territory had expanded from North Philly all the way up to Germantown and Logan. He even had a few blocks out Feltonville that were doing about a brick a week. We drove through every one of his spots, doubled back and laid them shits down. The back of Rahman's minivan was loaded like a mah'fucka, but I still wanted more. According to Beetle, the corners we hit were replenished every Sunday morning with a brick apiece. He also told us that because it was a Saturday night, the work that designated for distribution was being held at a stash house in Logan.

"That's the house right there," Beetle said, as we cruised up 11th Street, approaching Courtland. The house he pointed at was an old, two-story row house on the right side of the street. The location was perfect for a jux, as every house on the left side of the street was already abandoned, deemed unlivable by the city. The houses had been built over an old landfill that was beginning to sink, so the residence was forced to evacuate. I couldn't make this shit up if I wanted to. It was fucking perfect.

"And how much work you think is in there?" Rahman asked, as he turned right on Courtland Street. I was riding shotgun, and Beetle was seated in the back, wedged between Lil' Man and Jihad.

"Anywhere between six to ten bricks," Beetle propounded. "That's six bricks for the blocks we just hit, and that's not including the weight they gon' be selling out the house for the rest of the week."

"You keep saying *they*, who the fuck is they?" I looked back at Beetle.

"The nigga, Flames, and his brother, E-Matic. They the ones who be pumping out the house, moving all the weight for Mook."

"And you really think they got six to ten bricks in there?"

"At the very least," Beetle replied, as we circled the block for the second time. "Plus, you gotta take into account that Mook is outta town and won't be back until Friday. He prob'bly left them niggas wit' the mothaload. There's no telling what's in there, for sure, but more than likely it's sum'n heavy."

"How many people are usually in there?"

"Four or five. You got Flames and E-Matic, they baby mamas and the kids. These stupid-ass niggas be shitting where they eat."

"How many kids they got?"

"Flames has a daughter that's about ten, and E-Matic's baby mama just had a baby a few months ago. The baby mamas and the kids shouldn't be a problem. The only ones we gotta worry about is Flames and E-Matic."

"*What?*" I snarled at him, tempted to smack fire from his fucking face. "Nigga, let me worry about who the fuck we gotta worry about."

"You took the words right out my mouth," said Lil' Man, who was already indifferent towards Beetle. He didn't trust him, and was still feeling some type of way about the beef they had over the low-rises.

"Nah, A, I didn't even mean of like that," Beetle tried to clarify. "I was jus' saying."

"Yeah. Right," I cut that shit short.

I had Jesus clutched in my right hand and two extra clips stuffed down in my sweatpants' pocket. Rahman and Jihad both had choppas, and Lil' Man had the pistol-grip, sawed-off shotty that Rahman gave him when he saw the .38 he was packing.

"*Fuck is that lil' shit supposed to do?*" Rahman asked him before we left my moms' crib. Lil' Man was salty about the "*lil*" comment, but shook it off when Rahman gave him the sawed-off shotty from the bag of guns that was stashed in his minivan. And for good measures, to show Rahman that his gangsta was official, the first block we hit, Lil' Man hopped out and splashed three niggas at point blank range.

"*Yeah, big fella. Lil' Man get busy, huh?*" Lil' Man gloated when we hopped back in the van and we got ghost. He was smiling from ear-to-ear, looking like a black Chucky doll with short wavy hair.

"So, Beetle, how they usually do this shit?" I asked him, still looking over my shoulder towards the back seat.

"How they usually do what?"

"Nigga, how the fuck they run this jawn?" I snapped at him, beginning to lose patience. "You just walk up and knock on the door?"

"Oh, nah." Beetle shook his head. "I mean, you *can*. But if they don't know you, then chances are they won't open the door. It has to be somebody they know."

"Yeah. Somebody like you." Jihad pointed at him.

"*Like me?*" Beetle shot back, bitching. "I thought y'all just wanted me to show y'all where the house was. Y'all never said I had to be involved. These niggas know me. If they tell Mook, I'm done."

Clearly Beetle didn't know what time it was. Whoever was inside that mah'fuckin' house was getting they shit pushed back. I needed Mook to feel this shit. I needed to burn a spot in his brain and affect his judgement moving forward, and what better way than killing one of his top lieutenants, the nigga's brother, both of they baby mamas and they snot-nosed kids? Well, maybe not the kids. I figured we could tie them up and leave them locked in a room somewhere. Either way, when Mook learned about his blocks being hit, his men being killed, and his money and work being confiscated, this would surely knock him off balance. I was ready for war, and Pops had taught me well.

If waging war becomes necessary, then attack your enemy with utter resolve in order to divide his resources. Attack him from the East and the West; the North and the South. Attack his supply lines and attack his rest areas. You must always create diversions that will keep him off balance and dilute his defenses. You must attack from all angles, never giving your enemy the time he needs to rest and regroup.

"A'ight. So, this is how we gon' do it." I looked each man in his eyes. "Me, Rahman and Jihad are gonna lay in the cut while Beetle and Lil' Man go up on the porch. Beetle's gonna knock on the door, and Lil' Man, you just stand right behind him. You're little as shit, so they won't be able to see you."

"Fuck outta here wit' that lil' shit, yo. Straight up," Lil' Man warned.

"Nigga, calm ya ass down. I'm just going over the strategy," I shot right back, then I looked at Beetle. "So, all you gotta do is knock on the door. Them niggas know you, so there's no reason they won't open it. But as soon as you see that doorknob turning, get'cha ass out the way. Lil' Man is gonna step out from behind you and blast the nigga when he opens the door. The second Lil' Man let his shit blow, run ya ass back to the van and get behind the steering wheel. So that way if shit get funky and we need to get ghost, you'll already be in position to get us up outta here. Rahman and Jihad," I looked back and forth between the two hitters, "the second

Lil' Man splash the nigga at the door, I'ma bum-rush the spot. Y'all storm in right behind me."

"That's a good plan, but that shotgun blast is gonna draw too much attention," said Rahman as he parked his minivan at the bottom of the block. "Yo, Haddy, reach in the back and grab that duffel bag off the floor. There's a machete inside of it. Give that shit to Lil' Man, so he can stab the nigga at the door. If he shoots the shotty, or any gun for that matter while he's standing on the porch, the neighbors will hear it and call the cops. That's the reason we got these big-ass guns in the first place." He held up his AK-47, then he nodded at the choppa that Jihad was holding. "These big mah'fuckas command attention, so niggas gon' freeze when they see 'em. So, don't nobody shoot unless you absolutely have to. Y'all got that?"

"Yeah, we got it," we replied in unison.

Rahman looked at me to make sure I understood where he was coming from, and I nodded my head to assure him that I did. His know-how and guidance were right on point. He and Jihad were proving themselves to be valuable assets on my team, but I wasn't so sure about Beetle. I figured if he would flip on Mook for a measly nine ounces, then who's to say he wouldn't flip on me? Again, this was something that I learned from my pops.

When you seek to destroy your enemy, destroy him totally, including his allies who must be intimidated by your intensity. If they were once his allies, then clearly, they are not yours; at least not in the present. You must take time to watch them, study their moves and pay close attention to how they react to your war-time victories in contrast to your enemy's failures. Then and only then, can you truly determine if they are friend or foe.

"Aye, yo, A, one more thing," Beetle said as we climbed out of the minivan. "Y'all not killing the girls and the kids, right?"

"Just worry about knocking on the fuckin' door." I scowled at him, then I cocked back Jesus.

Click! Clack!

"Now, let's get it."

CHAPTER THIRTEEN

Knock! Knock! Knock!

"Who is it?" a voice sounded from the other side of the door.

"It's me, Beetle."

The porch light turned on, illuminating the sidewalk in front of the house. Rahman, Jihad, and me were crouched down behind the next-door neighbor's porch railing. We were dressed in all-black, so I was hoping the nigga at the door couldn't see us. But just in case he did, we were all locked and loaded, ready to get busy if shit got goofy.

"Beetle, what the fuck you want?" the voice questioned from behind the door.

"Mook ain't called y'all?" Beetle replied, improvising on the spot. "He was supposed to had called y'all. He sent me over to grab sum'n."

"Nah, nigga, Mook ain't called. He sent you over here to grab what?"

"We ran out of work down in the projects, so I called Mook and he told me to come through and see you. The block is jumping and niggas try'na eat. We need sum'n to hold us over 'til the morning."

I listened to Beetle kick game, and changed my mind about killing him. I didn't tell the rest of my crew, but I was planning on smoking his ass before we left the house. If only he knew how close he was to being baptized.

Lucky mah'fucka.

I could hear the door locks being unfastened, so I told Rahman and Jihad to get ready. I looked back on the porch at Beetle and Lil' Man. Beetle was rocking from side to side and cracking his knuckles, looking all suspicious and shit. Lil' Man was calm and quiet, ready to do his thing with the machete.

The front door opened up slowly, and I could see Flames standing in the threshold. His .357 was clutched in his left hand, down by his leg. A smoldering blunt was dangling from the right side of his mouth.

"Beetle, what the fuck is you doing?" Flames said when Beetle stepped to his left, and Lil' Man popped out from behind him. It happened so smooth and fast that Flames was stuck, frozen in disbelief like a deer caught in the headlights.

Thwap!

Lil' Man shoved the machete deep inside of Flames' torso.

Thwap! Thwap!

He stabbed Flames two more times, twisting the blade with his second thrust.

"Ugghhhh, *fuck!*" Flames grunted in disbelief. A shocked expression donned his face, as his eyes opened wide. He looked down at the machete blade protruding from his gut, then he dropped his burner. He looked down at Lil' Man, then he looked up at Beetle. "B—B—Beetle. You bitch—ass—nigga."

"Pussy, *shut* the fuck up," Lil' Man snarled as he extracted the blade. He heckled like a demon and stabbed Flames three more times.

Thwap! Thwap! Thwap!

"Yeah, mah'fucka, this how the *gangstas* do it," Lil' Man snarled some more, twisting the blade counter clockwise. "Now, get off my fuckin' knife!" He extracted the blade, ripping Flames' organs out of the front of his blood-covered shirt.

"Uuugggggghhhhh, shit!" Flames stumbled backwards, reaching for his guts with both hands. He coughed up a mouthful of blood, then his glossy eyes rolled into the back of his head. His body went limp and he crashed down hard on the living room floor.

Wham!

"Aaaaagggggghhhhhhh! Oh, my God! Oh, my God!" I heard a female scream.

Beetle hauled ass of the porch, as Lil' Man and me ran inside of the house. Rahman and Jihad ran in right behind us. I didn't see who, but one of them slammed the front door hard as shit.

Boom!

I scoured the living room looking for E-Matic, but I didn't see him. The only person I saw was a tall, fat, Luther Vandross looking bitch. Her fat ass was the one doing all the fucking screaming.

"Aaaaagggggghhhhhhh! Oh, my God! They killed Flames!" the fat bitch continued screaming, as she took off running towards the kitchen. She was fast as shit for a fat bitch, but not fast enough to outrun Lil' Man. He chased her down and jumped on her back. His tiny, little legs were too short to wrap around her waist, so he held on with his left arm curled around the front of her neck.

"*Leave me alone! Get off me! E-Matic, help!*" the fat bitch screamed even louder. Her arms flailed wildly, as Lil' Man began choking her. He was so small compared to how big she was that his little ass was looking like a book bag dangling off the side of her back.

"Bitch, calm ya big-ass down," Lil' Man snarled as he wrestled her to the floor, grunting like a pig.

I looked back at Rahman and Jihad, and saw they were already running up the stairs. A slight movement on the couch grabbed my attention. I swung Jesus in that direction, only to find it was a small infant stirring around on a fluffy, pink blanket. The baby awakened from the fat bitch screaming, and began to cry.

"*Waaannnnn! Waaannnnn! Waaannnnn!*"

I snatched the little girl by her ankles and pressed Jesus to the back of her head. By then, Lil' Man and fat girl were rolling around on the floor, wrestling for the machete. Her big-ass was getting the best of him.

"Don't just stand there, help!" Lil' Man shouted, looking at me with a crazed expression on his face. "This big mah'fucka strong as shit!"

Shaking my head, I ran over and kicked the fat bitch in her stomach.

Blam!

"Oww!" the fat bitch groaned, then she curled into a ball. She looked up and saw that her baby girl was dangling upside down with a gun to her dome, and broke down crying.

"Don't hurt my baby, *please?*"

"Well, then shut ya fat ass up," I barked at her.

She threw her hands up and spoke more calmly. "Whatever y'all want, y'all can have it. Just please don't hurt my baby."

"Waaannnnn! Waaannnnn! Waaannnnn!"

Hearing the baby crying, coupled with the pleas of her mother, sent cold chills rippling through my rotten, black heart. The last thing I ever wanted to do was hurt an innocent child, but I would if I had to. Money was power, and crack was strength. Both of them mah'fuckas were stashed somewhere in that fucking house, and were worth more to me than a human life—innocent or not.

"Here." I handed the fat girl the baby. "Shut this lil' mah'fucka up, 'fore I baptize her fuckin' ass."

"Ssshhh. Ssshhh. Ssshhh," she cooed into the baby's ear and caressed her back. "Mommy's here. Don't worry, baby, Mommy's got'chu. *Ssshhh. Ssshhh. Ssshhh."*

"Now, where the fuck is E-Matic?"

"Him, Latisha and Little Tish are upstairs," the fat bitch sobbed, clearly choosing the lives of her and her baby's over everyone else's inside the house.

"Upstairs, where?" Lil' Man asked her, then he wiped the blood from his machete on the back of her shirt.

Boca!

The thunderous blast of an AK-47 ringing out from the second floor answered the question. I could hear the loud shrieking of a woman screaming, followed by the thumping sound of a body being slammed.

"Yo, stay here and watch this bitch," I told Lil' Man. "Her fat ass even blink wrong, you chop her fucking head off."

"And you know I will," Lil' Man smirked, looking like a wild gremlin speckled with blood. He pressed the machete to the fat bitch's neck, then he leaned into her. "Fuck around if you want to, bitch. I'ma kill you *and* her." He pointed the machete at the crying infant. "Now, you fuckin' try me."

I ran up the stairs with my head on a swivel, not exactly sure what was up there waiting for me. My nerves began to settle when I locked eyes with Jihad. He was standing at the top of the stairs, posted in front of the bathroom door. His choppa was gripped tight, clutched in both hands. Huddled on the bathroom floor was a thick redbone chick and a little girl, who I knew had to be Flames' daughter. They were both crying, flinching every time they heard E-Matic scream. Rahman had his ass in the bedroom, fucking him up something vicious.

"Go 'head, A, do ya thing," Jihad said, pointing his choppa at the bedroom door. "I got this shit right here. Believe dat."

"Say no more." I nodded my head, but was mad as shit that he said my name. It was bad enough that none of us wore a mask. So, because he said my name in front Flames' daughter, my initial plan to spare the kids went right out of the window.

I pushed open the bedroom door with my left hand, and crept inside with Jesus clutched in my right. Rahman was hunched over E-Matic, who was balled up in the corner, raining down blows on his face and head nonstop.

Whop! Whop! Whop! Whop! Whop!

"Agh, shit! Nigga, chill!" E-Matic cried out, doing his best to block the blows. He was every bit of 5 foot, 8 inches tall and a buck-thirty soaking wet. Rahman was big-dogging his ass like a Bull Mastiff working on a Chihuahua.

Whop! Whop! Whop! Whop! Whop!

"Where the fuck is the money and the work at?" Rahman growled at him.

"I ain't got no money and work. I already told you that," E-Matic replied, spitting out teeth and blood. His skinny, long face had ballooned to the size of a pumpkin. Both of his ears were leaking out blood, and his broken nose was twisted like the letter *S*.

"Wrong fuckin' answer," Rahman snarled back. He punched E-Matic so hard that I could hear his bones crack.

Crunch!

"Yo, chill, Rock. I got this nigga," I said as I moved in between them.

Rahman grabbed his choppa from the foot of the bed. He clutched it like a baseball bat, then he cracked E-Matic on the top of his head.

Whop!

"Bitch-ass nigga. You gon' give us what we came for," Rahman snarled some more, pressing the choppa to E-Matic's temple.

"Come on, fam, I done already told you," E-Matic sobbed. He was rocking from left to right, dizzy as shit from being pummeled. "Flames is the one who be moving the work. I'm just the security."

"The *security*?" He pissed me the fuck off, saying that stupid shit. "Nigga, get'cha *punk*-ass up." I grabbed his throat and snatched him to his feet.

"Aaagghhh!" The nigga whined like a bitch.

I released my hands from his neck, and he crumbled back down. It was then, that I realized the gunshot I heard from the living room was Rahman blowing out his kneecap. His left leg was completely obliterated from the knee down, barely held together by his bloody red tendons.

"Nigga, bring ya ass on. I wanna show you sum'n." I drug E-Matic out into the hallway and pulled him towards the bathroom door. "You see this bitch right here?" I pointed Jesus at the redbone.

Blakka!

The blazing slug ripped through her forehead, blowing her gravy out the back of her biscuit.

Blakka! Blakka!

The next two bullets ripped through the little girl's chest, flipping her body into the bathtub behind her. "*Pussy, you think I'm playing?*" I shouted like a demon who'd been kissed by the devil. I pulled E-Matic towards me, then I pushed his face down inside of the bathtub. "You see this lil' bitch? *Look at her!*" I gave him an up-close view of his niece's dead body. She was covered in blood, twisted like a pretzel with her nerves still twitching. Her glossy, brown eyes were stuck wide open.

"I'ma ask ya ass one more time. Where the *fuck* is the money and the work at? And if you play me like I'm sweet, we gon' take this lil' party downstairs to ya bitch and ya baby. You decide."

"Come on, yo, please?" E-Matic cried like a baby. "Look at my fuckin' niece, yo. Look at my sis. Y'all niggas ain't have to do 'em like that. They was fuckin' innocent."

"So, downstairs it is."

I drug his ass to the top of the stairs, then I kicked him in his back. He lurched forward and tumbled down, crashing into the stair deck, face first. I ran down the stairs behind him. Rahman and Jihad followed suit. Kneeling down in front of his face, I pressed Jesus to the edge of his chin. I leveled the barrel, bringing his gaze to mines.

"Now, you sure this what the fuck you want?"

I waited for an answer, but he didn't reply. His right eye was completely swollen shut, but his left eye was still blinking. He looked at me with pure hated, and shook his head. I took it as a silent threat.

"You's a tough nigga, huh? I *like* that shit!"

I grabbed the back of his shirt and slung him across the room towards his baby mama. He reached out to grab her leg, but she kicked him away.

"E-Matic, what the fuck are you doing? Just tell 'em where y'all stashed the shit," she put him on blast. "Yeah, E-Matic. Tell us where y'all stashed the shit," Lil' Man antagonized him, smirking when he said it. His bloody machete was still pressed against the fat bitch's neck.

"Fuck these niggas, I ain't telling 'em nuffin!'" E-Matic snapped at his bitch. "They gon' kill us regardless. You see they ain't wearing no fuckin' masks. I ain't telling 'em shit."

"Yo, Rock, go in the kitchen and turn on the garbage disposal."

Rahman looked at me, then he looked down at the baby. A devilish smile spread across his face, as he headed towards the kitchen.

"And Jihad," I aimed Jesus down at the baby, "take her lil' ass in the kitchen and feed her to the garage disposal, one limb at a mah'fuckin' time. That'll make his ass talk."

"Ahn-ahn! No! *Hell no!*" the fat bitch shouted. She was leaned forward, clutching the baby like a football.

"Lil' Man," I gave the order without saying it. He raised the machete high above his head, then he swung it down hard on the fat bitch's shoulder.

Chop!

"Aaaaaaggggggghhhhhhhhhh!'" She hopped up on her knees, screaming at the top of her lungs. She dropped the baby and reached for her shoulder, but the only thing she felt was a gooey hot stump. "*My arm*! *My arm*! *My fucking arm*! *Aaaaaagggggggghhhhhhhhh*]!"

Her severed arm was laying on the floor, still wrapped around the baby. Jihad leaned over, snatched the baby, and stormed off towards the kitchen.

"*No*! *No*! *Not my baby, pleeeeeaaaaaassssssseeee*!" the fat bitch screamed for mercy. She swiped at Jihad's leg with her one good arm, but he was too far to grab. "*E-Matic, do sum'n*! *That's ya fucking daughter*!"

Her words must have struck a nerve, because E-Matic straightened up quick.

"A'ight, nigga, chill. Just calm down." He raised his hands in defeat. "I'ma tell y'all where it's at. Just please, man—please don't hurt my baby girl?"

"Well, talk, nigga. Time is money." I scowled at him, then I looked back towards the kitchen. Rahman and Jihad were standing beside the sink waiting for me to give the order. The crying infant was dangling from Jihad's left hand, just a few inches away from the garbage disposal.

Zzzzzzznnnnnnnnnnn!

"There's ten bricks in the kitchen," E-Matic finally confessed. "They're stashed in the cupboard, the one right next to the door. Just pull out the false bottom and reach inside."

"And where the fuck is the money?"

"It's upstairs in my bedroom closet. The two Timberland boxes on the top shelf. There's fifty-grand in each one. Y'all can have that shit. Just please, yo—please don't hurt my baby. I'm begging you."

"Yo, Rock, check the cupboard. The one by the door. He said it's ten bricks stashed at the bottom," I called out towards the kitchen.

Rahman went straight to work. He got down on his hands and knees, and reached inside of the cupboard.

"Jackpot!" I heard him announce after pulling out mad pots and pans. "Yo, ya man wasn't lying. These niggas was loaded like a mah'fucka." He held up one of the bricks and then tossed it to Jihad. Jihad the caught the brick and then turned off the garbage disposal.

He sat the baby inside the sink and continued watching as Rahman removed every brick.

"Lil' Man, go upstairs and grab the money from the closet."

"I got'chu, A. I'm all over the shit," Lil' Man replied as he ran up the stairs.

"And where the fuck is you going?" I walked over to E-Matic. He was squirming around on his stomach, trying to pull himself towards the door.

Blakka!

I blew his brains out the front of his face.

I looked down at the fat bitch, who was laying on the floor crying. The severed stump on her left shoulder was leaking like a mah'fucka. The shit was so bad, that even though her right hand was pressed against it, the heavy blood flow was gushing through the cracks of her fingers. I would had never guessed that a human body contained so much blood.

"Please—leave us—alone?" she lethargically panted, teetering on the brink of unconsciousness. Her eyelids were blinking nonstop, and it seemed as though she would check out at any given second.

Before I could say anything, the front door flew wide open. I stepped back ready to clap, but then I saw it was Beetle. He looked down and saw E-Matic's brains pouring out, and carefully stepped around them.

"Yo, Beetle, what the fuck is you doing? You 'posed to be waiting for us outside in the van."

"I know, A. I know," Beetle replied, struggling to catch his breath. "But them—gunshots—was loud—as shit. I could hear 'em—all the way down the street. That's the reason I ran up here to tell y'all. We gotta bounce before the cops come. *Oh, shit!* Yo, what the *fuck?*" He covered his mouth when he stumbled on the fat bitch's arm. It was laying on the floor right beside her, chunky and brown like a rump roast with the bone sticking out.

"B—B—Beetle," the fat bitch gasped, looking at Beetle with a face full of tears. "Tell 'em—to leave us—alone."

"Damn, A, what the fuck y'all did?" Beetle looked at me like he wanted to cry. "I thought we agreed the baby mamas and the kids were off limits. At least, that's the vibe you gave me. Why the fuck y'all had to do her like that?"

"Come here." I waved him over. He hesitated, then begrudgingly did like I told him. I spun Jesus on my trigger finger, presenting him with the handle. "Kill her."

Beetle shook his head. "Come on, A, man. You know I ain't no mah'fuckin' killer."

"Let's try this shit again." My eyelids became two dark slits. "Either smoke this bitch, or I'ma smoke you. The choice is yours."

Beetle sucked in a deep breath, then he reached out and grabbed the gun. He aimed the barrel at the fat bitch's chest and then closed his eyes.

Blakka!

"I got the money," Lil' Man said as he descended the stairs with a pillowcase in his hand. He held it up and showed me how bulky it was.

"That's good." I nodded my approval. "That's real good."

I grabbed Jesus from Beetle, then I looked back in the kitchen.

"Rahman and Jihad, y'all good?"

"Nigga, hell yeah," Rahman replied as he and Jihad emerged from the kitchen. "There were ten bricks, just like he said. I got 'em right here." He held up the trash bag in his hand.

"That's what I'm talking 'bout." I nodded my head, satisfied that our mission was complete.

I could hear the baby crying from the kitchen, so I looked at Beetle. I started to make his ass go in there and kill her, but the sound of police sirens blaring in the distance convinced me otherwise.

"Come on, y'all, we out," I said to my men, as I ushered them out of the house. I ran out last, slamming the door behind me.

The sirens grew louder as we hauled ass down the street. We hopped in the van and pulled off, just as the cop cars were pulling up. Those stupid mah'fuckas drove right past us.

Our getaway was clean, and the takedown was sweet. In total, we had $106,055.00, 10 bricks of coke—5 raw and 5 rocked up, and 48 bundles of crack worth $150.00 apiece. We split the money five ways, each receiving $21,211.

As far the work, I told my crew that I would hold on to it until it was time to link up with my papi homeboy, Raphael. I also told them to lay low for the rest of the night, and to keep Uzi out of the loop for the time being. I figured that because Mook had branched out to Germantown and Logan, then nine times out of ten, he was also serving Zion. So, if Uzi found out and then ran his mouth to Zion, there was a good chance that Zion would run his mouth to Mook. That shit was a train wreck waiting to happen, and would definitely undermine my war strategy.

I had every intention on forcing Mook's hand. But at that point, my best option was to stick and move, and attack him anonymously. By remaining anonymous, I could strike at will without any threat of retaliation. It would also give me the time I needed to weaken Mook's position and tarnish his image. This was yet again, another lesson that I learned from Pops.

A weakened enemy is an ideal rival. The weaker he is, the easier he can be conquered.

Askari

CHAPTER FOURTEEN

I was supposed to had went home, hopped in the shower, and then drove out Southwest to go see Kia. But somehow, I ended up in my moms' living room, smoking blunts and talking to Easy until the sun came up.

Rahman and Jihad were right about Easy, old head was a straight up G. He told me mad stories about his kingpin glory days—how he came up from the bottom and made it to the top, and how back in the eighties he was the first nigga to pump crack on the streets of Philly. Even more intriguing was the revelation that he and my pops used to be partners back in the day. They ran a crew of stick-up kids who called themselves the *Wolf Pack*. It was Easy, my pops, my Uncle Rayon, and this fake-ass chilly pimp I knew from down the projects named Beaver Bushnut. They started off robbing jewelry stores and check-cashing spots, then eventually graduated to robbing banks and taking down money-trucks.

I could see the excitement in Easy's eyes as he told me about the Wolf Pack and all of their felonious capers. But over time, and the more he spoke, his energy decreased from excitement to regret. I asked him why, and he told me that money and power were the root of all evil. He said the two of them together were a deadly mix, and when placed in the wrong hands, they could turn best friends into best enemies. His was referring to his and Pops relationship; how the bond they once shared turned from sugar to shit.

According to Easy, the rift between them first began on New Year's Eve 1985. Easy was down in Miami bringing in the new year when he crossed paths with Juan Nunes, a Columbian drug lord from the Medellin cartel. Juan introduced him to his brother Poncho, and Poncho was the nigga who fronted Easy his first brick of crack. Ironically, at the same time this was happening down in Miami, Pops was back in Philly plugging in with the boss of the Black Mafia, some old head nigga named Grip.

Pops and Grip had cut a deal that eventually evolved into the YBM, and by the time he and Easy linked back up, neither was willing to give up their new connect. Their only option was to go their separate ways while remaining friends.

The agreement between them was to set up shop in different parts of the city, with a clear understanding they would stay out the other's way. My pops had West, Southwest and South Philly, while Easy had North Philly and Uptown. Things went smooth for a while, as each man bubbled from a distance. But unfortunately, as time went on, it became clear the city wasn't big enough for the both of them. They ended up going to war, and the war led to Easy being kidnapped by the YBM. The old head, Grip, stepped in and revealed that Easy was his long-lost son. He told Pops to cut Easy loose, and then labeled him off limits from that point on. The shit was wild, and the more I sat back and listened, the more it felt like I was watching a movie. That shit could have been a blockbuster.

I asked Easy how my moms got caught in the middle, and the shit he told me, assuming it was true, had me seeing Pops in a whole different light. Easy and my moms had been creeping around for the past seven years. But when they first met, she never told him that Pops was her baby daddy. Eventually word got around to Pops, and he used it to his advantage. Him and Easy were still beefing over territory, but because Grip had labeled Easy untouchable, there was no way for Pops to kill him. So being the war lord he is, he devised a whole new strategy. He turned my moms out on crack, and then used her to turn out Easy. At first, I didn't want to believe it. But the more I thought about it, the more I knew it was true. It was actually one of the war principles that Pops had taught me through his letters—Total Destruction by Any Means Necessary.

Poison his food supplies. Disease his men with unclean women. Create a strain in his thinking and when he is flustered, drive in and destroy him.

As a young general equipped with the art of war, I understood exactly where Pops was coming from and why he did what he did. I just couldn't understand why he chose his own baby mama to do it. He deliberately brought harm to, and jeopardized the same earth where he planted his seed. The shit was ill, and I couldn't help but to feel some type of way about it.

Another thing that Easy and me spoke about were my aspirations of taking over the streets. I showed him the ten bricks of coke that we jacked from Mook's stash house, but I never told him where they came from. I just needed somebody to sample the work, and who better than Easy? He took a blast from one of the bricks that was already rocked up, and told me the coke was buttah. As far as the five bricks that were still raw, he told me that his man Mikey Bridges was the best chef in the city, and for a small fee he would take me to meet him. He said the raw was so good that a seven-on-one, meaning seven grams of baking soda on every ounce of raw, would stretch the five bricks into six and a quarter. I was cool with that, the more crack the better.

I called my niggas early that morning and told them to meet me at my moms' crib, so we could roll out together to meet Mikey Bridges. The only ones I didn't call were Uzi and Beetle, and for obvious reasons. But as far as Lil' Man, Rahman and Jihad, they were my main three hitters—the niggas who I knew I could count on in the clutch, come hell or high water, feast or famine. Everything that belonged to me, belonged to them, and I was determined to make sure they knew it. That was the reason I broke them off with the six pounds of smoke before we ever got shit rolling. I needed them to know without a doubt that my love and loyalty was real, and that my best intentions were centered around their well-being and security. Because once I established that, I knew my niggas would fight to the death for me. This was yet again, another lesson that I learned from my pops.

After choosing your men, your affections toward them must be shown through your actions. You must keep them at your breast, nurture them and care for them. But most important, you must establish a chain of command. You must separate them in ranks, keeping the strongest ones close to you. Take these principles to heart, and your men will not fail you. They will act accordingly.

So, there we were, parked outside of Mikey Bridges' house on 10th and Susquehanna. Easy and me were sitting in my Denali with the five keys of raw stashed in the back. Rahman and Jihad were parked right behind us in Rahman's minivan, and Lil' Man was standing across the street. Every last one of us were strapped.

"Yo, what's taking him so long?" I asked Easy, then I looked at the house where he knocked on the door about twenty minutes earlier.

"I 'on't know." Easy shrugged his shoulders. "He said that I caught him in the middle of sum'n, and that he'd be out to see us in a minute. Just be patient, it'll all work out. Mikey Bridges is the best. He used to cook up a hunnid bricks for me every first of the month. You know I wouldn't steer you wrong."

I was beginning to feel antsy. I trusted Easy, but I didn't trust Mikey Bridges. He was taking so long, that I began thinking he had us out there on some grimy shit. I was a grimy nigga my mah'fuckin' self, so I began thinking the worst shit possible. *What if he told us to wait outside, and then called niggas to come through and rob us?* I doubted that was the case, but then again who's to say? The city was vicious like that, and North Philly was treacherous, dangerous than a mah'fucka.

I readjusted Jesus on my lap, and then looked across the street at Lil' Man. He was standing at attention like a mah'fuckin' soldier—looking around from left to right, with his sawed-off shotty tucked down inside of his pants leg. He looked back at me and nodded his head, then I looked in my rearview mirror at Rahman and Jihad. Both men were on high alert, apparently thinking the same shit that I was thinking.

This nigga, Mikey Bridges, better not be on that bullshit.

Satisfied that my niggas had my back and that all was secured, I grabbed my flip phone from the center console. I still hadn't spoken to, or seen Kia since the day before, so I figured it was a good time to call her. I thumbed in the digits of her phone number, then I placed the phone to my ear.

Ring! Ring! Ring!

"Nigga, this better be you. And you better be calling to say you outside this mah'fuckin' door," Kia's attitude came through the phone.

"Nah, shorty rock, I'm just calling to tell you that shit got crazy last night. A situation popped up, and I'm still somewhat stuck in the middle of it. But as soon as I'm finished, I'ma shoot out there to come see you. Word. You know a nigga need somma that na-na."

"Fuck outta here, pa, you always the fuck lying," Kia replied. "My ass been out here doing everything I said I would, living up to my fuckin' word. But when it comes to *you*, and all the shit that *yo' ass* be kickin', you ain't been living up to none of it. Not a fuckin' thing. I'm telling you, AJ—"

"Bitch, you ain't telling me shit!" I snapped at her, knowing that thug shit turned her the fuck on. "Fuck you think you talking to? Ya ass better recognize."

"Nah, pa, I'm just saying," her decibel softened. "Like, fa' real, though. It's been two whole years since you been away from me. I'm just really fuckin' missing you, pa. I wanna see you."

"And I'm missing you, too. But not to the point I won't handle my fuckin' biz. You know me, Keys. You know the way I get down, and you know what I'm out here try'na do. I gotta stay focused out this mah'fucka, and keep sharp. You know that shit. The second I slip and these niggas catch me, I'm done. There's too much at stake for me to let that happen."

"So, where you at right now?" Kia asked me, then released a long sigh.

"I'm on 10th and Susquehanna. I gotta bust a move and then shoot out Kensington to holla at my man on D and Ontario. Everything should be straight after that."

"And when are you coming to see me?"

"Later on tonight, around ten or eleven. But that's give or take, depending on how much shit I get done."

"Do you want me to cook sum'n for you?"

The second she asked me, I knew she was referring to extra back up. Her and the two Spanish chicks that she rolled with had been secretly terrorizing the city for the past six months. The word on the streets was that a crew of young niggas were kidnapping and killing mad niggas for their paper. But really it was Kia and her two home girls, Maria and Michelle. The trio had pledged their loyalty to me prior to my release, but I honestly didn't take them seriously. If anything, I considered them my Plan *C*. But never my priority.

I looked in my rearview mirror at Rahman and Jihad, and then looked out the window at Lil' Man. I knew my niggas were ready for war, so I didn't need Kia and her mamacitas at that particular moment. I would, however, need them moving forward, so I gave her the green light to have shit ready when I got there.

"Yeah, ma, gawn and do that for me. Hook me up wit' some fried chicken. You know that's my shit."

"You want legs or drumsticks?" she asked me in code, referring to what kind of guns I wanted—handguns or choppas.

"Hook me up wit' both and throw in a couple of breasts wit' it too," I told her to make sure her girlfriends were present when I got there. "I'm hungry as shit."

"Say no more, pa. I got'chu."

"I already know that."

"You better know it." Kia chuckled. "I love you."

"Yup."

Click!

After disconnecting the call, I thumbed in the digits to Raphael's phone number. I had previously called him earlier that morning, but he was balls deep in some early morning cooch, and couldn't talk at the moment. He told me to call back later, and depending on where he was and what he was doing, I could fall through and check him out. That was three hours ago, around eight in the morning. I could have easily waited a few more hours before I called his ass back, but them ten bricks of yolk had my mah'fuckin' palms itching. Aside from that, my new plan moving forward was to have shit rolling before Mook returned from his Cali trip. So that way if shit went left and Pops had to intervene, at least he would see that I was already doing my thing. I figured that would tip the scale in my favor and show Pops that I was capable of holding down his legacy. In the meantime, I needed Raphael to show me around his hood so I could see the way it was flowing. That was the first step to taking over another nigga's hood. You had to *analyze, organize, deputize,* and *supervise.* The money came last. So above all else, I needed Raphael to show me around his hood. I needed to see who was who, and what was what.

Ring! Ring! Ring!

"Hola, papa. I'm glad ju call back," Raphael's voice came through the phone, laced with a thick Dominican accent. "I was jus' speaking to Mamacita about ju. I tell her all about ju, papa. How ju watch my back when ju and me was on lock. I never forget wha'ju do for me, papa. I never forget dat. Never."

"Aw, man. That shit wasn't 'bout nuffin'," I slowly replied, looking at Mikey Bridges' front door. It had just opened wide, and this old-ass Spike Lee looking nigga was standing in the threshold. His gray sweat suit was way too big for his scrawny frame, and his dicked pair of Nike Air Jordan's were scuffed up and leaned to the side. His eyeballs looked big as shit through his Coke bottle glasses, and his cheap-ass jewelry made a nigga want to scream. He had five silver necklaces bunched around his neck, and three silver bracelets bunched around both of his wrists. He even had a silver, five-finger ring on his left hand that spelled *MIKEY.*

Yo, what the fuck ol' head got going on? I thought to myself as I continued staring at him. *Easy got me out here on some bullshit, fuckin' wit' this weird-ass nigga. I was just starting to give him props on some cool shit, and then here he go, right back to the typical crackhead shit.*

I looked at Easy, then I shook my head and looked back at Mikey Bridges. He pressed his index finger to the bridge of his specks, and then gestured for us to come inside of the house.

"So, papa, wha'ju wan?" Raphael's voice came through the phone. I was so stuck on looking at Mikey Bridges, that I momentarily forgot Raphael was on the line. "Ju come and see me, or no?"

"Most def, I'm coming to see you. I've got a few things that I need to take care of, but after that I'm coming ya way. I should be there within the next hour or so."

"Ju know de address, papa. Ju come and see me when ju ready. I'll be right here waiting."

"That's a bet," I calmly replied, as I popped open the rear compartment and climbed out of the truck.

"Dat's cool, papa. I will see ju den. And Mamacita say she cook up for ju sum'fin nice."

"That's what's up, Raphael. Tell her I said thanks. I'll be there as soon as I can."

Click!

Easy and me were standing in Mikey Bridges' kitchen, watching him as he did his thing over the stove. He was whipping that coke like a mah'fucka, twirling the Pyrex pot with his right hand and dropping in ice cubes with his left. It wasn't even a full hour since he first began cooking, and two of the bricks were already rocked up and stretched out to two and a half. My initial assumption was that every brick would come back whole, compressed together in one big block like the five that were already cooked. But instead, they came back in buttery tan boulders. The large boulders were sprawled out on the dining room table, placed in front of a five-speed fan that was blowing on *High*. According to Mikey Bridges, it was the quickest way to dry off the water weight.

I took a pull on the blunt I was smoking, and continued watching as the liquid coke steamed up the Pyrex. The rancid odor that filled the kitchen made me sick to my stomach. I asked Mikey Bridges to open a window, but he wouldn't do it. He said he needed the coke fumes heavy and thick, because the contact high made his whip-game more efficient. Whatever the fuck that was supposed to mean.

"Damn, Easy, why it's looking like that?" I pointed at the foggy white liquid that was churning inside the pot. "It's all gooey and whatnot, looking like some hot-ass yogurt. It's supposed to look like that?"

"Don't ask me, ask him." Easy pointed at Mikey Bridges.

I looked at Mikey Bridges, who was standing there smiling at me. This nigga had more gums than Bubble Yum, not a tooth to his fucking name.

"Nah, youngin', this here ain't no mah'fuckin' yogurt. This that Peanut Butter Crunch," Mikey Bridges boasted. "That good ol' Toe-Tapper."

"*Toe-Tapper*?" I looked at him like he was crazy. "Ol' Head, what the fuck is you talking 'bout?"

"Youngin', this shit right *here*," he pointed at the Pyrex, "this the shit that make a mah'fucka start tap dancing. You know what I'm talking 'bout? They take one good blast and get to doin' like this." He backed away from the stove and started tap dancing like Sambo. "*Ta—Daaahhhh*!" He stopped on a dime with his arms stretched wide and his Bubble Yums on full display. He even had the nerve to be shaking his hands like two tambourines.

Easy and me cracked up laughing.

"Sum'n ain't right wit'cha man, Easy. This nigga's crazy as shit."

"Nah, youngin', I ain't crazy. I jus' tell it like it is," Mikey Bridges replied as he stood back over the stove and continued cooking.

I laughed at him some more, and then checked the time on his microwave. The digits read 11:54 a.m.

"Yo, Easy, I gotta make a run right quick. You gon' hold me down?"

"That's a fact." Easy nodded his head. "Do ya thing. I got'chu covered over this way."

"That's a bet," I told him, then I reached down inside of my pocket. I pulled out my stack of money and peeled off $1,500. "Here." I held the money out for Mikey Bridges, who was charging me $500 for every brick that he cooked. "That's fifteen hunnid. I'ma give you the rest when I come back."

"I can roll wit' that. Jus' sit it right there on the counter."

I placed the money on the counter, then I looked at Easy.

"I'll be back in about two hours. Keep ya eyes on this nigga." I nodded my head at Mikey Bridges, not caring one bit that he heard what I said. "Lil' Man, Rahman and Jihad are still outside. If you need 'em, they're ready."

"I got'chu," Easy said, then he patted the .38 that was bulging from his right hip. "I'm good wit' this here. Go handle ya business." With that being said, I was out.

CHAPTER FIFTEEN

It was only a ten-minute ride from 10th Street to D and Ontario, but I figured that I'd take a little detour. It was the second time that I found myself all alone since I touched down from the bing, so why not kick back and enjoy the solitude?

Fuck it.

The sun was shining, my rims were gleaming, and my system was knocking like a mah'fucka. I was leaned back in my plush leather seat, smoking out and nodding my head to 2Pac's new album, *All Eyez On Me*. The gangsta shit he was spitting on the *Heartz Of Men* had me feeling invincible. It felt like I was Tony Montana, John Gotti, and Bumpy Johnson all rolled into one.

911, it's an emergency, cowards tried to murder me. From hood to the 'burbs, every one of you niggas heard of me.

Shit, I'm legendary, niggas scary and paralyzed. Nothing more I despise than a liar. Cowards die. My mama told me when I was a seed. Just a vicious motherfucker while these devils left me free.

I proceed to make them shiver, when I deliver, criminal lyrics from a worldwide mob figure. Thug niggas from everywhere Mr. Makaveli. Niggas is waiting for some thug shit, that's what they tell me...

I slowed the truck at a red light on C and Erie, but I never came to a complete stop. I just tapped on the brakes long enough for the traffic to clear, then I murked out and banged a left on C Street. I floated past the *STOP* sign on C and Westmoreland, where a bunch of young jawns were standing on the corner. It looked to be about eight shorties all together. They were nodding their heads to the music and scoping out my truck, trying to see who was pushing it. My tinted windows were rolled down, so every chicken had a clear view of the handsome, young thug who was leaned back behind the steering wheel. There was one face in the crowd who seemed familiar. But before I realized who she was, I was already dipping past.

I turned left on Ontario Street and cruised up the block. I could see Raphael up ahead. He was standing in front of his house, wiping down the rims on a black Chevy Tahoe. My music was thumping, so the second he heard it, he stopped wiping and looked in my direction. He was scoping my truck, trying to see who was driving it.

Funny-ass nigga, I smiled at him, thinking about the first time we met.

It was two years ago and that Sambo, Judge Reynolds, had just sentenced me to twenty-four months. I was hoping to get one last visit before I left the Youth Study Center. But the second Reynolds banged his gavel, his bitch-ass deputies yoked me up and transported my black ass straight to placement.

When we pulled up in front of the New Castle Juvenile Correctional Facility, that faggot-ass Sheffield was standing at the front gate waiting for me. He scowled at me when I stepped out of the van, and I scowled right back.

I was tall and lanky and built like a bean pole, but my heart pumped the blood of a giant. Besides that, I was madder than a mah'fucka. I was ready to put my hands and feet on the first nigga that tried me. Sheffield must have seen the look in my eyes, because he simmered down quick. All the tough-guy shit he tried to chump me with flew right out of the window. Bitch-ass nigga.

I couldn't have done shit to him if I wanted to. My wrists and ankles were handcuffed tight, shackled together by a thick long chain that looped around my wrists. The ends of the chain were locked together and pushed through an iron box that was clamped over the handcuffs. The iron box was nutty like a mah'fucka. It was clamped on horizontally, and locked my hands right over left. That shit was way too uncomfortable.

The deputies turned me over to Sheffield, and Sheffield walked me inside of the facility. My first stop was the main building where the Intake Room was located. I was unshackled, stripped down and searched, and then given a set-up kit and a prison uniform.

After going through the intake process, I was led down a long hallway that branched off into separate housing units. We stopped in the chow hall where I was given a bagged lunch, and then continued walking down the hallway. The hallway was separated by a large rec room where a bunch of young niggas were hanging out, kicking it. Some of them were playing cards, while others were playing ping-pong and various board games. The entire room was loud as shit, and then suddenly everything went quiet. Every eye in the room was fixed on me. I was a Richard Allen nigga, so I knew the drill when a new face came on the set. They were sizing up the new fish. But little did they know, I was a full grown mah'fuckin' shark.

I slowed my stroll and ice-grilled every last one of them niggas. Sheffield tugged on my arm and told me to keep it moving, but the only thing he did was cause me to move slower. I carefully studied each face, checking to see if I recognized anybody. Strangely, I didn't.

I did, however, notice this one nigga who was seated at the card table. He was a dark-skinned, stocky nigga with his shirt sleeves rolled up and his Skelly hat on tilt. He appeared to be in his early twenties, which was way too old for a nigga to be locked up in Juvie. The only exception was a young nigga serving a Juvenile Life sentence, which stopped at twenty-one.

Fuck this nigga think he is? Adebisi from Oz? I thought to myself, as he and me locked eyes. There were three niggas seated at the card table with him, and four more standing around it. There was one nigga standing right behind him, a young, Spanish kid with two black eyes. He appeared to be flustered and way out of his element. His shoulders were sulked, his head was down, and both of his hands were stuffed down inside of his pockets. He reminded me of a small child who had just been chastised. He lifted his head for a brief second to look at me, then he looked back down.

"Come on, Rines. I said keep it moving," Sheffield hissed at me. He pulled on my arm for the second time, and my eyelids became two dark slits.

Cracker, you touch me again...

The fake-ass Adebisi smiled at me. He whispered something to one of his flunkies, then he looked away and continued playing cards.

After walking down the hallway and passing a few housing units, we stopped in front of F Block, the unit they assigned me to stay. The block officer met me at the door, and the first thing he said was that my work detail was sweeping and mopping the second tier. *"That's the tier you're gonna be staying on,"* he spoke with a slow, hill-billy drawl. *"You're expected to be awake bright and early for first count, then after breakfast you'll began working. Your assigned cell is 227. Now disappear."*

Again, my eyelids became two dark slits.

Disappear? Who the fuck this cracker think he talking to?

I carried my set-up to the second tier and strolled down to 227. When I reached the cell, it surprised me that someone else was already assigned there. He wasn't there physically, but his bed was made and his property was neatly placed throughout the cell. I noticed there were pictures on the wall, so I sat my set-up on the bottom bunk and then walked over to check them out. There were mad females in every picture, young and old. They each had a light-brown complexion, green eyes and curly black hair. They seemed to be on an island somewhere, like Puerto Rico or the Dominican Republic. I could tell from the palm trees and the white sand beaches in the background. There was one face in every picture that I recognized immediately—the young, Spanish kid with the two black eyes.

"Ain't that a bitch," I said to myself, shaking my head in disbelief. *"Out of all these niggas, why they had to put me in a cell wit' a fucking chump?"*

Based on the pictures, he seemed to be a cool nigga from a loving family. But shit like that didn't matter when a nigga was locked in the bing. Juvenile placement was gladiator school, and only two types of niggas existed: wolves and sheep. There was nothing in between, only predators and prey. I'd been taught by my pops to always be careful when choosing a celly, because the way they carried themselves would reflect on me. So, all that bitch-nigga shit, I wasn't having it. Not the fuck at all. Either papi was gon' stick his chest out and throw-down like a G, or his punk-ass had to move out and find a new celly. Straight like that.

The only personal property that I brought along with me were the six pictures that I stuffed in my pocket before I went to court that morning. I had one picture of my pops, one picture of my moms, one picture of my three little brothers, one picture of Daphney, one picture of Erica, and one picture of Kia.

I removed the toothpaste from the set-up kit they gave me, then I squirted globs of toothpaste on the back of each picture. My next move was pasting the pictures on the wall beside the bunk. So that way, whenever I laid down, I could roll over and see the faces of the people I loved, and who loved me back.

I felt the presence of somebody standing at the gate, so I hopped up from the bunk with the meanest ice-grill. The young, Spanish kid with the two black eyes was standing there looking shook, and standing right behind him was Adebisi and one of his flunkies. Adebisi and me locked eyes.

"Yo, excuse us for a minute, homie. We gotta handle sum'n right quick," Adebisi said as he stepped forward and stuck his head inside of the cell.

I looked at the Spanish kid, and he lowered his head. My assumptions about him were worse than I thought. Not only was he the prey, he was Adebisi's bitch. Adebisi and his homeboy were there to rape him.

"Nah, nigga, I ain't going nowhere. My celly ain't going nowhere neither. Aye, yo, celly, come on in here." I gestured for the Spanish kid to step inside of the cell. I could tell from the look on his face, he was terrified. He looked back and forth between Adebisi and me, then he looked back down not knowing what to do with himself.

"Yo, celly, you heard what I said? Come kick back and relax. Fuck these niggas."

"Say what?" Adebisi snarled, then he pulled his shank out from underneath his shirt. That shank shit didn't faze me. I took a step back and threw up my hands, ready to get busy.

"You only gon' get one swing wit' that mah'fucka. Then after that, I'ma knock you the fuck out and stick it up ya ass. Come on, nigga, bring that shit. YBM the fuck up! Nigga, what!"

Adebisi stepped forward, but his homie reached out and grabbed his arm. He pulled Adebisi back and whispered in his ear. Both of them niggas looked at me and squinted.

"*Yo, is Alvin Rines ya pops?*" The flunky asked me.

"*Yeah, that's my mah'fuckin' pops,*" I stated with my chest puffed out. "*But fuck all the bullshit. Y'all niggas want drama, then let's get it. I'm fit like a mah'fucka.*"

"*Nah.*" Adebisi shook his head, as he back pedaled away. "*I'm crazy, but I ain't that mah'fuckin' crazy. If Alvin Rines is ya pops, then Double R is ya uncle,*" he mentioned my Uncle Rayon, who the streets referred to as *Double R* or *Rayon The Reaper*, the craziest nigga to ever walk the streets of Philly.

"*I ain't even gon' play myself like that,*" Adebisi continued, as he and his flunky backed out the cell. "*You want this fuckboy?*" He pointed at the Spanish kid. "*You can have him. His lil' hoe-ass ain't the only hot pocket that's roaming around this mah'fucka. I can find me another bitch.*"

The Spanish kid and me stayed up that entire night talking. He told me that his name was Raphael Dominguez, and that he moved to Philly from the Dominican Republic. His pops was an immigrant who migrated to the U.S. in the 1970's, and made millions of dollars selling dope in the Bad Landz. The blocks he controlled were some of the most notorious in all of North Philly: 8th and Butler, 7th and Vernango, and D and Westmoreland. His pops moved him, his sister, his moms and his grandmoms to the States about three years earlier. Ironically, that very same year, his pops got smoked in a turf war by some Puerto Ricans who came for his territory. Raphael's uncles from the DR came to Philly to avenge his pops' murder. They settled the score with the Puerto Ricans, and regained control of his family's territory. Raphael told me that was the reason he was locked up and sent New Castle. He shot one of the Puerto Ricans who allegedly killed his pops.

According to Raphael, everything went smooth for the first two years of his bit. He was going to school to get a better grasp of the English language, and had obtained a barber's license so he could open his own barbershop when he came home from the bing.

I asked Raphael about his beef with Adebisi, and he told me that Adebisi had been doing him dirty since he first came to New Castle a few months earlier. I asked Raphael why he never fought back, and he told me that he had. But because Adebisi had his crew riding with him, they ganged up on him and helped Adebisi to do him dirty. I never asked Raphael about being raped. I just made him a promise that as long as he held his own, and didn't back down from any nigga who tried him, I would be there for him to hold him down and have his back. I also told him that in order to get his respect, he had to get his revenge on Adebisi. I told him I would make the first move, but after that he had to step up and do his thing. He promised that he would, but I wasn't quite sure if I believed him. Either way, I decided that I'd make my move the very next day.

It was 10:45 in the morning and the block officers were handing out commissary. Adebisi and two of his flunkies were standing against the railing on the second tier. They were looking down on the bottom tier at everybody who was standing in line waiting to receive their commissary. I was doing my work detail, sweeping the second tier, and could hear them pussies talking about who had what, and which inmates were the easiest to rob. They were so busy looking down on the bottom tier, that they never saw me walking towards them. Raphael was downstairs waiting in the commissary line. He had no idea what I was planning to do, but he damn sure was about to find out.

I slowly unscrewed the broomstick, as I moved towards Adebisi. I was one turn away from having it loose when I slid up beside him. The faggot-ass nigga must have felt my energy, because he turned around to face me. Unfortunately for him, I was seconds away from striking. I cracked the broomstick over my knee and it splintered in half with wooden shards sticking out.

Snap!

"*Yo, man, what the fuck is you doing?*" Adebisi asked, as his eyes opened wide. He tried to run, but it was too late. I stabbed him in his chest with the broomstick, and then grabbed his legs and threw his ass over the railing.

"Aaaaagggggghhhhhh!" Adebisi tumbled through the air with his arms stretched out, reaching for a railing that was no longer there.

Blam!

He came down hard on the metal tables that occupied the first tier. He bounced up and rolled off the side with the broomstick protruding from his chest.

His bitch-ass homies took off running, so I ran down the tier right behind them. They reached the tier's end and hauled ass down the stairs, so I ran down the stairs right behind them. I dove over the railing when I was halfway down, and landed on the closest one to me. We both hit the floor, but I landed on top. I stabbed his ass with the second half of the broomstick and began whipping him like he stole something.

Whop! Whop! Whop! Whop! Whop!

"Agggghhhhhh, shit! Somebody get this nigga off me!" His punk-ass screamed like a bitch. *"C.O.! C.O.! Agggghhhhh, shit! Get this crazy nigga off me!"*

"Nigga, shut the fuck up!" I snarled at him, then I caught him with a heavy right hand. It connected on the right side of his jaw and left his bitch-ass snoring.

I looked up and saw that Raphael was fucking up Adebisi. He was cracking him over the head with the half of broomstick I left in his chest, and kicking him in the face.

"Ju fuck wit' me?" Raphael screamed at him. *"Fuckin' punto! Ju die now! Ju fuckin' die!"* He stabbed Adebisi in his face with the broomstick, and then went down hard when the block officer tackled him.

"Inmate Rines!" The block officer shouted my name when Sheffield and ten more officers stormed the block. *"Lock him down! That sonofabitch is the one who started it!"*

Sheffield and the ten officers ran straight towards me. I threw my hands up and began swinging, but Sheffield had a trick for me. He sprayed me with mace and I went down coughing. I could barely breathe, and it felt like my face was on fire.

Adebisi was fucked up bad, but he didn't die. His man that I fucked up had two broken eye sockets, a broken nose, and a fracture jaw. I broke that pussy's whole fucking face. Bitch-ass nigga.

In the end, Raphael and me spent the next six months in the hole. I didn't even give a fuck. My nigga got his revenge, and I established myself as the new nigga who was not to be fucked with on the compound. Raphael and me grew mad tight during those six months in the hole. He was close to the end of his bit, so he went home a few days after we returned to population. But before he left, he gave me his phone number and told me to call as soon as I touched down. He said he had a block for me.

"Damn, Raphael, calm down. It's only me." I smiled at him, as I stuck my head out of the window. I pulled up behind his Tahoe, killed the engine and climbed out of my truck.

"AJ! It's so good to see ju, papa. Welcome home," Raphael said as he met me halfway and shook my hand. "Ju put on weight, papa. Ju look like Debo from de Friday." He cracked up laughing and punched me on the arm.

"I was giving them niggas hell up that jawn after you left," I told him with a smile. "Remember that bitch-ass Adebisi? I had that pussy washing out my boxers and socks. Punk mah'fucka was walking around wit' black eyes on the regular."

At the mention of Adebisi, Raphael's demeanor changed. He was still mentally scarred from the months of abuse that Adebisi and his crew had inflicted on him.

"But fuck all dat," I changed the subject. "This you right here?" I pointed at the Tahoe. The large truck had a glossy paint job, 20" rims, and dark tinted windows. "This mah'fucka's hot right here."

"It's okay." Raphael smiled. "I jus' buy it a few days ago. But look at ju and de way ju roll up." He pointed at my Denali. "Ju doin' pretty good ju'self. No?"

I smiled at him.

"I'm doing a'ight, nah mean? My pops hit me off wit' a little *welcome home* gift. My next move is the Lexus Bubble that's about to come out, that RX-300. I can't rest until I get me one. Word."

I looked around and noticed right away that his block was deserted. There were row houses on both sides of the street, but not one person was outside hustling. The entire block was a mah'fuckin' ghost town. The only thing missing was a big-ass tumbleweed rolling down the street.

"So, what's up wit' the block? You told me it was jumping out here."

"Not now, papa." Raphael waved me off. "We talk about de business later. For now, I wan' for ju to meet mi mamacita, mi sister and mi grandma-ma. Dey inside de house, dey waiting for see ju. Mi mamacita, she cook up for ju sum'fin nice. Come on, papa, let's go inside de house." He gestured for me to follow. "We relax, ju know? Get us sum'fin to eat and relax, papa. De business, we do later."

CHAPTER SIXTEEN

I could tell off the rip that Raphael's crib was different from the average three-story row house. When we stepped through the front door and entered the vestibule, instead of another door that led to the living room, the only thing I saw was a wide staircase about twenty stairs deep. We headed down the stairs which led to a hallway, and at the end of the hallway, we stepped into a large foyer.

"What the fuck?" I looked around in amazement. "How the fuck is this even possible?"

"Mi papa," Raphael smiled at me, "he make it like dis before he die. Come on, papa, lemme show ju around. Dis is what I like to call—*paradise*—in de slums." He continued smiling and gestured for me to walk with him.

I began walking, but was still trying to make sense of everything that I was seeing.

The large foyer had three ivory beams that ran from the floor to the ceiling, and the thirty-foot-high ceiling was crowned in gold. Luxurious statues and exotic artworks decorated the walls, and the white, marble floor had a sliver of red carpet that trailed into another hallway. We followed the carpet until we reached another room that was just as opulent as the first.

The large room was white like a crystal. The all-white furniture had platinum trimmings, and the coffee table and light stands were platinum and white gold. A white, marble fireplace with a glass door and platinum handles was situated against the far-left wall, and placed on the wall directly across from it was a large oil painting of a young, Spanish man who resembled Al Pacino. The young man was dressed fresh in a white linen suit, with a red lapel and a matching red dress shirt. He was seated behind an oakwood desk, and leaned back in a brown leather a high-back chair. The look on his face was all business, and the diamond ring on his right pinkie had real diamonds blinging from it.

"Dat's mi papa right dere." Raphael pointed at the picture. "Wha' he do was, he buy up every house on dis side of de street, and den buy up every house on de same side de next block over. He bring in he workers who do de construction for him in Los Angeles. Dey transform all of de houses into one big house, wha'ju see now. Dey knock out de *waaalls* dey lay de *maaarble,* de *gooold,* de *plaaatinum.* Papa make it perfect for he familia when he bring us over from de Dominican. De best of all is dat nobody know we live like dis, except for ju now. Dat's how we do it, papa. We hide in plain sight. Never forget dat."

"Damn, Raphael, this some fly-ass shit right here. Word."

Raphael chuckled and waved me off.

"Now, come on." He began moving down another hallway that branched off from the all-white living room. "It's time for ju to meet mi mamacita, mi sister, and mi grandma-ma."

I followed Raphael down the hallway and could smell the savory aroma of some bomb-ass Spanish food being cooked. We continued walking until we came across a four-way divide. Raphael stopped and began telling me more about the house.

"Down de hallway here," he pointed to the right, "is de movie theater, de weight room, and another lounge area for mi familia. And dis way," he pointed straight ahead, "is de elevator dat take us back upstairs to de bedrooms and mi papa's office. And dis way," he pointed towards the hallway on the left, "is where de kitchen and de dining room is located. Come on, papa, dis de way we go." He took off in that direction and gestured for me to follow.

When we reached the hallway's end, it branched off into two additional hallways. The shit was like a fucking maze. I looked down the hallway on my right and could see that it led towards the kitchen. The hallway on my left led towards the dining room. That's exactly where Raphael led me.

The dining room was just as large and eye-pleasing as the first two rooms that Raphael showed me. It had the same high ceiling, the same ivory beams, the same statues, and similar artwork. The only difference was the large, oakwood table that occupied the center of the room, and the high-back chairs that surrounded it. The high-back chairs were a dark stained version of the oakwood table, and had burgundy, suede padding.

The delectable food spread that occupied the table made my mouth water. There were platters full of fresh fruits and vegetables, various wines and exotic cheese, large dishes that were loaded with meat, and two large bowls that were overflowing with rice and beans.

I rubbed my stomach and licked my lips, and then looked down at the far end of the table where an old, Spanish woman was seated at the head. Another Spanish woman, who I assumed was Raphael's moms, was standing on the old woman's right-hand side, while a younger, Spanish woman was standing on the old woman's left. The three of them looked at me and smiled.

"Come on," Raphael said as he began walking towards them. "Come meet mi mamacita, mi grandma-ma, and mi sister, Azriela."

I followed behind him, feeling nervous as shit. I had never in my life received such a great level of respect and honor, so I really didn't know what to say or do.

When we reached the table, before I could even say anything, Raphael's moms was already hugging me. His sister came over and did the same. They welcomed me into their home and gave me mad thanks for having Raphael's back and for making sure he made it home safe from the bing.

"And dis one here," Raphael pointed at the old, Spanish woman, "is mi grandma-ma."

"Hola, grandma-ma. I'm AJ." I smiled at her and slightly bowed my head. I waited for a reply, but the old woman just looked at me and continued smiling.

"Mi grandma-ma, she no talk," said Raphael.

I looked at Raphael, then I looked back at his grandmother. She had a smooth brown complexion, and wavy black hair that was pulled back into a bun. Her beautiful eyes were a hazel light green. Her daughter and granddaughter shared the same exact features. The three of them were drop dead gorgeous.

Grandma-ma stretched her hands out to me. The gesture confused me, so I looked at Raphael. He gave me the head nod to move in closer. I swallowed the lump in my throat, and then did as Raphael told me. I moved in closer, not knowing what else to do.

Grandma-ma giggled, then she waved for me to come in closer. I looked at Raphael, then I looked at his moms and his sister. They each gave me the nod to move in closer. I was already standing so close to grandma-ma, that I towered above her. So, the only thing I could think to do next was lower my head. Grandma-ma placed her hands on both sides of my face, and then reached back behind her neck and unclasped her gold necklace. It was a thin gold necklace with a diamond pendent of St. Christopher. She removed the necklace from her neck and then fastened it around mines. She returned her hands to my face and then softly kissed my forehead.

"Okay." Raphael smiled, as he patted me on the back. "Let's eat."

The food that Raphael's family prepared for me was the best cuisine I had ever tasted in my entire life, even to this very day. But what stuck with me the most from that entire experience was Raphael's sister, Azriela. She was by far the most beautiful girl I had ever laid eyes on. The entire time I was there, she was looking at me and smiling. I was so embarrassed, that all I could do was smile back and lower my head. Grandma-ma noticed and smiled at the two of us flirting. Raphael's moms was quick to notice, as well. She said something in Spanish that I couldn't understand, causing Azriela to scoff at her and blush. Raphael also noticed that his sister and me were flirting, but he didn't seem to mind. He just continued eating and insisted that I try every dish.

★★★★★

"Yo, thanks, Raphael. That was love right there," I told him as we left the house and returned outside. "You got a beautiful family, homie. And the food ya moms' made was all that." I patted my stomach.

"I'm glad ju enjoy ju'self," Raphael replied as he sparked up a cigarette. "Now, let's get down to de business."

"Let's do it." I rubbed my palms together, eager to hear about the block he promised me.

"Come on, we go around dere now. We take mi papa's car," Raphael said, then began walking towards a Pepsi-blue IROC-Z that was parked in front of his Tahoe. The blue coupe had black rims, dark tinted windows, and black air vents on the hood.

"De corner I got for ju, papa, is D and Westmoreland," Raphael said as we climbed inside of the IROC-Z and pulled off with the engine humming. We turned left on D Street and cruised up the block.

The intersection of D and Westmorland was popping like a mah'fucka. The traffic was so thick it reminded me of a free-cheese line. There were White fiends, Black fiends, and Spanish fiends, all huddled into different crowds throughout the intersection copping their drug of choice. Some were there for the heroin that Raphael supplied, while others were scoring dime bags of crack and powder. I already knew the difference between a crackhead and a dope fiend, so it was easy to see who was buying what. The crackheads were huddled on the northwest corner, while the dope fiends were crowded around on the southwest corner. The crackheads stood out the most, looking like the zombies in the Michael Jackson *Thriller* video.

What the fuck? I thought to myself, as I recognized the nigga who was serving the smokahs. *That's the young bul, Meekos, from down the towers. That nigga hustle for Big Jabby.*

No sooner than I recognized him, I spotted Big Jabby's Q45. It was parked in front of a house on the right side of the street. I also saw Dev and Kyle, who were standing outside on the sidewalk. They were looking up at the second story window talking to Big Jabby, who was sticking his head out.

This sneaky mah'fucka, I continued thinking, as Raphael drove through the intersection. *His ass ain't never say nuffin' about no mah'fuckin' Kensington. He made it seem like Bartram Village was the only trap he had his hands on outside of the projects. How the fuck are we 'posed to be partners, and he's already holding out on me? Sucka-ass nigga.*

Raphael turned left on Erie Avenue, made another left on C Street, and then turned left on Ontario, pulling back up in front of his house.

"So, dis is de thing, papa. Most of de dope traffic ju see around de corner, dat's mi familia's shit. But de rest of de dope, de coke and de crack, dat belong to de puntos I'm having de problems wit'."

"Oh, *yeeeaaah*?" I looked at him like I really gave a fuck. "Problems, like what?"

Raphael took a deep pull on his cigarette, then he rolled down the window and flicked it out of the car.

"Ju already know about de beef I had wit' de Puerto Ricans. How dey kill mi papa, and how I shoot one of dem and go to jail for dat."

"Yeah, I'm hip. But how do the Ricans play into this problem of yours? I thought that was already handled."

"It *was* handled, papa. At least to an extent. Ju know wha I mean?"

"Nah, not really. Put me on."

"A few months ago, somma de Puerto Ricans dat I go to war wit', dey come home from jail and try to move in once again. I call mi uncles in de Dominican to come back over and help wit' de aggression, but dey tell mi no. Dey say de only thing dey do is send mi de dope, and how I move de dope, dat's all on mi."

"A'ight, so what about the problem?" I asked him, even though I already knew the deal. Big Jabby and his crew were Richard Allen niggas just like me, and our second nature was to roll out and conquer the next nigga's shit. So, before Raphael even told me, I already knew Big Jabby was slowly moving in on his territory; especially since the towers were shut down and them Bartram Village niggas were beginning to push back. For a brief second, I entertained the thought of revealing to Raphael that I knew Big Jabby and had him tucked away in my back pocket. But then Pops' voice rang clear in the back of my mind.

"Knowledge is power, Trap. So, when you play your cards, you gotta always keep 'em close to your vest. If you reveal your hand

too soon, you could risk the chance of giving your opponent the up-
per hand. When you play the game, you play to win. Don't ever for-
get that."
As always, Pops words were right on point. If I told Raphael
about my inside line with his opposition, that would take away some
of my leverage. I needed Raphael to think that solving his problem
would be a difficult task for me. So that way when it was time to
negotiate and make my demands, I could better position myself.
Raphael was my boy, no doubt. But fuck friends. I was trying to get
that money.

"So, what's up wit' these niggas making problems for you? You
still ain't told me nuffin'."

"One of dem, de leader, he got a girl dat live on Westmoreland.
He was out dere one night when de Puerto Ricans try to jump mi.
He run dem off. He tell mi he name Jabby. He say he got a crew of
young ones who could work on de block for mi, and can hold mi
down against de Puerto Ricans. I tell him yeah, let's do it. I let de
young ones work on de block, which ju already know is a dope
block. I no fuck wit' de coke. I only fuck wit' de heroin, dat's wha'
mi papa do, so I honor he. But den de next thing I know, de young
ones, dey out dere wit' de rock and de powder. I go to Jabby. I tell
for him to tell his young ones dat dey no move de rock and de powder, only de dope. But den Jabby ask mi if de young ones can move
de rock and de powder for he, while dey also move mi dope. Ju
follow wha' I say?"

I nodded my head. "Yeah, I hear you."

"Okay. Good." Raphael nodded back and then sparked up another cigarette. "So, I tell Jabby go 'head. De young ones can move
de rock and de powder, so long as dey move mi dope. Things go
good for only like a month, papa. Den de next thing I know, de
young ones, dey tell mi no. We no more move for ju de dope, we
only move de dope and de powder for Big Jabby. I figure I have no
choice, ju know? Dey keep de Puerto Ricans away, so I go wit' it. I
bring in mi own young ones from de Dominican to move mi dope.
But den de next thing I know after dat, Jabby tell de young ones dey
can also move de dope. But only for he."

145

I gritted my teeth.

"So, that's the problem? You need me to get these niggas out the way?"

"Exactly, papa. I hoping ju can fix it. Den after dat, ju move in and take over de rock and de powder. But de dope, papa, ju leave de dope to mi and mi familia."

"I can handle that," I told him, as I cracked my knuckles. "But I'ma need a lil' more than that, nah mean?"

"A lil' more, like wha'?"

"I'ma do my thing wit' the coke only, so let me make that clear. I just need the same lead way on the two other blocks that your family controls. If my memory serves me correct, that's 7th and Venango and 8th and Butler. I wanna move my shit out there as well, nah mean? And at the same time protect your interest wit' the gwalla-gwallas, keep they asses in check. What'chu think about that?"

"Ju no think dat's a lot to ask?" Raphael's brow shot up.

"Not at all." I shook my head. "I'm the one taking all the risk. I could possibly have to go war wit' these niggas, the Ricans, included. So, the way I see it, that's more than fair."

Raphael caressed his goatee and squinted his eyes. After doing some deep thought, he looked at me and nodded his head.

"Ju know wha', ju got a deal, papa. But only wit' de coke. I can have it no other way."

"Absolutely," I said with a smile. "And that problem of yours, just gimme a few days and I'ma handle that shit."

"I know ju will, papa. If anybody can hold me down, it's ju."

Ring! Ring! Ring!

My Motorola flip phone rang from my pocket. I pulled it out and held up my index finger for Raphael to give me a moment.

"Yizzeah. Who dis?"

"Twin, it's me," Daphney's voice came through the phone. "Where you at?"

"I'm around. Why, what's up?"

"Hey, boo!" I heard Erica's voice in the background. "Me and Daphney are parked outside of your mom' house. Are you any-where around here?"

"Yeah, I'm not too far away. Why, what's up?"

"Well, come around here. I need to see you about sum'n," said Daphney. The tone of her voice made my palms sweat. I couldn't explain why, but for some reason I had the feeling that she knew about the stash house robbery and that me and my crew were the ones responsible.

"You need to see me about sum'n? See me about what?"

"Not over the phone. It's better that we speak in person."

"A'ight. I'll be around there in like twenty minutes."

Click!

"Everything good, papa?" Raphael asked when he saw the look on my face.

"Yeah, man, everything's good. I gotta swing past my moms' crib and take care of sum'n. In the meantime," I cracked open the passenger's side door and stuck my leg out, "no more worries about this problem of yours. All I need is a few days, and it's done."

"Say no more, papa. I'll be waiting to hear from ju."

CHAPTER SEVENTEEN

The first thing I noticed when I pulled up in front of my moms' crib was the cocaine-white Mercedes-Benz S600 that was parked across the street. The V12 coupe had an AMG kit, dark tinted windows, and low-pro Pirelli tires on deep-dish rims. The Delaware license plate on the back read *DAPHNEY*, so there was no need to wonder who owned the car.

"Damn, Twin, you out here doing it like that?" I said to myself, as I pulled in behind the Benz. I threw the transmission in *park*, and then killed the engine. Jesus was laying on the leather console, so I reached over and grabbed him. I placed him on my hip, then I popped open the driver's side door and climbed out slowly.

Looking down the street, I saw my three little brothers and the four young buls they introduced to me the day before. They were playing basketball with a milk crate hoop that was dangling from a telephone pole in the middle of the block. Lucifer was sitting on the curb watching them like a hawk. I whistled three times and pounded my chest, causing Lucifer to look in my direction. His cropped ears stood at attention, then he hopped off of the curb and ran towards me.

"What's up, lil' nigga? You miss me?" I asked him, then I leaned forward and caressed his head. My young bul was a fucking monster—two feet tall, two and a half feet long, and fifty-five pounds of nothing but rock-solid ferociousness. His head, neck, and chest were bulky and stout, and his massive shoulders were wide and stocky like a bulldog's. My lil' nigga was a top notched Pit, and the best part about him was that he followed my every command.

I was still leaned forward, caressing Lucifer's head and chest, when Daphney and Erica stepped outside on my moms' front porch. Erica was all smiles when she seen me, but Daphney's demeanor appeared to be somewhat agitated, perplexed even. I already knew why, so my cap-game was ready for her. And not just her, but for anyone else who tried to link me to the stash house robbery.

I 'on't know shit. I ain't seen shit. I ain't heard shit. And if you feel otherwise, then prove it. Other than that, get the fuck outta my face. Straight like that.

I watched Erica and Daphney as they walked off of the porch and descended the steps that led to the sidewalk. Daphney was looking fly, as usual. She was dipped down in a soft-colored Coogi dress that stopped mid-thigh, a white Coogi handbag, and some fly-ass spaghetti strapped, peep-toe pumps. The blinged out diamonds on her neck, wrists, and ears were the perfect contrast to her chocolate brown skin. She was talking on her flip phone and walking a few steps behind Erica.

I looked at Erica and gritted my teeth. I was still in my feelings about the fuck shit she said on my first night home, when she told me that she wouldn't kill for me. Hearing her say that, made me feel as though she truly didn't love me, and that her so-called loyalty came with a limit. I swear, that shit rubbed me the wrong way. And the more I thought about it, the more I contemplated on whether or not I should cut her the fuck off. The only thing that had me stuck, was that I really did love her. She had a crazy hold on me that I just couldn't shake, and for every reason that I wanted to leave, there were five more reasons that made me want to stay. That ghetto love was a mahfucka, yo. Straight up.

Goddamn, this a bad mah'fucka, I thought to myself, as I licked my lips and studied Erica's body from head to toe. The skin-tight dress she wore hugged her body like a glove. Her ass was so phat that I could see it from the front, and her juicy plump titties had a jelly-like bounce. If I could, I would have fucked her right then and there. I was just about to tell her how good she looked, but Lucifer's growling grabbed my attention. He was peeking around my right leg, keyed in on something behind me.

"What's up, boy? What'chu looking at?" I asked him, then I looked over my shoulder.

Aww, fuck! My heartbeat seized. I couldn't believe my fucking eyes. Cruising down the street was the war van that shot up my party. It was right up on me, just an arm's length away, and cruising so slow it was barely moving. Its tinted windows were too dark for me to see inside, but what I did see was the barrel of an AK-47. It was sticking through a small crack in the door and aiming straight at me.

Dizzamn. These punk mah'fuckas caught me slipping, I thought to myself, as I sucked in a deep breath and accepted my fate. I couldn't have done shit if I wanted to, them bitch-niggas had me.

Lucifer was going crazy—barking and growling, and jumping up and down.

Uggggrrrrrrr Urf! Urf! Urf! Uggggrrrrrrr! Urf! Urf! Ugggg-grrrrrrr! Urf!

My nostrils flared, as I stood there ice-grilling the van. I was waiting to hear the gunfire, knowing it was coming at any given second. But instead of wetting me up, the van jerked forward and sped down the street.

Scurrrrrrr!

Thinking about my three little brothers, I yelled for them to get out of the street. But as I looked down the block, I noticed they were no longer there. They had dipped inside the Chinese store on the opposite corner. I could see Jahlil through the window, ordering candy at the counter.

"Who the fuck was that?" Erica said as she came over and wrapped her arms around my waist. Her and Daphney were walking on the opposite side of the street when the van rolled through, so they never saw the choppa sticking out the door. "They was Joe as shit, driving all crazy like that."

My heartbeat was thumping nonstop, and my brain was moving at a thousand miles per second. I looked at Erica, then I looked at Daphney, who was standing beside her Benz. She looked at me and rolled her eyes.

Yo, I know this bitch ain't just try to line me the fuck up, I began thinking the worst about my own flesh and blood. Daphney had already shown me she would take Mook's side over mines, so who's to say he didn't send her to set me up? *This bitch gon' call me and tell me to come around here. Then as soon as I pull up, that fuckin' van gon' slide through right behind me? Yeah, though? Just like that?* My nostrils flared, as I continued thinking the worst.

"And what's your problem? Why you looking at me like that?" Daphney's voice was mad saucy.

"What'chu mean? You looking at me the same way," I shot right back.

"Boy, don't play wit' me." She rolled her eyes. "Now, come here. I need to holla at'chu about sum'n."

I didn't respond, I just stood there staring at her.

"Fuck is you standing there looking stupid for?" She continued popping fly, as she moved around the back of her Benz and climbed in the driver's side. "Come on, Twin, I ain't got all day." She stuck her head back out and waved me over. "This shit is serious."

I shook my head and sucked in a deep breath, realizing that I played myself. The same lessons that Pops taught me, he had also taught Daphney. I figured that was the reason she told me to come through, and then sent the war van right behind me. She was checking my temperature, looking to see if my guilty conscience would shine through. That was probably the reason them niggas didn't smoke me. It was all a test, and I failed like a mah'fucka.

"Go 'head, boo. Holla at Daphney, and then come upstairs to see me," Erica said, then she stood on her tippy-toes and kissed the right side of my neck. She patted my dick through my jean shorts and smiled at me seductively. "I needs that, so hurry up. I'm try'na drive that dick. Then after that, I'm try'na drive that truck." She pointed at my new Denali. "I'm try'na come through stunting on these dumb bitches."

I patted Erica's ass, and told her to take Lucifer inside of the house.

"Come on, Lucifer. Come with Mommy," Erica told him.

Lucifer looked at her, but he didn't budge. He was still turned up from the war van and determined not to leave my side.

"Dominoes," I gave him the command word to go inside the house. He looked at me and whimpered, but followed my order, nonetheless.

Erica kissed my neck once more, and then told Daphney she would call her later that night.

I watched Erica's phat ass jiggle as her and Lucifer headed up the steps, then I walked over and climbed inside of Daphney's Benz.

"Yeah, Twin, what's up?" I asked her, as I settled back on her plush leather seat.

"Twin, you're my brother, and I love you. But I need you to tell me the truth," Daphney said with a serious look on her face.

"Tell you the truth about what?" My Poker face was game tight. I exposed my hand prematurely, but not to the point I couldn't fix it.

"I received a call from Mook this morning," she looked me straight in the eyes, "and he told me that of few of his blocks were robbed last night. Eight of his runners were either shot up or killed. You wouldn't know anything about that, would you?" She squinted her eyes, still staring into mines.

"Not at all." I shook my head *no*, thinking of a slick way to throw her off my trail. "How would I know about sum'n that happened down the projects? Pops told me to lay low and keep my ass from around there, and that's exactly what I'm doing."

I could tell from the look on her face that she wasn't buying it.

"That's on the real, Twin. I ain't been down there since the party."

"I'm not talking about Richard Allen. I'm talking about the blocks that were hit in Feltonville, Germantown and West Oak Lane."

"Come on, Twin, is you serious right now? I just came home after being on lock for two whole years. How the fuck would I know if Mook had different blocks all throughout the city? The only blocks I knew about were the low-rises. Anything else, I couldn't tell you."

Daphney sucked in a deep breath and exhaled slowly.

"There was also a house in Logan that was hit. Ten bricks were taken, and four people were killed. I'm guessing you don't know nothing about that either, huh?"

"Hell naw, I 'on't know nuffin' about that," I slowly replied, while at the same time doing some math in my head. She said that only four people got smoked, but I was more than certain we killed five. Lil' Man bodied Flames at the door. I smoked Flames' baby moms and his daughter in the bathroom, and then I smoked E-Matic's bitch-ass in the living room. That fat bitch should have bled out from her arm being chopped off, and even if she didn't, the chest shot that Beetle gave her should have killed her for sure. So, what the fuck was Daphney talking about? That was five bodies, not four.

"And you're absolutely sure about this?" Daphney asked, and then folded her arms across her chest.

"You mah'fuckin' right, I'm sure. I ain't have nuffin' to do wit' that shit. Fuck I gotta rob somebody for? I still got the ten stacks and the ten pounds of Hydro you gave me. Then on top of that, I got a brand-new truck. I'm winning right now. The only thing I'm doing is waiting on Pops. Other than that, I'm just out here chilling."

"Well, *whoever* it was," she paused for a second, being extra dramatic, "the muthafucka who *did* do it, shit is about to get real fuckin' ugly for him."

"Aye, yo, dig right, I really don't give a fuck *who* did it. All I know is that it wasn't me," I reinforced my stance. "But speaking of the mah'fucka who *did* do it," I used my fingers to indicate quotation marks, "what'chu mean it's about to get ugly for him?"

Daphney's Poker face was just as strong as mines, so it was hard to tell whether or not she bought my story.

"The house that was robbed in Logan, the stupid muthafuckas who did it, they fucked up. They fucked up *bad*. They thought they killed everybody inside the house, but they didn't. The nigga who worked the spot, his baby mama was there. They chopped the bitch's arm off and shot her in the chest, but she didn't die. The cops made it to her just in time, and they rushed her to the hospital.

"Mook is flying back from Cali later on tonight, and he's going to the hospital to see her. Apparently, she told somebody close to Mook that she recognized one of the niggas who ran up in the house. It must have been an inside job. Because who else would have known about the stash house, other than someone from his crew? Eventually, Mook is gonna find out who done it. And that loose thread, *whoever* he is, is gonna tell Mook everything he knows—who was with him, who done what and why. So, whoever *did* do it, and I'm not saying it was you. But *whoever* it was, they better double back and tie up that loose thread. Because if they don't, not only will they have to face Mook, they're also gonna need to shake the cops."

"The *cops*?"

"Yeah, Twin, the muthafuckin' cops. Do you really think that girl is gonna keep her mouth shut? She's gonna tell the cops everything she knows, and that's the reason Mook is going to the hospital to see her. He's try'na see what he can do to keep the bitch quiet."

Fuck, man! This fuckin' nigga, Beetle! I should have known better than to fuck wit' his dumb ass. Stupid mah'fucka. Why the fuck he couldn't just shoot the bitch in her fuckin' head?

"Twin?" Daphney reached across the leather console and placed her hand over mine. "I love you, and I'm here for you. But you seriously need to be more careful."

"And I love you, too." I looked back at her, and lowered my head. It was clear that she knew I was the one who done it, so there was no need to keep fronting. I just appreciated the fact she gave me the heads up. As far as Mook finding out that it was us who done it, I really didn't give a fuck. My only concern was the cops. If the fat bitch snitched on Beetle and got him locked up, there was a good chance he would rat us out to save himself.

"Well, alright." She took another deep breath and sighed. "I gotta make a few runs, and then pick up Mook from the airport. His flight is scheduled to land at 10:30 tonight."

"Aye, yo, Twin, keep it a hunnid," I said as I cracked open the door and climbed out the Benz. "How the fuck did you know it was me?"

Daphney looked at me and scoffed.

"You better start paying attention to these niggas you be running wit'. Especially Lil' Man, wit' his itty bitty, tiny, little ass. Because the second the fat bitch said that a midget chopped her arm off, I *knew* it had to be him. There's only like a million and one midgets roaming around," she stated sarcastically. "So that's how I knew it was you. Because you, Lil' Man, and Uzi are always together. And who the *fuck* goes on a mission wit' a *fucking* midget?

I swear, Twin, you're just as smart as you are stupid. And If I was you, I'd be tying up that loose thread. Know what I'm talking 'bout?"

"Yeah, Twin, I got'chu. And good lookin', you heard?"

"Umm-hmm. You just tie up that loose thread."

★★★★★

As I stood there watching Daphney's Benz drive away, I noticed that my phone was ringing. I grabbed it from my pocket, flipped it open and accepted the call.

"Yizzeah. Who dis?"

"This is Becky," a white girl's voice eased through the phone. "May I please speak to Cocoa?"

"Cocoa? Who the fuck is Cocoa?"

"Umm, she's the girl whose number I just called."

It took a couple of seconds, then I realized she was one of Daphney's weed customers. The last thing on my mind was some fucking weed, so I snapped on the bitch. I told her not to call anymore and then I banged on her dumb ass. I stuffed the phone back inside of my pocket, but before I could run in the house and handle my business, the fuckin' phone started ringing again.

Ring! Ring! Ring!

"Yo, didn't I just tell you not to call this fuckin' number no more?"

"Woah, homie. Cool out. It's just me. It's Beetle."

"*Beetle*?" The hairs on the back of my neck stood up straight. "Yo, where you at? You been laying low like I told you?"

"Yeah, man. I'm just out here chilling."

"Chilling where?"

"I'm out West Philly, at my grandmama's crib on 60th and Landsdown."

"Have you spoken to, or seen anybody from down the 'jects?"

"Nah, A, I ain't heard from nobody."

"Not even Mook?"

"Nizzaw. I ain't heard nothing from Mook. Not from him, or nobody else. But dig, right, the reason I'm calling is that I came up on a nice lil' block for us."

"Oh, yeah? Where at?"

"Right out here, on my grandmama's block. My cousins and nem got this shit jumping. But the work they selling is some straight up garbage. I broke him off wit' two of them ounces you gave me, and the fiends is out here loving it. I was thinking we could break him off wit' somma that buttah we took last night. Nah mean? Have these niggas out here pumping for us."

"Oh, yeah?" I slowly replied, thinking about what to say next. I had a strange feeling that someone else was on the line, listening to our conversation. I wasn't sure if it was Mook's crew or the cops. But whatever the case, it seemed as though Beetle was trying to get me to implicate myself in the stash house robbery.

"Nah, fam, the only thing I got right now is some greenery. And you know I 'on't fuck wit' these phones like that. So, if you wanna holla, we gotta do it in person."

"I feel you, my nigga. I feel you." Beetle chuckled. "That's my bad. I'm just hoping we can talk sooner rather than later. Nah mean? These niggas got this shit jumping out here, and I'm try'na get parts."

"You can pull up on me later tonight, as soon as the sun goes down."

"A'ight. But where at?"

"Just meet me at the old hangout."

"That's a bet," Beetle confirmed, then he disconnected the call.

Askari

CHAPTER EIGHTEEN

The plan was to run in my moms' crib, grab the two bundles that I owed Easy, and then shoot back to Mikey Bridges' spot. But shit didn't work out that way. I went upstairs to my bedroom where the five bricks of hard and forty-eight bundles were stashed, and was stuck on stupid when I laid eyes on Erica. She was laying on my bed butt-ass naked, watching a porn video and finger-fucking her pussy at the same time. Not to mention the look she gave me when she noticed that I was standing there watching. She bit down on her bottom lip and squinted her eyes, looking at me like she wanted to rip me apart.

"Come get it, boo. Come get up in this pussy. Uhhhhnnnnn!" She closed her eyes and leaned back, finger-fucking her pussy even faster.

I should have been more disciplined and stuck to the plan, especially after hearing about Beetle and the possible identification of Lil' Man. But seeing how wet Erica's fingers were as she plunged them in and out of her neatly-trimmed pussy, the only thing on my mind was digging in them guts.

Man, fuck all the bullshit, I thought to myself as I slipped out of my clothes and approached the bed. *Some bomb-ass pussy is exactly what I need right now. I can deal wit' the rest of this shit later.*

Completely naked except for my socks, I climbed on the bed and buried my face in Erica's pussy. She arched her back and grabbed the back of my head, and then slowly fucked my tongue in a circular motion. I grabbed her thighs, then I rolled over and flipped her body on top of mine. She popped her pussy up and down on my face, and then spun around slow. I continued licking her pussy while she sucked on my dick.

"Ummmmm!" Erica moaned as she brought me to the depths of her throat. She deep-throated my dick nice and slow while her two hands jerked me up and down. "Pfft!" She spat on my juicy bulb, and then twirled her tongue around the tip. She moved her hands from my shaft to my sack and massaged my balls steady and deliberately.

"Umm, damn." My body became tense. I was sucking on the box like a mah'fucka. I dipped my tongue deep inside of Erica's pussy hole, and then licked up and down her creamy wet slit.

"Ummmmm," Erica moaned on my dick some more and massaged my balls just a tad bit harder. Normally, a feeling so good would have made me cum. But this time, the more she did it, the more she was turning me off. Shaking my head, I stopped licking her pussy and laid back on the pillow.

"*Ummmmm!*" Erica moaned more aggressively, agitated because I stopped sucking her box. She dropped her pussy back down on my mouth, and I turned my head. "Ummmmm! Ummmmm! Ummmmm!" She sucked my dick even faster, and moved her hips around so she could find my tongue.

This stankin-ass bitch, I thought to myself, as the left side of my face became soaked with her juices. *Ain't no way in the world this bitch wasn't out here fuckin'. She was damn near a virgin before I got knocked. So, how the fuck she get so experienced all of a sudden?*

The thought of another nigga fucking my bitch, had me mad as shit. I started to question her about it, but then a devious thought crossed my mind. Since her ass wanted to be all experienced and shit, I figured that I'd find out just how experienced the bitch really was. I lifted her body from mines, and then got up on my knees and bent the bitch over.

"Ummmmm, yeah! *Fuck* yeah!" Erica looked back at me, fiending for the dick. "Gimme that rough shit, nigga. Beat this pussy the fuck up."

"You want that rough shit, huh?" I shoved my dick deep inside of her tunnel, then I grabbed her shoulder and pulled her back towards me. Balls deep, I thrust my hips and long-dicked the pussy hard as shit.

Clap! Clap! Clap! Clap! Clap!

"Yes, baby, yes! Just like that! Uuuuhhhhhnnnnnn, *Shit!* Fuck this pussy, daddy! Fuck this pussy!" Erica cried out, throwing the pussy back at me.

Clap! Clap! Clap! Clap! Clap!

I pounded the pussy until her legs began to shake and her creamy cum dripped down between my thighs. She jerked forward and buried her face in the pillow, but was still throwing the pussy at me.

"You want that rough shit, huh?" I growled at her. "Well, take it, then!"

I pulled my dick from her pussy and jammed it up her ass in one quick motion. I gave her the whole thing, hoping I would rip her wide open. But instead of hurting her, the bitch went crazy and threw it back even harder. I couldn't believe it. I was long-dicking her bootyhole, and the bitch seemed to like it.

Clap! Clap! Clap! Clap! Clap!

"Eeeeewwwwwww! That's what the fuck I'm talking 'bout!" She cried out in ecstasy. "Fuck my ass, daddy! Fuck my ass! Gimme every inch of that dick! *Uuuuuuuuhhhhhhhhhhhnnnnnnnn!*" She grabbed the headboard and threw her ass back just as hard as I was pounding her.

No fuckin' way! I shook my head in disbelief, watching Erica's body tremble and jerk. She was cumming so hard, that the bed began to shake. It fucked my head up seeing that she liked getting fucked in the ass. I was so disgusted that I pulled my dick out and plopped down on the edge of the bed.

This stankin-ass bitch. I scowled at her and gritted my teeth. She was still moaning and squirming around the bed like a fish out of water.

After going through the motions, Erica sat up and wrapped her arms around my shoulders. She kissed my neck and earlobe, and then traced her tongue along the grooves of my back. She laid her face on my shoulder, and continued rubbing my body.

"Boo, what's wrong? What happened?" Erica asked me. "You didn't even cum, did you?"

"Nah, yo, I couldn't even concentrate. My mind was on some other shit. Matter of fact," I shrugged her away and stood to my feet, "I'm 'bout to hop in the shower. I still got mad shit that I need to do."

"I'm down wit' that." Erica said with a smile, then she climbed off of the bed. "I'ma take a shower wit'chu. We can do it under the water."

"Under the water, huh? You just full of surprises, ain't you? All of a sudden ya ass wanna be all freaky and shit."

"Huh?" Erica gave me the stupid face. "What are you talking about?"

"Nuffin'. I just wanna take a shower. *Alone.*"

I grabbed my bathrobe, washcloth and towel from the closet, and then stormed out of the room. The bitch had me pissed off something serious.

Ol' grimy-ass bitch!

After taking a quick shower, I returned to my bedroom so I could get dressed and leave. I slipped out of my bathrobe and let it fall to the floor. Erica got up from the bed and picked it up. She was dressed in a pink bathrobe and had a polka dot shower cap covering her head. I didn't even know she had clothes and shit stashed in my bedroom. It seemed like every other second, the bitch had something new with her, and the more time I spent with her, the more I realized she was no longer the same innocent girl who had stolen my heart years earlier.

"Huhn." Erica passed me the blunt she was smoking. "You need somma this, 'cause you trippin' right now. Straight up, boo, you on some other shit."

"Oh, yeah?" I took the blunt from her and placed it to my lips. "The only one trippin' is you. All of a sudden ya ass done got all freaky and shit. You wasn't like that before I got knocked. So, what's the difference between then and now? I'ma tell you what the difference is, you done let one of these niggas turn ya ass out on some freaky shit, 'cause it damn sure wasn't me."

"Say what?" Erica cracked up laughing. "Hold up, boo. Hold that thought." She held her hands out to me and laughed some more. "That's the reason you're acting all stank? Because I spent the last two years learning my own body, try'na make sure you were sexually satisfied when you came home? Are you serious right now?"

My eyelids became two dark slits.

"You damn right, I'm serious. You was out here fuckin' niggas. I know you was, so don't even front. We ain't fucked in two whole years, so how the fuck is you able to take the dick so good? You even let me fuck you in the ass, and you fuckin' liked it. What type of freak body shit is that?"

"Aye, *yooooo!*" Erica laughed even harder. She leaned forward and held her stomach.

"Fuck is you laughing for? Ain't nuffin' I said was fuckin' funny. You lucky I 'on't punch you in ya fuckin' mouth."

"Hold up, boo, lemme show you sum'n," Erica said, as she looked at me and shook her head. She reached up on the top shelf in the closet and pulled out a black velvet box. "Huhn." She handed me the box. "Open it."

My nostrils flared and my jaw muscles pulsated.

"Fa' real, boo. Open it."

I opened the box and looked inside. The first thing I saw was a nine inched dildo. There was also a bottle of KY Jelly and a half-empty bottle of Johnson & Johnson's baby oil.

"Fuck is up wit' this?" I looked back at her.

"That's my side nigga." Erica smiled, then mischievously licked her lips. "I've been using it to pleasure myself and to make sure my fuck-game was on point when you came home. I knew these hoe-ass bitches would be all on ya dick, try'na get'chu. So, because I wasn't all that experienced, I figured that I'd step my game up for you. Where do you think all of these pornos came from?" She pointed at my big screen TV where a bunch of porn videos were stacked on top. "I've been watching Heather Hunter, Janet Jackme, and Vanessa Del Rio damn near every night. Trust me, boo, everything that I am belongs to *you*. I've never been with anyone else."

"Damn, ma, that's like sexy and weird all at the same time." I looked back and forth between the porn videos and the dildo inside of the box. "That's crazy, yo. You could have at least said sum'n. I was starting to think you turned into a hoe on me."

"Nope." Erica shook her head. "I turned myself into a hoe *for* you."

"Yeah, I'm trippin'. That's my bad." I closed the velvet box and gave it back to her.

"Umm-hmm." Erica smiled at me. "So, what's up wit' a second round? You never got'cha shit off, and a bitch ain't feeling that."

"Nah, ma not right now. I've got mad shit that I still need to handle. But we can get together and do sum'n tomorrow."

"Umm-hmm." She gave me an incredulous look. She returned the velvet box to the closet and then grabbed me a pair of boxers, a wife-beater, and a pair of socks from the dresser. "And what'chu feel like wearing?" She moved back over to the closet.

"Just grab me sum'n that's all black."

"All black?" She turned around to face me. "All black for what? I hope you're not thinking about doing something crazy."

"Nah, not at all," I lied through my teeth, knowing damn well the plan was to go out and catch another body. "That's just how I'm feeling right now. I'm in an all-black mood. Nah mean?"

"Umm-hmm," Erica replied. She reached inside of the closet and pulled out a black pair of Guess jean shorts and a black Polo shirt. "Huhn." She handed me the clothes. "And what else you want? Sneakers or Timbs?" "Gimme a pair of sneakers. The all-black Air Forces."

She grabbed the sneakers and handed them to me.

"Now, gimme my blunt back." She giggled and stuck her hand out.

After taking a deep pull, I passed her the blunt and began dressing. The only thing I didn't wear were the white socks she gave me. I threw them back in the drawer and exchanged them with a black pair of Nike socks. I threw on the socks and then slipped on my Nikes.

"And wear somma this," Erica said as she sprayed me down with the Polo Sport cologne she grabbed from the dresser. "I love the way this cologne smells on you. I think about you every time I smell it."

"A'ight, and just so you know, I prob'bly won't be back until the morning. So, are you sleeping over, or going back down the 'jects?" I asked her, as I headed towards the door.

"Nah, boo, I'll prob'bly just take a shower and call a cab to take me back home. I was supposed to be linking wit' Daphney tonight, anyway. So, I'll prob'bly just do that. Maybe in the morning we can go out for breakfast or sum'n."

"Yeah, I'm wit' that." I leaned forward and kissed her on the lips. "A'ight, ma, I'm out. I gotta go."

"I love you, boo, and be safe."

"I love you back," I told her, as I headed out the door.

"Hold up, boo, wait. You forgot sum'n," Erica called out behind me. "Huhn." She held out Jesus with one hand, and my flip phone with the other. "You left 'em on the floor beside the bed."

"Good lookin', ma." I kissed her lips once more. I tucked Jesus on the small of my back, and then looked down at Lucifer who was sitting outside of the door.

"Come on, boy." I patted the crown of his head. "I need you to handle sum'n for me."

Askari

CHAPTER NINETEEN

Mikey Bridges' house was only five blocks away, so I figured that I'd take Lucifer and walk him around there with me. I grabbed his leash from the living room closet, clipped it to his collar, and walked him out of the door. He was still on tilt from when the war van slid up, so by the time we reached the street he was barking and going crazy—growling at every car that drove past and tugging on his leash so hard that he damn near broke the mah'fucka.

Uuuurrrrrrrrrrrrr! Urf Urf! Urf! Uuuurrrrrrrrrrrrr! Urf!

Lucifer's aggressive aura trickled over to me, and before I knew, I was scouring the street from one side to the other. I pulled Jesus from the small of my back and tucked him under the front of my shirt. If drama was in the air, then Lucifer sensed it.

Uuuurrrrrrrrrrrrr!   Uuuurrrrrrrrrrrrr!   Urf!   Urf!
Uuuurrrrrrrrrrrrr!

"Shamooyah!" I commanded Lucifer to calm down. But instead of heeding, he looked back at me and continued tugging. His disobedience was highly unusual, so whatever he felt it must have been warranted. He was tugging on his leash so hard, that I couldn't tell if he was struggling to get to something, or struggling to get me away from it. Either way, I was super on point. My right hand was wrapped around Jesus and my trigger-finger was pushed through the trigger-guard. The first nigga to bust a move was getting baptized. Straight like that.

"*Shamooyah!*" I commanded Lucifer once again. He was still lunging forward, barking and growling, and tugging on his leash so hard that his razor-sharp claws were scratching the pavement. I snatched the leash back, and the swift change of velocity made him stand up on his hind legs. "Calm down, boy, damn. I got us covered. Trust me."

Lucifer settled down and began walking like he had some sense. But even then, he was still growling at everything around us that moved.

Uuuurrrrrrrrrrrrr!

Approaching the corner of 10th and Susquehanna, I saw that my niggas were still on point. Lil' Man was standing across the street, posted in front of the Chinese store. Rahman and Jihad were standing outside of Mikey Bridges' front door. The AK-47s that were tucked under their garments were slightly bulging out, and both men appeared to be on high alert. Jihad was looking up the block towards Dauphin Street, and Rahman was looking down the block at the Chinese store where Lil' Man was standing. His left eye was locked on me, but his lazy right eye was aimed at Lil' Man. He nodded his head and tapped his chest, insinuating that everything was secured.

I tapped my chest and nodded back, and then looked at Lil' Man, who was slowly walking towards me. His sawed-off shotty was sticking out the bottom of his right pants leg. He was so short, the double barrels made him walk with a limp.

"Yo, AJ, man, where the fuck you was at? You took long enough," Lil' Man said, then he gave me some dap. "You said you was coming back in two hours. That shit was four hours ago. Niggas was out here worried about you."

"Worried about me?" I stopped walking. I looked back and forth between Rahman and Jihad, and then I looked down at Lil' Man. "Fuck you mean, y'all was worried about me? Worried about me for what?"

Lil' Man sucked in a deep breath and exhaled slowly.

"Remember them niggas who came through in the van? Them bitch-ass niggas who killed Black Mooch?"

"Of course, I remember. Why, what's up?"

"Them sucka-ass niggas popped back up. They drove through the block about three times since you left."

"They drove through where? *Here*?"

"Yup." Lil' Man nodded his head. "Them niggas ain't try to hop out or do nuffin'. They just cruised through the block on some super slow shit. The first time I seen 'em, they was driving up Susquehanna. The last two times, them niggas came down 10th Street. It was almost like they knew we was out here, like somebody put 'em on us. That's the reason Rahman and Jihad is up there looking like that." He pointed up the street where the two hitters were standing on point. "We was waiting for them pussies to drive back through, so we could air 'em the fuck out. And that's the reason we was worried about you. The last time we seen 'em was two hours ago, around the same time you told us you was coming back. But when you *didn't* come back, and the van never came back, we was thinking they might'a ran into you on the way over here. I called ya phone like ten times, but you never answered."

I started to tell him about the situation that happened in front of my moms' crib, but there was no reason to stir the pot. Whoever them niggas were, if they really wanted some smoke, they could have popped off when they caught me slipping. And besides that, I still had the notion they were somehow connected to Daphney. In regards to the missed calls, I had turned my phone off during the time that I spent with Raphael's family. Had it not been for that, I would have answered.

"Man, fuck them niggas. All that rec-chasing shit can wait. The only thing I'm worried about is making sure this mah'fuckin' work got cooked."

"But what if them niggas slide back through?" Lil' Man asked, as we continued walking up the street.

"That's a fact." I nodded my head. "We gotta get to this nigga before the cops do. The good thing is that I already talked to Beetle. He's hiding out in West Philly at his grandmama's crib."

"You didn't tell him about the fat bitch, right?"

"Nizzaw." I shook my head *no*. "I just told him to meet me down the 'jects as soon as the sun goes down, so I can break him off wit' somma this work. It's going on three o'clock, so we still got time. We gotta make sure the work is straight, stash it, and then lay low for the next few hours. But the second the street lights come on, we gotta shoot down the 'jects. I'ma knock Beetle's head the fuck off."

"But down the 'jects, though? Down the 'jects, where?" Lil' Man asked me. He knew Richard Allen just as well as I did, so he knew how crowded it would be on a nice summer night.

"I told him to meet me at the perfect place. The one spot where nobody can see us, or hear this nigga scream."

"And where the fuck is that?" Lil' Man shot back.

"The old hangout."

"The *towers*?" Lil' Man cracked a smile.

"Without a doubt. We're gonna lure his ass right up on the mah'fuckin' roof. Now, take Lucifer." I handed him the leash. "I'ma go in the house and see what's up wit' this work."

When I stepped inside of the house, Easy and Mikey Bridges were seated at his dining room table, drinking beer and talking shit. Sprawled out across the table were seven mounds of crack wrapped in cellophane. Each mound was bulky and tan, and had a twist-tie fastened at the top. At first glance, they appeared to be a fresh batch of sugar cookies broken apart. But even then, there was no denying the cooked coke smell. The acrid odor was so strong that it seeped through the plastic and permeated the room.

"So, what's up Easy? How we looking?"

"Oh, this that sho' nuff tapper right here," Easy replied, then he took a swig from his Budweiser can. "I told you Mikey Bridges was the best."

I looked at Mikey Bridges, who was leaned back in his chair smiling at me. His Bubble Yums were on full display, and his skinny arms were folded across his chest.

"Say now, youngin', why you ain't tell me Alvin Rines is yo' daddy? Boy, we damn near family," Mikey Bridges claimed.

"Yeah, that's my pops." I smiled back at him. "I didn't know you and him was close like that."

"You damn straight, we close like that. Yo' daddy and this crazy muthafucka right here," he pointed at Easy, "they done brought me so much snow over the years, if I had it all together at one time, I'd need me a snowplow just to walk from here to the kitchen. And since you cut from that same cloth, I'm assuming you'll be doing the same thing."

"That's the plan," I told him, then I dug down inside of my front right pocket. I pulled out my thick wad of cash and then peeled away ten Benjis. "Huhn." I handed Mikey Bridges the money. "That's the stack I owe you."

"And I appreciate it," he said as he accepted the money and sat it down on the table. "But from here on out, just gimme two-fifty a wop. Five hunnid is the price I be charging these meatballs. You Alvin's boy, so that makes you premium steak. You jus' make sure you tell yo' daddy that ol' Mikey Bridges took care of you."

"I most definitely will," I told him, then I peeled away three more Benjis from my knot. "Easy, this you right here." I gave him the money. "That other thing we talked about, I forgot to bring it wit' me. But I still got'chu when I get back to the house."

"Don't even sweat it." Easy waved me off, then he leaned over and stuffed the money inside of his back pocket. "Whenever you need me, I'm here for you."

"That's what's up."

"And Lil' Alvin, take this here to load 'em up," Mikey Bridges said, then he handed me the duffel bag he pulled from the top drawer of his China cabinet.

"That's what's up. Good looking, OG."

I loaded up the seven mounds of crack, and then left the house with the duffel bag clutched in my hand. The second I stepped outside and Lucifer saw me, he lunged straight towards me.

"Agh, shit! Lucifer, calm down!" Lil' Man shrieked, as Lucifer drug his ass across the street. Lil' Man let go of the leash and hit the ground hard, rolling over twice before he popped back up. "Stupid-ass dog."

Lucifer ran up to me and stood on his hind legs. His massive paws landed on my shoulders. But before he could lick me, I pushed him away.

"Here, Rock, take this." I handed Rahman the duffel bag.

As he stashed it in the back of his minivan, the rest of us climbed inside.

"Yo, A, man, what's up wit' this dog of yours?" Rahman asked as he climbed down inside the van. "I 'on't be having no dogs in my ride, homie."

"Nah, fam, this my mah'fuckin' nigga right here. Wherever I go, Lucifer can go. And on top of that, I got a lil' job for him." I reached back and caressed Lucifer's head. "Ain't that right, lil' nigga?"

Urf!

Rahman shook his head and left it alone.

For the next few hours, we bagged up and weighed most of the work, and when the night came, we headed down the projects. It was time for Beetle to get his issue.

CHAPTER TWENTY

"Where the fuck is this nigga at?" Rahman looked over and called out to me. We were standing on the roof of the 10th Street tower. Rahman was posted on the right side of the building, and Jihad was posted on the left. Lil' Man was posted in the front, and I was posted in the back. We were all looking over the ledge trying to see if Beetle was coming, and checking to see if he came alone or if someone else had come with him. Specifically, the niggas from Mook's crew, or the fucking cops if they just so happened to grab him.

"I on't know, Rock. His ass should'a been here by now. I told him to come as soon as it got dark," I shouted back to him.

I looked across the roof at Lil' Man, thinking about what Daphney said about doing dirt with a midget. There were only three midgets in the city who were known for getting busy: Lil' Herb from J Street, Midget Mike from Berks Street, and Lil' Man from Richard Allen. So being as though the fat bitch told the cops that a midget had chopped her arm off, there was no doubt the three gangsta elves would be rounded up and questioned.

I loved Lil' Man like we came from the same nut sack and womb. But I still couldn't see myself going to jail for him; especially for a quadruple homicide.

I highly doubted that Lil' Man would snitch, but then again who's to say? There were mad niggas who I swore up and down would have never told, but they ended up snitching. There were also niggas who I *thought* would snitch, but when the pressure came they stood tall and kept it G. I figured that Lil' Man was somewhere stuck in the middle, so I was still debating on whether or not I should kill him. Beetle, on the other hand, was a different story. Even as kids, he was never as rough and tough as the rest of us. He used to run home bitching every time we had beef and had to rep for the Allen. Besides that, he was still a member of Mook's crew and could flip sides at any given time. So, yeah, this nigga had to die. No doubt.

"AJ, what's up?" Lil' Man called out when he turned his head and saw that I was standing there watching him. I had Lucifer's leash clutched in my left hand, and Jesus gripped in my right. Both of them mah'fuckas were ready to wreak havoc.

"Nah, I ain't say nuffin'. Why? What's up?"

"Ain't shit," Lil' Man replied. "I just looked back and saw you was over there looking at me. I thought you had called my name or sum'n."

"Nah, homie, we straight," I called back and then shook away my thoughts of killing him. I looked back over the ledge and continued watching for Beetle.

Looking down over the ledge, I had a bird's eye view of the entire projects. There were mad niggas standing outside on Poplar Street hustling. The constant flow of crackheads coming and going had me thinking about the money that I planned on making. In addition to the smokahs, there was also a steady flow of fly whips pulling up and parking outside of Kim's Deli. They were Mook and Big Jabby's weight clientele, a bunch of niggas from out of town who had come through to cop nothing less than a brick. Unfortunately for them, the young wolves who were parked across the street in their tinted-out hoopties, were waiting for them niggas to cop their weight and leave. The second they did, the young wolves would pull off right behind them. They would follow the fly whips at a safe distance, waiting for the right time to pounce. Then as soon as them niggas were far enough away from the projects, the young wolves would pull up beside their cars and box them in at gunpoint. They would rob them niggas for whatever money and jewelry they had, confiscate the weight, and then bring it back to either Big Jabby or Mook. The young wolves would keep the money and jewelry, and then wait for the next playa to come through and grab.

Typical Richard Allen shit, I thought to myself, as I continued watching the whole scene play out. A sick thought came to mind, then a wicked smile spread across my face. *What's the purpose of paying niggas to hustle for me? All I gotta do is kidnap a bunch of fiends and lock 'em in trap houses all around the city. I can feed 'em crack and dope and have 'em moving all the work for free. That would cut my overhead tremendously. My word, the streets ain't*

never seen a nigga like me. Fuck having a slice, I'm coming for the whole fuckin' pie.
I smiled at the thought, knowing it would fortify my position in Pops' empire. But that was later on down the line. The issue at hand was Beetle's bitch-ass. Not only did he pose the threat of possibly snitching, he was still one of Mook's soldiers. So, I figured that I'd kill two birds with one stone. Smoking Beetle would eliminate the threat of him snitching, and twisting his top on some extra raw vicious shit would send Mook another message—that he and his crew were no longer safe on the streets and a new King was taking his throne.

"Yo, AJ that's him! It's Beetle!" Lil' Man called out, as he pointed down the front of the building.

Rahman, Jihad, and me walked over to the ledge where Lil' Man was pointing. I looked down at Beetle and saw him moving through the tent city that now occupied the basketball court. He was creeping through the crowd with a black hoody pulled up over his head. He looked around from side to side, then he looked up at the roof.

Lil' Man, Rahman and Jihad leaned back so Beetle couldn't see them. I remained cool. I waved my hand in the air to get his attention, then I gestured for him to come upstairs to the roof. Beetle nodded his head, then he pulled open the lobby's front door. The lock on the door was already picked.

"Y'all see anybody else creeping through the crowd?" I asked my niggas. I was looking down at basketball court, but all I could see were a bunch of smokahs and dope fiends roaming around like zombies.

"Nah, that nigga came by his'self," said Lil' Man. "If somebody else was wit' him, we would'a seen 'em by now."

"A'ight. Go meet his ass downstairs in the lobby." I said to Lil' Man, then I handed him the flashlight that I brought with me. The entire building was dark as shit.

"I got'chu." Lil' Man nodded his head, then he pulled out his shotgun from his right pants leg. "Fuck all the bullshit. Why I can't just kill him downstairs in the lobby?"

"Nah, don't do that. I've got sum'n else in mind," I shot back at Lil' Man. "I'ma break his ass off sum'n proper."

"A'ight, AJ, if you say so." Lil' Man shrugged his shoulders. He tucked the shotty back inside of his pants leg, and then took off walking towards the door.

"Yo, one of y'all gimme a light," I said to Rahman and Jihad, then I grabbed the twisted blunt that was stuck behind my ear.

"I got'chu right here, Lil' A," Rahman said, then he handed me his lighter.

I placed the flame to the tip of my blunt and inhaled deeply. That 'dro smoke hit my ass right away. I coughed a couple of times, and then passed the blunt to Rahman. My flip phone began ringing as I exhaled the smoke. I pulled it out, flipped it open and held it against my ear.

"Yizzeah. Who dis?"

"Twin, it's me," Daphney's voice came through the phone.

"Yeah, Twin, what's up?" I said as I backed away from Rahman and Jihad. I walked over and stood beside the pigeon coop that was stationed about ten feet away from the ledge. The old wooden cage stank like bird shit and had four pigeons flopping around inside of it.

"That situation we talked about? That loose thread? It's already taken care of, so don't worry about it," Daphney told me.

"Don't worry about it?" My eyebrow shot up. "But I thought you said—"

"I know what I said," she cut me off mid-sentence. "But don't worry about it, it's already handled."

"You sure?"

"Damnit, you's a hardheaded ass. Fuck I just tell you?" she snapped at me. "Now, leave that shit alone. There's no need to create more problems than we already have. You've done enough already."

"And what the fuck is that supposed to mean?"

"Just do like I told you, and leave that shit the fuck alone."
Click!

"What's rockin', Lil' A? You good?" Rahman said when he walked over towards me.

I looked at him, debating on whether or not I should tell him about the phone call. But before I could choose, Beetle chose for me. He stepped through door chiefing on a blunt, strolling all calm and cool like shit was sweet.

Stupid mah'fucka. You just stepped into ya own crime scene, I thought to myself, as Lil' Man stepped out from behind him.

"Damn, A, what's up?" Beetle looked at me like he shitted on himself, realizing that death was upon him. Jihad's choppa was aimed at his grill, and Rahman was scowling at him and cracking his knuckles. His one good eye was locked on Beetle, but his lazy right eye was fixed on me. His big ass was standing there looking like a grizzly bear with a bald head.

"Come on, A, man. Please?" Beetle said when he looked back at me. His eyes began to water when Lil' Man cocked his shotty.

Click! Clack!

"Come on, A, man, what the fuck is this? I thought we was squad," Beetle said, then he groaned like a bitch. He damn near buckled and dropped to his knees when Lil' Man's shotgun jabbed him in the back.

"*Squad?* I looked at Beetle and gritted my teeth. "Nigga, you the mah'fuckin' enemy."

"The enemy? How the fuck am I the enemy? I ain't even did shit," Beetle whined. He was standing about eight feet away, looking back and forth between Jesus and Lucifer. I could tell from the look in his eyes he was wondering which weapon would hurt the worst—my pit or my pistol.

"Bitch-ass nigga, stop whining," I snapped him.

Lucifer looked back at me, then he looked at Beetle. He must have felt my energy, because he started going crazy—barking and growling, and biting at the air while he tugged on his leash trying to get to Beetle.

Urf! Urf! Urf! Uuuurrrrrrrrrrrrrr!! Urf! Urf! Uuuurrrrrrrrrrrrr!

"Yo, A, man, get'cha dog!" Beetle screamed like a bitch.

"Lil' Man, get out the way," I ordered my soldier.

Lil' Man smirked and backed away shaking his head. I uncoiled Lucifer's leash, giving him more room to get at Beetle. Lucifer lunged forward and leaped in the air, trying to bite Beetle's face off. *Urf! Urf! Urf! Urf! Urf!*

"Yo, A, get him off me!" Beetle shouted, as he stumbled backwards and fell on his ass.

I ran over to Beetle, so Lucifer could lock on his ass. But then I snatched him back before he could bite. *Uuuurrrrrrrrrrrrr! Uuuurrrrrrrrrrrrr!*

"What the fuck did I do?" Beetle cried out, scooting back on his ass. "I ain't done shit! I swear, I ain't done shit! Come on, A, you gotta believe me! *Please?*"

"Pussy, get'cha faggot-ass up," I snarled at him, showing no mercy whatsoever. My black heart wasn't built that way. I gave him a few seconds to stand back up, and when he didn't, I shot him in his fucking shoulder.

Blakka!

"Agggghhhhh, *shit!*" Beetle screamed as he rolled over clutching his shoulder.

"Pick his ass up, Rock."

"Dickhead, that's one of the reasons you up here now," Rahman growled at him, then he grabbed Beetle by the back of his hoody and snatched him the fuck up. "Agh, shit," Beetle cried as he hunched forward holding his shoulder. "Come on, A, don't kill me, man. I knew you my whole life. Lil' Man, you too. Don't do me like this, man. Please don't do me like this? We know each other's whole family!"

"Nigga, fuck you," Lil' Man snarled, then he jumped up and cracked Beetle upside the head with the butt of his shotty. Beetle dropped, but Rahman snatched him back up.

Lucifer was still going crazy, so I tightened my hold on his leash. I walked down on Beetle, forcing him towards the ledge on the left side of the building.

Uuuurrrrrrrrrrrrr! Urf! Urf! Urf! Uuuurrrrrrrrrrrrr! Urf! Urf!

"Nigga, you got three options. You can meet Jesus." I aimed the .40 dead in his grill. "You can meet Lucifer." I uncoiled Lucifer's leash and my little nigga lunged at him, "or you can jump ya ass off this mah'fuckin' roof. Matter fact, there's a fourth option, you can get all three. But either way ya ass gon' die tonight. Now, how the fuck you want it?"

Instead of replying, Beetle took off running towards the door. He only made it two steps before Rahman punched him in the back of his head.

Whop!

"Agggghhhh, fuck!" Beetle screamed in pain when he crashed down hard on the asphalt.

"Pick his ass back up," I told Rahman.

Rahman snatched him to his feet, then he jumped out the way when I let Lucifer loose on his punk ass. My little nigga went to work. He buried his head between Beetle's legs, chomping on his dick and balls.

"*Aaaaagggggghhhhhh! Get him off me! Get him off me!*" Beetle screamed as he stood on his tippy toes and grabbed Lucifer's head with both hands. Lucifer slung him from side to side, forcing him closer to the ledge.

"Shamooyah! *Rah!*" I commanded Lucifer to let him go. Lucifer released his bite, then ran back towards me and sat down quietly. I looked at Beetle and smiled like a demon. He was leaned forward, shaking and crying, and clutching his private parts with both hands. He looked up at me with tears in his eyes. His bottom lip quivering, as he begged me not to kill him. His pleas for mercy fell on death ears, though.

"So, I see you met Lucifer," I told him, then I aimed the .40 right between his eyes. "Now, it's time to meet Jesus."

Blakka!

Beetle flew backwards and flipped over the ledge with his arms flapping wildly. We leaned over the ledge and watched his body as it tumbled through the air.

Ka-Whap!

He splashed against the ground, laying on his back with his limbs stretched out. I looked at Jesus, then I looked back down at Beetle.

"Ain't that a bitch?" I looked at my niggas and started laughing. "Jesus got him looking like he's stretched out on a cross. Bitch-ass nigga."

After taking care of Beetle's bitch-ass, I felt like kicking back and blowing off a little steam. So, after dropping off Lucifer at my moms' crib, Lil' Man and me hopped in my truck and then drove up Germantown to kick it with Uzi. Rahman and Jihad returned to the stash house so they could finish weighing and bagging up the coke. The plan was to link back up first thing in the morning.

"Damn, yo, look at how young we was," Uzi said, then he handed me the photo album he pulled out. We were chilling in his living room, smoking blunts and drinking 40s. Uzi was seated on the sectional, and Lil' Man was leaned back in the rocking chair with his baby legs hanging off of the side. I was a few feet away from him, stretched back on the love seat. My flip phone and Jesus were laying on the coffee table.

"Yeah, fam, we was young as shit right here," I nodded my head, looking at a picture of Lil' Man, Uzi, Black Mooch, and me. "Yo, Lil' Man, look." I handed Lil' Man the photo album. "Look at how young we was."

"Yeah, man, them was the days right there," Lil' Man said with a smile, then he took a swig from his 40 bottle. "I just wish Black Mooch ain't have to go out like that. Nah mean?"

"Most def. I feel the same way," I said, then I took a puff from the blunt I was smoking. I hit the blunt a few more times, and then I passed it to Lil' Man.

"Ohhhhh, shit!" Lil' Man perked up, showing us a throwback picture of him and Meesha. "You even got a picture of me and my 'roni in this jawn. That's crazy, yo. This was our ninth-grade grad-uation. Meesha gave me the draws for the first time that very same day. Ain't that a bitch?"

"Them must'a been some big-ass draws." Uzi cracked up laughing. "Even back then, Meesha was big as shit!"

"Fuck you, Uzi." Lil' Man scowled at him. "I'll bust ya ass in here, talking about my mah'fuckin' 'roni. Fuck you think this is?"

"Nigga, puff the blunt or pass it," I told him, then I took a swig from my 40 bottle.

Lil' Man placed the blunt to his lips and hit it mad hard, looking like a smokah taking his first blast of the morning. I shook my head, and then looked down at my flip phone ringing. I picked it up, flipped it open and placed it to my ear.

"Yizzeah. Who dis?".

"Cocoa?" A white boy's voice came through the phone.

"Nah, this ain't no mah'fuckin' Cocoa!" I snapped at him, al-ready knowing he was one of Daphney's weed clientele. They'd been calling my phone all throughout the day, and the shit was start-ing to burn me out. "Cocoa's black ass got locked up. Don't call this mah'fucka no more."

Click!

"Damn, A, you over there sounding like me and shit." Uzi laughed at me, then he knocked down the rest of his Olde E. "I be the same way when these young jawns be blowing up my jack."

"Nah, man, it's this fuckin' phone that Daphney gave me. These fuckin' weed heads been calling me all day. I gotta change the num-ber on this jawn, yo. Fa' real."

No sooner than I sat the phone back down, the shit started ring-ing again. I looked at Uzi and shook my head.

"See what I'm saying? This the nut shit I'm talking 'bout."

I snatched my phone back up, but then I realized it wasn't my phone that was ringing. It was Uzi's. His black Nokia was laying on the coffee table right besides mine.

"This ain't even me." I grabbed Uzi's phone and tossed it to him. "That's yo shit."

Uzi smiled, looking all stupid.

"That's prob'bly one of my young jawns, I was telling you about. She must want somma this diiiyyyyock."

"Fuck outta here, nigga. Answer the phone." I laughed at him.

Uzi accepted the call and held the phone to his ear. He looked at me and squinted his eyes. "Yeah, he's here. He's sitting right across from me. AJ, huhn." He handed me the phone. "It's Erica."

"Erica?" I looked at him sideways. "Fuck is she calling you for?"

"How the fuck would I know? Don't ask me, ask her," Uzi said, then he leaned back on the sectional, mumbling under his breath. "*She prob'bly want somma this diiiyyyyock.*"

"Yeah, a'ight, nigga." I laughed at him, shaking my fist. I placed the phone to my ear, but I didn't hear anything. The line was completely silent.

"Erica? This you? Why the fuck you ain't saying nuffin'?"

"The bitch can't talk wit' a gun in her mouth," a muffled voice came through the phone.

"*What?*" I hopped up and snatched Jesus off of the coffee table. "Who the fuck is this?"

"Don't worry about who the fuck this this," the voice growled back. "Ya lil' ass wanted drama? I'ma bring it to you, starting wit' this bitch. You got twenty-four hours to drop off a hunnid stacks. And if you don't, I'ma send this bitch back to you, dripping nut wit' her brains blew the fuck out."

"Pussy, you touch my fuckin' girl..."

"Nigga, squash that shit. Just keep ya ass by the fuckin' phone. I'ma call back tomorrow night at the same time. Either have my money, or schedule this bitch a funeral."

"*Aaaaaaagggggggghhhhhhhh!* Oh, my God! AJ, help!" I heard Erica scream before the line went dead.

"These bitch-ass niggas!" I shouted in frustration.

"Yo, A, what's wrong? What happened?" Uzi said, as he and Lil' Man jumped up from their seats. "Who the fuck was that? I thought it was Erica."

"It *was* Erica. Mook and them niggas kidnapped her."

CHAPTER TWENTY-ONE
An Hour Later

I was pacing back and forth in Uzi's living room, from one side to the other. Lil' Man, Uzi, and Uzi's brother, Zion, were huddled in the dining room loading the hammas that Zion had brought through a little while earlier. I really didn't know Zion all that well, except for the fact he was Uzi's brother, and that he and his crew, the *Haines Street Mafia*, had the city on smash from Germantown to Mt. Airy. It was clear from the way he rolled up, the nigga had paper. His brand-new Range Rover 4.6 was parked outside sitting on dubs, and his platinum jewelry had more carats than Bugs Bunny's shit. The look in his eyes was the look of a boss, something that I hadn't seen since the day my pops went to prison. I had known Uzi my entire life, but this was my first time actually meeting Zion. He stepped to me on some real nigga shit, shaking my hand and telling me that he had my back.

"Uzi told me that y'all came up from the sandbox together, so my hands is ya hands. However you wanna handle these niggas, me and mines are riding wit'chu," were the words he professed to me. The nigga wasn't lying neither. He had a Gucci duffel that was loaded with hammas, and had another bag that was filled to the rim with extra clips and bullets. The ten niggas that he brought with him were posted outside on the porch, and just like him, they were all driving brand new Range Rovers. I didn't know it until Zion told me, but the Haines Street Mafia were YBM affiliated.

"You good, fam?" Zion asked when he stepped back inside of the living room. He offered me a hit from the blunt he was smoking, but I shook my head *no*. Shit was too real to be getting high. There were too many questions that were left unanswered, and the future of my takeover depended on me making the right move. The weed smoke would have only clouded my thoughts more than they already were.

"Don't even stress that shit. We gon' make it right," Zion said, then he plopped down on Uzi's sectional. "In the meantime, I wanna run a few things past you. Nah mean? No judgement or nuffin' like that, I just wanna know what'chu think."

"A'ight." I looked at him skeptically, trying to figure out which angle he was coming from. "Go 'head, I'm listening."

"So, dig right, I've been doing some thinking. I really don't know the bul, Mook, like that, but what I *do know* is that he feeds his family the same way that I feed mines."

"A'ight. And?"

"And what if it wasn't Mook who kidnapped ya peoples? And I see the way you're looking at me, but hold on, just hear me out. Have you ever considered that someone else might have taken her? Or that somebody from Mook's crew might have did it, and he doesn't even know?"

I stopped pacing and looked at him like he was crazy.

"Fuck you mean, what if wasn't Mook? Who else could have taken her? Mook is the only nigga I'm out here beefing wit'."

"I'm just saying, like, from what I know, you and the nigga had words and all dat. But was it serious to the point he would shoot up his own trap, and then double back and kidnap your girl? We gotta be missing sum'n."

"Nah, fam, I ain't missing shit. I dissed him in front of his crew, and now he's try'na save face. He's intimidated by me, because he sees my potential. He knows that I'm the only nigga out here wit' enough juice to knock him from his spot. So now he's try'na show everybody that he's still that nigga, and that his boss hand ain't to be tested."

"In theory, that could very well be the case," Zion said as he leaned forward and caressed his goatee. "But killing a cockroach wit' a sledgehammer? And I'm not saying that to disrespect you," he quickly clarified when he saw the look on my face. "I'm only try'na get'chu to see things from another perspective. There's levels to this shit, and niggas in Mook's position, they usually don't move this way."

"Aye, yo, dig right," I began cracking my knuckles, "fuck that nigga, and fuck you, too, if ya ass ain't feeling me. I ain't the one who called you niggas, Uzi did. If ya ass ain't down to ride, then step the fuck off. Straight like that."

Zion smiled at me. He stubbed out his blunt in the ashtray on the coffee table, then he stood to his feet. I looked him up and down, ready to bust his ass if he wanted some smoke.

"Yo, Uzi, I'm outta here, bro," Zion called into the dining room, ice-grilling me just as hard as I was ice-grilling him.

"You're leaving?" Uzi asked when he stepped back in the living room. "For what? What happened?"

"Ask him," Zion replied as he headed towards the door. "This nigga ain't nuffin' but a funeral waiting to happen, too smart for his own fuckin' good. If I was you, I'd leave his ass where you found him."

"Fuck you say?" My nostrils flared. "Pussy, I'll twist that top."

"See what I mean?" Zion smiled, then he opened the front door. "He 'on't even realize where the fuck he at, or even worse, who the fuck he talking to. Stupid mah'fucka."

Zion shook his head, then he left the house and slammed the door behind him. Uzi looked at me, vexed.

"Yo, A, man, what the fuck? That's my fuckin' brother."

"Fuck that nigga. Him and his bitch-ass crew. I 'on't need them niggas. They can smoke a dick and choke, for all I care."

"Nigga, we *need* Zion. Him *and* his crew. How the fuck we 'posed to go to war without a *fuckin'* army?"

"Them niggas is cream puffs." I waved him off, then I grabbed the blunt that Zion left in the ashtray. I told myself that I wouldn't smoke, but fuck it. I sparked the blunt back up, placed it to my lips and inhaled deeply.

"If anything, that nigga served his purpose," I spoke through a thick cloud of smoke. "He ain't take back none of them hammas he brought wit' him. I'm cool wit' just that. I 'on't need no half-assed niggas riding wit' me. Ol' sucka-ass nigga. He should have taken my side when he had the chance. 'Cause when it's all said and done, and *I'm* the nigga who's running shit, his ass is gonna *wish* that he did. You mark my fuckin' words. Believe that shit, nigga!"

The front door opened, and Rahman stepped inside of the house. Jihad stepped in right behind him. I called them after finding out that Erica was kidnapped and told them to come through, asap.

"Yo, what's up wit' Zion?" Rahman asked with a confused look on his face. He was facing Uzi, but his lazy right eye was locked on me. "I was just talking to him before he pulled off. He told me y'all was in here on some weirdo shit. Fuck was that about?"

"Fuck that nigga, Rock. Ol' half-assed mah'fucka. He gon' step to me wit' a soft spot for the enemy. We 'on't need them niggas. We can handle this shit on our own."

"Yo, AJ, dawg, you gon' *stop* disrespecting my brother," Uzi warned, then he stepped into my chest like he wanted some work.

"Yeah, though?" I stepped forward, pressing my forehead against his. "You absolutely right."

Whop!

I snuffed him with a short-right hook, and his knees buckled. He fell back on the sectional and tried to get back up, but I was already on his ass. I reached down and grabbed him by his throat, and then shook him in the air like a rag doll. He clawed at my hands trying to pull them away, so I squeezed even harder.

"*Uggghhhhh!*" Uzi gasped with his legs kicking wildly. His eyeballs bulged out and his tongue sprang from his mouth.

"Lil' A, chill!" Rahman shouted, trying to break us apart.

"Yo, AJ, what the fuck?" Lil' Man shouted as he ran into the living room. His little ass hopped on the sectional and jumped on my back. "Naw, cuz, we ain't going out like that! This the home team! We squad! We already lost Black Mooch!"

Between Rahman tugging on my arms and Lil' Man hanging from my back, I slammed Uzi down on the sectional. I released my hands from his neck, and he rolled over coughing and gagging.

"Nigga, you ever step to me again, I'll *bite* cha fuckin' head off." I leaned down and growled in his ear. "And Lil' Man, get the *fuck* off my back!" I slung his ass across the room with one good thrust. He landed on the love seat, rolled over the side, and crashed into the wall behind it.

I looked at Rahman and Jihad, who were standing there in total silence.

"You mah'fuckas got sum'n to say? *Say it!*"

Jihad shrugged his shoulders and looked away. Rahman's one good eye was locked on mines.

"I just need you to keep in mind what niggas is out here try'na do," Rahman stated. "The last thing we need is inner strife between us. A house divided won't stand."

"Is that all," I quickly shot back, already discounting Uzi as a member of my squad.

"Pretty much," Rahman replied. "I just wanna see you win. I wanna see *us* win. But a cell is only as strong as its nucleus, and a body can't function wit' just a brain. It also needs the heart. The heart is what makes the blood flow. Don't ever forget that."

I looked down at Uzi, who was still coughing and gagging, then I looked down at Lil' Man.

"Goddamn, AJ, ya ass strong as shit." My little nigga smiled at me. "So, what's next?"

"Go in there and grab them hammas from the table. We up out this mah'fucka."

The drive back to North Philly was quiet as shit, as Lil' Man and me were sifting through our own thoughts. At least that's what I was doing, Lil' Man was more or less following suit. He was leaned back in the passenger's seat chiefing on a blunt and staring out of the window.

I replayed the conversation that I had with Zion, and some of the things he said were beginning to make sense. What if it wasn't Mook who kidnapped Erica? The beef between us, like Zion pointed out, wasn't really that deep. If anything, I was the one working angles trying to force his hand against me. But even then, I still hadn't done anything that would make him bring the drama at such an extreme level. He couldn't even link me to the corners we hit and the stash house we robbed, because I killed Beetle before he could implicate me. So, Zion was right, I had to be missing sum'n.

"Ya lil' ass wanted drama? I'ma bring it to you, starting wit' this bitch," the kidnapper's voice echoed throughout depths of my mind. I thought long and hard trying to see if I recognized the voice, but I didn't. The sound was too muffled. Whoever the nigga was, he must have had something covering his mouth.

Damn, yo. I shook my head, thinking of all the niggas who could have possibly taken her. *What if it was Adebisi, or one of them niggas back at the jail? A few of them niggas beat me home, so what if they was out here laying on me? Maybe it was them who came through in the war van and shot up my party. But nah, that doesn't make any sense. If that was the case, they would have smoked me in front of my moms' crib. And that brings me to Daphney. What if it was her? I was so caught up when she told me about the loose thread, that I never asked her about the war van. And Erica definitely said sum'n about the two of them linking up later.*

"Fuck!" I pounded my fist on the steering wheel. Lil' Man looked at me and scowled, mad because the loud sound startled him. I scowled right back at his ass, then I leaned back in my seat and continued thinking.

Nah, man, there's no way that Daphney could have done it. For one, that's my fuckin' sister. And two, if that was the case, then why the fuck would she tell me about the loose thread? Fuck, man! I've gotta be missing sum'n. What the fuck am I missing?

"Yo, AJ, you see that Crown Vic behind us?" Lil' Man said as he stood up on the seat and leaned over the headrest. "Look in the rearview mirror. It's a black Crown Vic. I'm not sure, but I think it's following us."

I looked in the rearview mirror, and just like Lil' Man said, a black Crown Victoria was two cars behind us. We were riding down Germantown Avenue, a block from Cambria Street. I stopped at the corner and turned right on Cambria. The first car behind us continued going straight, but the Crown Vic also turned right on Cambria. It was creeping up behind us, but keeping an unsuspected distance.

"See what I'm saying?" Lil' Man said, as we cruised past the playground. "The first time I peeped him was back at the Stinger Bar. The second time was at the red light on Germantown and Erie. I really didn't pay it no mind until we drove past Carmen's, and the nigga was still on us. I'm telling you, AJ, that Crown Vic is following us."

Instead of replying, I just kept my eyes on the Crown Vic.

"Fuck around and be one of Zion's peoples," Lil' Man suggested. "Uzi might'a called him and told him what happened, and now he's try'na get us hit."

"Nah, Lil' Man, I doubt it. Especially, since he know you in the truck wit' me. I could see if I was by myself," I slowly replied, still watching the Crown Vic through my rearview mirror. "You still got the strap?"

"You mah'fuckin' right, I got the strap," Lil' Man replied, then he pulled his shotty from his right pants leg. "And don't forget about the bag of guns that I stashed in the back. Them mah'fuckas is loaded and ready."

"A'ight. I'ma pull over across the street from the bar," I told him, then I grabbed Jesus from the center console. "Hop ya ass in the back seat. 'Cause I'm shooting through the door if he roll up beside us."

Lil' Man did exactly as I told him.

The traffic light on 11th and Cambria turned red, but I drove straight through it. I pulled over across the street from the bar, while the Crown Vic stopped at the light.

"You think it's one of Mook's peoples?" Lil' Man asked me. He was standing on the back seat, watching the Crown Vic through the window.

"I 'on't know, but we damn sure about to find out."

The street lights on the corner were bright enough for us to see inside the Crown Vic. A young, light skinned nigga was seated behind the steering wheel. He appeared to be riding by himself. He was talking on his cell phone and looking around the intersection, scoping the scene.

"So, what'chu want me to do?" asked Lil' Man. He looked at me, and then looked back at the Crown Vic. "You want me to hop out and start blasting?"

"Nah, let's wait and see what he does, first. For all we know, he's a choir boy driving home from Bible study. But I'm telling you now, *whoever* he is, if he pull up beside this truck, that's his ass."

I rolled down the passenger's side window and aimed Jesus at the door panel. I was ready to bust right through that mah'fucka.

The traffic light turned green, and the Crown Vic lurched forward. It was coming straight toward us. The young nigga behind the steering wheel was nodding his head to whatever music he was listening to, and I could see that his windows were rolled up. I wasn't exactly sure what I was looking at—who the nigga was and what he was up to, if anything at all. The only thing I knew was that my bitch got 'napped, and that this nigga in the Vic seemed to be following us. It crossed my mind that maybe it was all coincidence. But then I remembered what my pops had taught me about coincidences, he told me they didn't exist. So, if the nigga stopped or slowed down anywhere near my truck, I was baptizing his ass. Straight like that.

We were parked on the left side of the street, so the Crown Vic rolled up on the right. My heartbeat intensified as it drove right past us. It stopped at a *stop* sign one block up, and then turned left on 12th Street.

"Lil' Man, what the fuck?" I looked back and scowled at him. "You almost made us kill a mah'fucka for nuffin'. Man, get'cha ass in the front seat."

Lil' Man shrugged his shoulders, looking all stupid and shit. He climbed his little ass in the front seat and plopped down on my buttah-soft seat.

"You can say what'chu want, AJ. That mah'fucka was following us."

"Man, that nigga wasn't following us," I shot right back and then pulled away from the curb. I made a left on 12th Street, another left on Indiana Street, and then came back out on Germantown Avenue. I cruised down Germantown and then turned right on Susquehanna.

"I'ma shoot past my moms' crib real fast. I wanna make sure everything is good over there," I told Lil' Man, as I turned left on Franklin Street.

"Yo, what the fuck is this?" My eyelids became two dark slits.

It was 10:45 at night, and my three little brothers were standing outside. Had I not known any better, I would have thought they were out there hustling.

"Yo, ain't them ya lil' brothers?" Lil' Man pointed out.

"Yeah, that's them. What the fuck is they doing outside?"

Askari

CHAPTER TWENTY-TWO

"Yo, what the fuck is y'all doing outside? Where Mommy at?" I looked at Jahlil, as I hopped out of the truck with the engine still running.

"I 'on't know." He shrugged his shoulders. "We been standing out here since we left from Horsey and Boo-Boo's house. We knocked on the door, but Mommy never let us in."

Jahlil had a look on his face like he didn't care, and Jabril's facial expression was the same. Jacobi, on the other hand, was looking at me like he wanted to cry. He ran up and wrapped his arms around my leg.

"We think sum'n bad happened to Mommy," Jacobi said, then he looked at Jahlil. "Right, Jahlil? Right?"

I sucked in a deep breath and inhaled deeply.

"Come on, y'all. Let's go in the house and see what's up."

I reached back inside of my truck, grabbed my keys, and then led my brothers up the steps. I was just about to open the front door, but my moms' voice made me turn back around.

"Poe? Poe? Where y'all going? Lemme get some money."

"Mommy, where you went?" Jacobi asked, then he ran over and wrapped his arms around her waist.

"Eeww, boy, get off me. Being all touchy and feely and shit." She shooed him away. "Poe?" She looked back at me and stuck her hand out. "Gimme some money. I need to go food shopping right quick."

"Bitch, is you—*ummmmm!*" I caught myself and bit down on my bottom lip. I started to grind her ass to dust, but for the sake of my brothers I held my composure. The last thing I ever wanted to do was disrespect our moms in front of them, and then have them thinking it was okay to do the same.

"Yo, where you was at?" I asked her in a tone that was calmer and more civil.

"I was around the corner." She scratched her head, as her eyes opened wide. She was clearly high on crack. "You gonna gimme some money, or what?" She stuck her hand back out. "I need to go shopping for food, and the boys didn't eat nuffin' yet."

"*They didn't eat yet?*" I screwed my face at her.

"Ahn-ahn, AJ, we ain't eat yet. The only thing we ate was some cereal and the candy we got from the store," Jacobi said, then he looked at Jahlil. "Right, Jahlil? Right?"

"That's the truth. We had a bowl of KIX this morning, and some Jolly Rancher sticks," Jahlil replied, sounding more mature than his six years of living.

"Take them in the house. I'ma come back wit' some food," I told my moms.

"And what about my money?" she asked me, still holding her hand out. She clearly didn't care about my brothers and the fact they were hungry. The only thing she cared about was buying some more crack.

"We'll talk about that when I come back wit' the food."

She sucked her teeth and rolled her eyes.

"Bring ya asses!" she snapped at my brothers, then she un-locked the door and stormed inside the house. "AJ, let us come wit'chu," Jabril said.

"Nah, yo. Go in the house wit' Mommy. I'ma be right back."

Jabril lowered his head, then he took off after Jahlil, who was already trucking up the steps. Jacobi whined and followed behind our brothers.

"Aye, yo, come back. Front and center," I called out to my brothers.

Their three bodies stopped, spun around and marched back to me. I had trained them well.

"Jahlil, who are you?"

"I'm powerful," he answered like a G with his chest poked out.

"Jabril, who are you?"

"I'm powerful," he replied with the same intensity as Jahlil.

"Jacobi, who are you?"

"I'm powerful," he slowly replied, then he wiped the tears from his eyes.

"Jahlil, *what* are you?"

"I'm powerful."

"Jabril, what are you?"

"I'm powerful."

"Jacobi, what are you?"

"I'm powerful."

"And together, what are we?"

"*Powerful*!" We shouted in unison, and then came together for a group hug.

"I love y'all lil' niggas," I told my brothers. "If don't nobody else got y'all, just know that I always will. Now, go in the house. I'ma bring y'all back some food and sodas."

"You promise?" Jacobi asked me.

"Yeah, Cobi, I promise. I'ma get us some Chinese food."

I watched my baby brothers go in the house, and fought like hell to keep from crying. I hated the fucked-up cards that life had dealt them. I needed to find a way to change that shit, and I needed to change it fast.

★★★★★

The Chinese Store on Germantown and Lehigh was the only food spot in the hood still open, so that's where we went to get some grub for my brothers. Under normal circumstances, I would have never gone to this particular spot. The food was nasty as shit, and the place was a death trap, responsible for mad niggas getting they shit pushed back on the late night.

"Now, you know we gotta be on point out this mah'fucka," I told Lil' Man as we left the store and climbed back inside of my truck. We had already placed our orders and the Chink behind the bulletproof glass told us we had a ten-minute wait. I ordered three chicken wing platters with French fries, two 40 ounces of Olde E, and a box of blunts so Lil' Man and me could get our chief on while we waited for the food.

It was 11:05 p.m., so the intersection was all but deserted. But even then, I knew that looks could be deceiving. I had a weird feeling that something wasn't right, like more drama was just a breath take away. It was a weird feeling that I couldn't shake, and as Lil' Man and me sparked up the blunts we had just rolled, the craziest shit happened to me. An image of God popped up in the back of my mind, and my heartbeat seized. He was up in heaven looking down on me, and shaking his head in contempt.

"Thou shalt not kill!" His booming voice rang loud in my ears, reminding me of Exodus 20:13. I remembered the Bible verse because Erica's grandmother, Big Mama, had taught it to us when we were little kids running around the projects.

If only we had listened to, and accepted the gift she tried to give us.

I wasn't even religious, but I swear that shit had me shook. It had me feeling like Erica's kidnapping was God's way of punishing me for the people I killed. I reached for the necklace that Raphael's grandmother had given me, and slowly caressed St. Christopher.

"Yo, AJ, look. It's Top Cat and J-Dawg. They just pulled up in front of the Chinks."

"They just pulled up where?"

"Right there." Lil' Man jabbed his finger, pointing across the street at a pearl-white Bonneville sitting on dubs. "They 'on't even know it's us sitting here. They ain't never seen ya truck before."

"And how you know it's them?" I looked back at him, still clutching the gold pendant of St. Christopher. "You can't even see through the tints."

"Ain't no question, that's them. I know that bullshit-ass Bonnie from anywhere. I remember the day Top Cat bought that piece of shit. And you know that nigga, J-Dawg, is wit' him. Top Cat don't never go nowhere without J-Dawg. I'm telling you, AJ, that's *them.*"

No sooner than Lil' Man said it, the driver's side door popped open and Top Cat climbed out slowly. J-Dawg climbed out of the passenger's side a few seconds later.

"I *told* you!" Lil' Man perked up, being way too hyped. "Is you thinking what I'm thinking?"

My breathing intensified and my nostrils began to flare. I looked at Lil' Man, and then looked across the street at Top Cat and J-Dawg. I kissed St. Christopher's wings, and then snatched him off *my* neck and threw him out of the window. I was too far gone to turn back, and to make shit worse I was just getting started. So whatever punishment God had planned for a nigga, then so be it.

"So, what's up? We gon' smoke these niggas, or what?" Lil' Man asked me.

"You mah'fuckin' right, we gon' smoke 'em." I grabbed Jesus from the center console. "But first we gotta wait until they come out of the store. We was just in there, so the Chinks can identify us if we go back in and blaze up the spot."

"So, how you wanna do it then?" Lil' Man smiled, looking like a troll with his tiny little baby feet hanging off of the seat. His sawed-off shotty was clutched tightly in both of his hands.

"Climb ya lil' ass in the back compartment. I'ma pull up on 'em when they get back in the car, and then pop open the back doors. You hop out and give it to 'em."

"And you know I will." Lil' Man smiled some more, eager to kill. "This shit is for Black Mooch," he rolled over the back seat and crouched down in my back compartment, "and for Erica, too. These bitch-ass niggas is finished. I'ma show 'em how the lil' one get down."

We waited for five more minutes with the engine running. We were parked up the street from the store, facing Broad Street. The white Bonneville was facing the Avenue.

Top Cat and J-Dawg emerged from the store talking shit. Top Cat was eating from his purple bag of Chumpies potato chips, and J-Dawg was drinking from a 40 bottle that was tucked inside a brown paper bag. I unlocked the back-compartment doors, as they climbed inside of the Bonneville.

"Don't push the doors open until we're right up on 'em," I called back to Lil' Man.

"I got'chu, AJ. I got'chu," Lil' Man said as he leveled his shotty. The pistol-grip was clutched in his right hand, and the back-door's handle was slightly ajar in his left.

The headlights on the Bonneville came to life, and I pulled away from the curb. I banged a U-turn in the middle of the street, and then sped up in front of the Bonneville.

Sccuuurrrrtttt!

I mashed down on the brakes, and then looked back over my seat as Lil' Man pushed open the doors. He hopped out of the back of my truck and landed on the Bonneville's hood. Top Cat and J-Dawg never seen it coming.

Boom! Boom! Click! Click! Boom! Boom! Click! Boom!

The windshield crumbled from the force of gunfire, peppered with five bullet holes that were large enough to push an apple through. Top Cat must have died with his foot on the gas, because the Bonneville rammed into the back of my truck.

Vrrrrmmmmmmm! Wham!

"You bitch-ass mah'fucka!" Lil' Man shouted as his little ass went flying through the air. He flew back and bounced off my speaker box, and then landed back on the Bonneville's hood.

Ta—Doom!

"Lil' Man, come the fuck on! We gotta go!"

Boca!

"Yo, what the fuck?" I looked around confused, flinching from the gunshot that penetrated my windshield.

Boca! Boca! Boca! Boca!

Four more bullets ripped through the windshield, airing out the passenger's seat. A swift burst of glass sprayed me in the face, so I closed my eyes and ducked down behind the steering wheel. I aimed Jesus over the dashboard and shot back blindly in the same direction the bullets were coming from.

Blakka! Blakka! Blakka! Blakka!

"Yo, who the fuck is that shooting at us? And where the fuck is it coming from?" I shouted to Lil' Man, who was climbing over the back seat.

198

"It's the same nigga from the Crown Vic! He's standing over there on the corner!" Lil Man shouted back, then returned fire from the back seat.

Click! Boom! Click! Boom! Click! Click! Boom! Boom!

"Run his ass over!" Lil' Man shouted, as more bullets penetrated the windshield.

Blakka! Blakka! Blakka!

I threw some more of my hot shit at him. I was still crouched down behind the steering wheel, but could see out the windshield enough to drive. I floored the gas pedal and the tires began screeching.

Scurrrrrrr!

The truck leaped forward, gunning straight for the nigga who was shooting at us. I was trying like shit to run his ass over, but he let off a few more rounds and then dove out of the way. He popped up, ran across the street, and then jumped inside of his Crown Vic. The fucking car was parked on the corner with the engine running.

Blakka! Blakka!

I blazed off two more bullets, tearing up the Crown Vic's headlight and fender. I tapped on the brakes, turned right and then sped down the Ave. Looking in the rearview mirror, I saw that the Crown Vic was chasing us. Even worse, I saw the blue and red lights that were glowing from its dashboard and grill.

"Yo, Lil' Man, you see this shit? This nigga's a fuckin' cop!"

"I on't give a fuck! Fuck the cops!" Lil' Man replied as he fumbled with the pumpkin-head bullets he was using to reload the pump. "Fuck I care about the mah'fuckin' cops? Them pussies get they tops popped, too!"

I veered right on 10th Street, which was bumpy as hell from the trolley tracks and potholes. Lil' Man was standing on the backseat, so every time I hit a pothole he stumbled backwards and dropped the bullets he was trying to load.

"Yo, AJ, what the fuck?" Lil' Man snapped at me, reaching down for the bullets he dropped. "Stop hitting all these mah'fuckin' potholes! You see me back here try'na reload this fuckin' pump!"

"Nigga, fuck that pump!" I shouted right back. "You got a whole bag of guns on the back seat! Grab one and get busy!"

Lil' Man was so nervous and turned up, that he momentarily forgot about the Gucci duffel that was full of guns. The fucking bag was laying on the seat right beside him.

"And I told you this nigga was following us!" Lil' Man said as he reached down inside of the bag. He pulled out a black Mac 11 with a ladder sticking out, and then cocked back a live round.

Click! Clack!

"Lil' Man, stop talking! *Blast!*"

Tat! Tat! Ttttttttat! Ttttttttat! Tat! Tat! Ttttttttat!

The rapid fire from the Mac 11 lit up the Crown Vic's windshield and hood. The headlights were shot out and the front grill was dangling from the bumper. But even then, it was still chasing us.

"Whoooooh, *shit!*" Lil' Man screamed like a wild cowboy. His little ass was jumping up and down on the back seat, waving the Mac around. "This a bad mah'fucka right here! I should'a *been* got me one of these!"

"Lil' Man, what the fuck is you doing?" I spazzed on him. "Stop fuckin' around, this nigga's still on us!"

"I'ma get him up off us, A! I'ma get him up off us!"

Lil' Man aimed the Mac out of the window and continued clapping.

Ttttttttat! Ttttttttat! Ttttttttat!

Still speeding down 10th Street, I looked back and saw that the Crown Vic had turned right on Dauphin Street. I blew past Susquehanna and gunned the truck at top speed. Lil' Man was still turned up in the back seat, hopping around with the Mac in his hand.

"*Whooooo—oooh!*" Lil' Man shouted. "The lil' one strikes again, baby! Richard Allen mah'fuckin' Mob! *Raaaam Squaaad!*"

We blew past the Diamond Street projects and continued heading south towards Richard Allen. Not once did I slow down or stop at a *stop* sign. The chrome grill on the front of my truck was husky and wide and ready for impact. So, any bullshit car that got in my way was getting rolled the fuck over.

Finally, we reached Girard Ave and a calm feeling washed over me. We were two blocks away from the Allen, without a single cop in sight. I thought we had gotten away Scott free. But then the second we crossed Girard Ave, the Crown Vic popped back up from out of nowhere. It was speeding straight towards us, coming eastbound on Girard. Lil' Man was the first one to see it.

"Fuck is up wit' this mah'fuckin' cop? This bitch-ass nigga won't quit!" Lil' Man lashed out, then he looked at me. "Gun this mah'fucka, A! We can shake him in the low-rises!"

I floored the gas pedal and the truck lurched forward. The Crown Vic spun the corner, but we were already two blocks away about to turn right on Poplar Street. I whipped the steering wheel to the right, and mashed down on the brakes. The tires burned rubber, as the truck spun clean.

Scurrrrrrr!

I pressed my foot back down on the gas, but not a damn thing happened. The engine roared, but there was no acceleration.

Vrrrrrrrrrrmmmmmm!

"Fuck is up wit' this mah'fuckin' truck?" I looked around confused, trying to figure out what happened. I pressed back down on the gas, but instead of taking off we just rolled down the street like the gear was stuck in *Neutral*.

"Fuck all the bullshit, A. We gotta bounce," Lil' Man said, as the wailing of police sirens rang in my ear. He popped open the back door and hopped out with the Mac in his hand. The Crown Vic spun the corner, and Lil' Man gave it heat.

Tat! Tat! Ttttttttat! Ttttttttat! Tat! Tat! Ttttttttat!

The Crown Vic's hood flew up, and the car lost control. It skirted sideways and fish tailed into a light pole at the corner.

Wham!

"Come on, nigga, we out!" Lil' Man shouted as he took off running. He darted past Kim's Deli and dipped through Reno, moving so fast that his little legs became a blur.

I hopped out of the truck with Jesus in my hand, and all I could think about were the fingerprints I was leaving behind. I took off running towards the towers, ducking when a bullet whizzed right past me. The bitch-ass cop was dumping at me.

Boca! Boca!

I back aimed Jesus, and squeezed the trigger.

Blakka! Blakka!

The two bullets missed their target, as the cop continued chasing me. He seemed to be about fifty yards away, but was catching up quick.

Blakka! Blakka!

I let off two more shots and continued running. I didn't know why, but my plan was to hide inside the 10th Street tower. I was halfway toward the building's front entrance, when I tripped over something and crashed down hard. I looked back to see what I tripped over, and saw that it was Beetle's dead body. It was twisted and splattered, leaking out blood like a pig in a slaughterhouse. He'd been laying there since I shot him off of the roof. I shook away the image, then I popped up and continued running.

Boca! Boca!

The cop threw some more of his hot shit at me. The bullets whizzed past my ear and blew a large chunk of brick from off of the building. My instincts were to shoot back, but I couldn't. I fucked up and dropped Jesus when I tripped over Beetle. I turned the corner and hauled ass towards the entrance. The front door was still ajar from when we stripped the locks a few hours earlier. I dipped inside the lobby and looked around, not knowing where to go. I thought about hiding on the roof, but I refused to die the same way that Beetle had, flying over the ledge with a bullet stuck in my head.

I was running out of time, so I had to think fast. The lobby was dark as shit, so I could barely see. But because I was born and raised in the towers, I knew exactly where to hide. I ran across the lobby and dipped inside of the elevator shaft. I was hoping the cop would run in behind me, dart past the elevator and run up the stairs. If he did, I could slide out and get away.

CHAPTER TWENTY-THREE

"Philadelphia Police Department!" The bitch-ass cop shouted from the door. I could see him through the small slit between the elevator's doors. He appeared to be about six-foot-one with a stocky build. I squinted my eyes trying to see his face, but I couldn't. The flashlight he held in his hand was too bright to see behind it.

"I know you done ran up in this mah'fucka, 'cause I seen you!" The cop continued shouting, sounding more like a street nigga than he did a cop. "Real shit, dawg, this ya last mah'fuckin' warning. If you make me come up in this mah'fucka looking for you, the same place I find you gon' be the same place I leave you. I done told you project niggas, but clearly y'all ain't understanding my mah'fuckin' message. It's a new day and time, and I ain't playing wit'chu niggas. Ain't *shit* going down 'round this mah'fucka unless *I* say so!"

Yo, this nigga ain't no mah'fuckin' cop, I thought to myself, as I continued watching him. The way he talked and the way he dressed, had my head fucked up. He appeared to be in his mid-twenties, and had the swag of a hustla. The gold chain that hung from his neck had an iced-out Jesus piece, and the gold watch around his wrist had an iced-out bezel. The diamonds were so bright that I could see them in the dark.

"The irony," he blurted out, and I didn't know why. He looked back over his shoulder, and mumbled something under his breath. A few seconds later, another person walked up behind him. He was a tall, white man with a medium build. A bulletproof vest was strapped on over his shirt, and a silver detective badge hung from his neck.

Now, that's a mah'fuckin' cop, I continued thinking, watching both men as they stood outside the entrance. I listened closely, as the two men conversed.

"So, how many ran inside?" The white cop asked the light-skinned nigga. "Was it both suspects, or just one?"

"It was only one. The other bastard got away," the light-skinned nigga told him, then he stepped aside so the white cop could step inside of the lobby.

"These little bastards. They usually run to either one or two places—the pussy they came out of, or the pussy they're cumming in," the white cop stated. "But running inside of an abandoned building? Where nobody can hear him screaming? *Really?*" His cracker-ass chuckled, then he pulled out a .357 Magnum. "Well, damnit, I'd have to say he's the dumbest sonofabitch in the whole, wide frickin' world."

I watched him closely, looking at his nickel-plated .357 Magnum. It shimmered in the dark with his every movement. The fake hustla stepped into the lobby behind him. He waved his flashlight from left to right, illuminating the lobby.

"And the perp, he's a one-eighty-seven suspect, correct?"

"Affirmative," the black nigga stated. It was the first time he sounded like a cop since I heard him speak. "I've been following him and the one who got away for the past hour or so. The two victims they murdered were Top Cat and J-Dawg. The two perps were parked outside of the Chinese store on Germantown and Lehigh, when Top Cat and J-Dawg pulled up in Top Cat's Bonneville. The two vics went inside of the store and when they came back out and climbed inside of their vehicle, the two perps pulled up in front of them. The perpetrator who got away, who's name is Lil' Man, jumped out of the back of AJ's Denali and landed on the hood of Top Cat's Bonneville. He used a shotgun to murder both victims."

What—the—fuck? My mind was blown when the black cop mentioned Lil' Man and me by name.

"And this AJ kid, he's Alvin Rines' son, correct?" The white cop asked.

"Affirmative. He's the one we've been waiting for."

"And now it's time to pay the fucking piper," the white cop chuckled.

This shit is fuckin' crazy. I shook my head in disbelief. *Even if I get away now, these pussies still gon' book me. Fuck.*

"And another thing, there's a dead body on the side of the building," said the black cop. "His name is Antonio Robinson, but his nickname is Beetle. From the looks of him, it seems as though somebody *shot him in the head and then* pushed him off of the roof."

"And this AJ kid, do you think he's responsible? Most perps return to the scene of their crimes, you know."

"I can't say for sure, but he *did* drop this," the black cop replied, then he pulled Jesus from his waistband. "It's a Smith & Wessin 40 caliber."

"A 40 caliber, huh? I wonder if it's somehow connected to the massacre in Logan last night." The white cop rubbed his chin. "From what I've gathered, there were 40 caliber shell casings left at the scene. So, make sure you tag and bag it. It's a far reach, but who's to say? It could very well be our murder weapon. I'm gonna have my guy in ballistics take a look at it."

Fuck, man! I'm fuckin' finished. I'm done. I continued thinking, knowing damn well that Jesus had at least five bodies on him.

"So back to this AJ kid, how do you wanna play it? We could kill his ass and get away with it."

"Well, killing him is always an option." The white cop smiled. "But let's give him a chance first. Hey, *dickhead!*" he shouted out loud. "You've got exactly five seconds to come out with your hands up! If not, we're gonna *fucking* kill you! The choice is yoo-ouuurrrs!" he stated in a sing song voice, sounding like a schmuck.

Damn, yo! What the fuck I'ma do? I looked around for an escape route that didn't exist. *There's no way out this mah'fucka.*

"Five! Four! Three! Two!"

"A'ight, man, y'all got me." I stuck both of my hands through the slit, making sure they could see that I wasn't strapped. "I'm coming out, man, don't shoot me."

Both men approached me with their guns drawn. They snatched me from the elevator shaft, handcuffed me, and then led me outside to another Crown Vic that was parked the wrong way on 10th Street. The black cop walked away scowling at me, and the white cop smiled. My word, I had the craziest shit running through my mind. Shit was about to get real fucking dark for me.

"Alvin Rines Jr, huh?" The white cop continued smiling, as he shoved me in the back of his Crown Vic. "Boy, oh boy, do I sure have plans for you."

I scowled at him and curled my lip. "Smoke a dick and choke on it. *Pig!*"

It didn't take long before I realized that something strange was happening. I had been arrested more times than I could count, and not one time was I ever handcuffed, thrown inside the back of a cop car, and driven around aimlessly by the pig who arrested me. The police station that governed my hood was the 26th District, which was located in Fish Town, on East Girard Avenue. But instead of making a right turn on Girard towards the precinct, the white cop turned left.

"Yo, my man, where the fuck is you going? You going the wrong way."

Instead of replying, he looked back at me with a stone hard face. He gritted his teeth, and then slammed shut the fiber glass window that separated the front seat from the back.

These bitch-ass niggas, I thought to myself, as I began to realize exactly what was happening to me. *These mah'fuckas ain't arresting me. They fuckin' kidnapping me.*

The white cop drove us to Logan and cruised past the stash house that me and my crew had invaded the night before. The next destination was Germantown. He drove past the house where Uzi lived, and then drove back to North Philly and did the same thing to Mikey Bridges' house. The next place he took me was Kensington. He circled Raphael's block, then he turned left on D Street and drove past D and Westmoreland.

My brain was completely fucked, seeing all the places he had just taken me. Each one was directly linked to my ultimate goal of a hostile takeover. So, clearly, my enemy was two steps ahead of me. Either he or someone else had been tracking my moves that entire day.

Damn, yo, I fucking played myself. I lowered my head in defeat. I thought I had the game figured out, but clearly, I didn't. Shit was way deeper than my young mind could have ever imagined. I had underestimated the strength of my enemy, and now I had to pay the consequence.

"Always remember, Trap, you're not the only student of war," I could hear Pops voice in the back of my mind. *"There's always the possibility your enemy is just as sharp as you are, and could be maintaining his power the same way that you maintain yours. So, never be too confident when engaging in battle. The perfect enemy is capable of defeating you."*

Thinking about Pops, I shook my head and sighed. Not only did I let myself down, I had also let Pops down. He had high hopes for me and big-time dreams. My entire life he'd been training me to take his empire to new levels and heights. But I fucked up. I blew it, and all because I came home and moved too fast. My bloodthirsty way of thinking and deadly desire for trap money and fame became my two worst enemies. I should have been more observant. I should have been more patient. But instead, I went chasing after something that was already mines: *my father's crown.*

I picked my head back up and looked out of the window. We were back in North Philly, headed westbound on Girard. I had no idea where the white cop was taking me, but I assumed it was West Philly. He turned left on 34th and Girard, and pulled over at the Philadelphia Zoo.

My heartbeat quickened and my palms began to sweat. My nostrils flared and my breathing intensified. There was no doubt in my mind that death was around the corner. My only hope was that whoever kidnapped me would kill me right there on that dark, shadowy street. Because if he didn't, I'd be taken to another location and tortured to death.

The white cop looked back at me and gritted his teeth. His Motorola cell phone was placed to his ear. He nodded his head and calmly affirmed that he and I were parked outside of the zoo.

"Stankin-ass pig," I mumbled under my breath, as a pair of headlights came cruising down the block.

It fucked me up when I looked out of the window and saw the car was my Yukon Denali. Right behind it was a cocaine-white Mercedes-Benz S600. My bullet-riddled Denali pulled over and parked across the street. The white Mercedes-Benz pulled up in front of the Crown Vic. I looked at the Benz and squinted my eyes. The license plate on the back read *DAPHNEY*.

CHAPTER TWENTY-FOUR

"*Daphney?*" I said to myself, as I reread the license plate. The V12 coupe was the same exact car that my sister was driving earlier that day. Daphney told me that she was picking up Mook from the airport at 10:30, which was over an hour ago. So, I figured it was then, that shit got crazy for her. Mook must have somehow learned that it was me and my crew who invaded his stash house and robbed his blocks. But instead of grabbing his pistol and popping off like a G, he was paying me back by kidnapping and killing the closest people to me.

I wasn't afraid of death, because real gangstas were *born to die and bred to kill.* So, dying in the streets was inevitable for a young, thug nigga like me. My only concern was Daphney and Erica. I couldn't shake the feeling they were already dead, chopped to pieces and stuffed inside of Daphney's trunk. My sister and boo were completely innocent of my treacherous savagery. But even then, they'd been forced to deal with the consequences of my actions.

My gangsta betrayed me, and fresh tears flooded my eyes. The Angel of Death had taken the souls of my sister and bitch. My dark, hollowed life force was next. There was nothing I could do to stop him, so a nigga said fuck it. My only hope was that Double R would strike back and give Mook the ghetto justice he deserved.

The white cop must have read my mind, because he looked back at me and smiled. I shook away my tears and scowled back at him, refusing to acquiesce defeat. If he thought I would die like a bitch-nigga begging for my life, then his cracker ass had the game fucked up. Because even behind tears, handcuffed and waiting to die, my cold, black heart pumped the blood of a gangsta.

"You see this shit, you little fucking bastard?" the peckerwood antagonized. "Had you come home and done as you were told, you wouldn't be in this position. So, now you's gotta answer to the fuckin' boss. You silly, little sonofabitch."

"Nigga, fuck ya boss," my tongue spat acid. "Both of y'all can suck a dick."

No sooner than the words left my mouth, a third pair of headlights sliced through the dark. I looked out of the window and saw the car was a cherry-red, convertible 5.0 Mustang. The top was down, and I could see Mook leaning behind the steering wheel. His Motorola flip phone was pressed to his ear, and his blinged-out pinky ring sparkled in the dark. I had seen this ring many times before, as every captain in my pops' army had one. The ring was a 24-karat gold nugget; the letters YBM were scripted across the crown in VS1 diamonds.

"Bitch-ass nigga. You ain't worthy to wear that ring," I mumbled under my breath.

The 5.0 pulled over and parked in front of Daphney's Benz. The white cop climbed out of the car and approached the Benz. Two envelopes were passed to him through the driver's side window. He stuffed the envelopes inside of his pocket, then he waved his hand at my bullet-riddled Denali. My tinted windows rolled down, and the dome cut on. The black cop who chased me down and tried to smoke me, climbed out slowly. Still dressed like a hustla with his gold smothered in diamonds, he moved with the smooth calm of a certified gangsta.

This fuckin' clown. I shook my head in contempt.

The two cops conversed for a minute, then the trunk of Daphney's Benz popped open. I leaned forward, pressing my face against the fiber glass divider. I was looking to see if my sister and boo were chopped up and stuffed inside the of trunk, like I grotesquely imagined.

"Please, Allah. Please don't let 'em be in there," I mumbled a quick prayer, despite knowing that God wasn't fucking with me. My human morale was lower than whale shit, and God knew it. Aside from that, my trigger finger had amassed a small graveyard. More bodies would surely drop if I somehow survived my predicament.

Still looking inside of Daphney's trunk, a deep sigh of relief washed over me. The dead bodies of my peeps weren't stashed inside, just a speaker box and a red gasoline can. The black cop removed Jesus from the small of his back and extracted the clip. I remembered the white cop telling him to tag and bag it, but clearly that was not the case. The black cop stuffed the clip in his back pocket, then he reached down inside of the trunk. He placed Jesus on the speaker box, and pulled out the red gasoline can. The white cop closed the trunk, as the black nigga strolled back across the street.

"Fuck is he doing that for?" I asked myself, as he raised the gasoline can, and began dousing my front and back seats. After shaking away the last few drops, he tossed the can inside of my truck and then pulled from his pocket a white handkerchief and a shimmery gold lighter. He lit the handkerchief and then tossed it through my rolled down window.

Whoosh!

An orange, fiery glow illuminated my truck's interior. Billows of dark smoke wafted into the air, as my leather seats crackled and burned.

The fake-ass hustla stepped away from my cooking truck. He nodded his head at the 5.0., and then Mook stepped out. Seeing this nigga, made my blood boil. My nostrils began to flare, and just that quick I was right back in G mode.

I gathered up a mouthful of phlegm to spit in Mook's face when he pulled me out the Vic. But instead of walking towards me, he moved around the front of Daphney's V12 coupe and climbed in on the passenger's side. A few minutes later, the driver's side door popped open. I couldn't believe my fucking eyes. The driver was *Daphney*. She said something to the white cop, and then pointed at me through the windshield. The white cop looked at me and nodded his head. Smiling like the schmuck he was, he walked over and pulled me out the Vic.

"C'mere, you little fucking bastard. The boss lady wants you," he snarled at me, then he slammed me against the car.

The boss lady? I looked at Daphney, confused. *What the fuck?*

The white cop leaned against me, talking mad shit as he un-locked the handcuffs. "You'll be seeing me again, just when you least expect it. And guess what, I'm gonna stick my foot right in your fucking ass."

"Not if I catch you first," I spat back at him, looking at Daphney when I said it. She was still wearing the same Coogi dress from earlier that day. Her Coogi handbag was dangling from her shoulder, and both arms were folded across her breast. The look she gave me was stank.

The black cop scowled at me, as he moved around the back of the Vic. He pulled open the passenger's side door and climbed inside.

"Don't forget what I told you, AJ," the white cop said as he climbed in behind his partner. "I'm gonna be on your ass like flies to shit."

"Fuck outta here, nigga. Milk a dick."

The white cop shook his head, then he drove away laughing at me.

"Yo, Twin, what the fuck is this?" I looked at Daphney and began walking towards her. "Where the fuck is Erica? I know you got her."

"Hold that thought," Daphney said, then she reached inside of her handbag. For a brief second, I thought she was reaching for a burner. But instead of a gun, she pulled out her Motorola cell phone. She flipped it open, thumbed in seven digits, then she placed the phone against her ear.

"Gimme a few more minutes, and then bring y'all asses around here," she dictated like the boss I never knew she was. She closed the phone and stuffed it back inside of her Coogi bag.

"Damn, Twin—it was you this whole fuckin' time," the tone of my voice was laced with pain. "And I felt that shit. I *told* myself it was you. But I disregarded every sign, telling myself, nah, not Twin. Ain't no way she would cross me like this, no fuckin' way. *Kidnapping my bitch? Setting me up?* You outta pocket, Twin. Straight up."

"First of all, it wasn't my call," Daphney claimed.

"You think I 'on't know that. It was this nigga." I pointed at the Benz where Mook sat.

"It wasn't Mook either." Daphney scoffed.

"Well, then who the fuck was it?"

"It was Daddy."

"*Pops?*" I looked at her like she was crazy.

"Umm-hmm." Daphney nodded her head. "And I vouched for you, Twin. I told Daddy that I could keep you on the straight and narrow. I laced you with a brand-new truck. I gave you ten pounds of Hydro. I fucking gave you money."

"*Money?* Man, fuck that money!" I snapped at her. "I 'on't give a fuck about none of that shit! You my fuckin' sister! I fuckin' trusted you!"

"Don't even go there, Twin. You didn't trust me. Because if you did, you would have listened to me. I told you to fall back and leave shit alone. *Daddy* told you to fall back and leave shit alone. But you being you, wit'cha hard headed ass, you just *had* to go out and do whatever the fuck you wanted. Typical AJ shit, can't nobody tell you nuffin'."

I placed my hands on the back of my head and sucked in a deep breath. It took everything inside of me not to smack that bitch. I needed something to rip apart and break, so I figured that I'd make Mook the scapegoat. His ass was the one responsible.

"Yo, tell ya bitch-ass boyfriend to get out the car. Pops ain't the one behind this shit. It's *him!*"

"See, there you go assuming shit. You're too smart to be this stupid," Daphney hurled back. "Yeah, he's my man and all dat, but money grip don't run nuffin'. He works for me."

"He works for *you?*" My face grew tight. "Fuck you mean, he works for you? He's the one who Pops left in position."

"Do you hear ya'self right now? You know Daddy just as well as I do. And you *really* think he would leave his empire to an out-sider? I've been groomed for this shit my entire life. But at the end of the day, I'm still a *bitch*, controlling a deadly game that's domi-nated by men. So, who better to watch my back, while at the same time being my front, than Daddy's most trusted soldier?"

Hearing these words as they left my sister's mouth, made my stomach churn. Once again, Pops had chosen Daphney over me. It was the first time in my life that I truly felt like a *Trap Bastard*. My mind traveled to a dark place, recalling every time Pops had called me that. He made it seem jocular. But the more I listened to Daphney, the more I realized that Pops wasn't joking at all. He really saw me as his Trap Bastard.

Seeing the hurt look in my eyes, Daphney's hard exterior softened. She stepped in closer and placed both hands on my shoulders.

"Listen, Twin, I can only imagine how you're feeling right now," Daphney spoke softly. "But I'm pretty sure I know what you're thinking."

"Oh, yeah? And what's that?"

"You're thinking that Daddy doesn't love you; that he overlooked you and doesn't have any plans for you. So, I'm telling you now, as your sister, and somebody who loves you more than I love myself, you're wrong. Not only does Daddy love you, he's personally told me you're the future of our family. But before you can take your rightful place as the next king, first you gotta prove ya'self."

"Prove myself? Fuck I gotta prove myself for? Did Pops make you prove ya'self before he put you in charge?"

"There's no need for me to prove myself," said Daphney. "My only job is to keep shit afloat and help Mook groom you. And when the time is right, the stage is yours."

I sucked in a deep breath and exhaled slowly.

"And how am I supposed to prove myself? What I gotta do?"

"Well, that's between you and Daddy," Daphney replied. "He's expecting to see you first thing in the morning. And here." She pulled out two items from her handbag and handed them to me. The first item was a set of keys to the 5.0, and the second item was a small, black box.

"And what the fuck is this?" I held up the black box. It resembled a beeper with two lights sticking out. One light was green, and the other was red.

"That's the tracking device and kill switch that was placed on your truck." She pointed at my burning Denali. "That's how I knew you was out here going crazy, doing everything that I told you not to do."

Damn, it's like dat? It fucked my head up when Daphney said that shit. *A tracking device? So, that's the reason that war van kept popping up—and why my truck stalled out when that sucka-ass cop was chasing me. Ain't that a bitch.*

"And Daddy?" Daphney's eyebrows shot up. "Yo, that nigga was *pissed.* Especially when you robbed our stash house in Logan. Fa' real, tho, Twin—that was some *dumb-ass* shit you did. Those ten bricks were already yours, so you killed them people for no reason. But I'ma leave that alone. That's for you and Daddy to talk about."

"And what about the fat bitch? Do I still need to worry about her?"

"See what I'm saying?" She playfully doinked me on the forehead. "Didn't I tell you that was already handled?"

"I know, but how?"

"I told Daddy, and Daddy sent them boys at her. They slipped inside of her hospital room and slit her fucking throat. But you ain't heard that from me, though."

"A'ight. So, what about Erica? Where is she, and why did Pops want her kidnapped?"

"Again, that's for you and Daddy to talk about. But Erica's fine, so don't worry," Daphney said, as she walked back to her car. She pulled open the driver's side door, and then looked back at me. "Twin? Don't forget. First thing. In the morning. Daddy."

"Stop talking to me like I'm retarded," I quickly replied.

"Nah, you're far from retarded. Ya ass is just crazy." Daphney laughed.

"Aye, yo, Twin? Hold up," I called out when she stepped one foot inside of her Benz. "Whats up wit' my burner? I need that jawn. The cop bul left it inside ya trunk."

Daphney didn't reply. She looked back at me one last time and then sank down inside of her car. The V12 pulled off a few seconds later.

Shaking my head, I walked over to the Mustang and climbed inside. That fuck-nigga Mook was tall as shit, so the driver's seat was pulled back far. I pulled the seat forward and readjusted the mirrors. But before I could stick the key in the ignition, the loud sound of screeching tires grabbed my attention.

Scurrrrrr!

What the fuck? I looked over my shoulder and spotted the war van. The fucking thing had somehow crept up beside me. The dome light was off and the van was mad dark, so I couldn't see inside. The only thing I saw was the double barrel shotty that was aimed at me through the rolled down window. Them niggas had the drop like a mah'fucka.

Damn, Twin, you sent these niggas to come smoke me? The griminess in me had me thinking the worst; that Daphney had thrown me to the wolves. I figured that was the reason she ignored me when I asked her to give my gun back. It didn't even matter that the cop bul extracted the clip. Her black ass didn't see him do it. As far as she knew my shit was still loaded. So, there I was, assed out and stuck without a pistol.

"Ya little ass wanted drama, I'ma bring it to you, starting wit' this bitch," a deep, raspy voice spoke in the dark, echoing the same exact words the kidnapper spoke on the phone.

"Fuck you, nigga! Bring that shit!" I shouted back, preparing for death.

I waited for a blast, but the blast never came. The dome light cut on, and I squinted my eyes. A full-fledged monster was seated behind the steering wheel. His dark-skinned face was twisted like the killer he was, and his sawed-off shotty was one blast away from sending me to Satan.

"*Double R?*" I said my uncle's name, completely caught off guard and stuck on stupid. He gritted his teeth and then turned off the dome light. The van's side door swung open wide and three niggas jumped out quickly. They were dressed in all-black and had bone-white skull masks sticking out the front of their hoodies. They each had a choppa, and all three barrels were pointed at my fucking wig.

Bddddddddoc!

To Be Continued...

COMING SOON

TRAP BASTARD 2: TEARDROPS & CLOSED CAS-KETS

Submission Guideline

Submit the first three chapters of your completed manuscript to ldpsubmissions@gmail.com, subject line: Your book's title. The manuscript must be in a .doc file and sent as an attachment. Document should be in Times New Roman, double spaced and in size 12 font. Also, provide your synopsis and full contact information. If sending multiple submissions, they must each be in a separate email.

Have a story but no way to send it electronically? You can still submit to LDP/Ca$h Presents. Send in the first three chapters, written or typed, of your completed manuscript to:

LDP: Submissions Dept
Po Box 944
Stockbridge, Ga 30281

DO NOT send original manuscript. Must be a duplicate.

Provide your synopsis and a cover letter containing your full contact information.

Thanks for considering LDP and Ca$h Presents.

<u>Coming Soon from Lock Down Publications/Ca$h Presents</u>

BOW DOWN TO MY GANGSTA

By **Ca$h**

TORN BETWEEN TWO

By **Coffee**

THE STREETS STAINED MY SOUL **II**

By **Marcellus Allen**

BLOOD OF A BOSS **VI**

SHADOWS OF THE GAME II

TRAP BASTARD II

By **Askari**

LOYAL TO THE GAME **IV**

By **T.J. & Jelissa**

IF LOVING YOU IS WRONG… **III**

By **Jelissa**

TRUE SAVAGE **VIII**

MIDNIGHT CARTEL IV

DOPE BOY MAGIC IV

CITY OF KINGZ II

By **Chris Green**

BLAST FOR ME **III**

A SAVAGE DOPEBOY III

CUTTHROAT MAFIA III

DUFFLE BAG CARTEL VI

HEARTLESS GOON VI

By **Ghost**

A HUSTLER'S DECEIT III

KILL ZONE **II**

BAE BELONGS TO ME III

A DOPE BOY'S QUEEN III

By **Aryanna**

COKE KINGS V

KING OF THE TRAP II

By **T.J. Edwards**

GORILLAZ IN THE BAY V

3X KRAZY III

De'Kari

THE STREETS ARE CALLING II

Duquie Wilson

KINGPIN KILLAZ IV

STREET KINGS III

PAID IN BLOOD III

CARTEL KILLAZ IV

DOPE GODS III

Hood Rich

SINS OF A HUSTLA II

ASAD

KINGZ OF THE GAME VI

Playa Ray

SLAUGHTER GANG IV

RUTHLESS HEART IV

By Willie Slaughter

THE HEART OF A SAVAGE III

By Jibril Williams

FUK SHYT II

By Blakk Diamond

TRAP QUEEN

By Troublesome

YAYO V

GHOST MOB II

Stilloan Robinson

KINGPIN DREAMS III

By Paper Boi Rari

CREAM II

By Yolanda Moore

SON OF A DOPE FIEND III

By Renta

FOREVER GANGSTA II

GLOCKS ON SATIN SHEETS III

By Adrian Dulan

LOYALTY AIN'T PROMISED III

By Keith Williams

THE PRICE YOU PAY FOR LOVE III

By Destiny Skai

I'M NOTHING WITHOUT HIS LOVE II

SINS OF A THUG II

By Monet Dragun

LIFE OF A SAVAGE IV

MURDA SEASON IV

GANGLAND CARTEL IV

CHI'RAQ GANGSTAS III

By **Romell Tukes**

QUIET MONEY IV

EXTENDED CLIP II

By **Trai'Quan**

THE STREETS MADE ME III

By **Larry D. Wright**

IF YOU CROSS ME ONCE II

ANGEL III

By **Anthony Fields**

FRIEND OR FOE III

By **Mimi**

SAVAGE STORMS III

By **Meesha**

BLOOD ON THE MONEY III

By J-Blunt

THE STREETS WILL NEVER CLOSE II

By K'ajji

NIGHTMARES OF A HUSTLA III

By King Dream

THE WIFEY I USED TO BE II

By Nicole Goosby

IN THE ARM OF HIS BOSS

By Jamila

MONEY, MURDER & MEMORIES II

Malik D. Rice

CONCRETE KILLAZ II

By Kingpen

HARD AND RUTHLESS II

By Von Wiley Hall

LEVELS TO THIS SHYT II

By Ah'Million

MOB TIES II

By SayNoMore

BODYMORE MURDERLAND II

By Delmont Player

Available Now

RESTRAINING ORDER **I & II**
By **CA$H & Coffee**
LOVE KNOWS NO BOUNDARIES **I II & III**
By **Coffee**
RAISED AS A GOON I, II, III & IV
BRED BY THE SLUMS I, II, III
BLAST FOR ME I & II
ROTTEN TO THE CORE I II III
A BRONX TALE I, II, III
DUFFLE BAG CARTEL I II III IV V
HEARTLESS GOON I II III IV V
A SAVAGE DOPEBOY I II
DRUG LORDS I II III
CUTTHROAT MAFIA I II
By **Ghost**
LAY IT DOWN **I & II**
LAST OF A DYING BREED I II
BLOOD STAINS OF A SHOTTA I & II III
By **Jamaica**
LOYAL TO THE GAME I II III
LIFE OF SIN I, II III
By **TJ & Jelissa**
BLOODY COMMAS I & II
SKI MASK CARTEL I II & III
KING OF NEW YORK I II,III IV V
RISE TO POWER I II III
COKE KINGS I II III IV
BORN HEARTLESS I II III IV

KING OF THE TRAP

By **T.J. Edwards**

IF LOVING HIM IS WRONG…I & II

LOVE ME EVEN WHEN IT HURTS I II III

By **Jelissa**

WHEN THE STREETS CLAP BACK I & II III

THE HEART OF A SAVAGE I II

By **Jibril Williams**

A DISTINGUISHED THUG STOLE MY HEART I II & III

LOVE SHOULDN'T HURT I II III IV

RENEGADE BOYS I II III IV

PAID IN KARMA I II III

SAVAGE STORMS I II

By **Meesha**

A GANGSTER'S CODE I &, II III

A GANGSTER'S SYN I II III

THE SAVAGE LIFE I II III

CHAINED TO THE STREETS I II III

BLOOD ON THE MONEY I II

By **J-Blunt**

PUSH IT TO THE LIMIT

By **Bre' Hayes**

BLOOD OF A BOSS **I, II, III, IV, V**

SHADOWS OF THE GAME

TRAP BASTARD

By **Askari**

THE STREETS BLEED MURDER **I, II & III**

THE HEART OF A GANGSTA I II& III

By **Jerry Jackson**

CUM FOR ME I II III IV V VI

An **LDP Erotica Collaboration**

BRIDE OF A HUSTLA **I II & II**

THE FETTI GIRLS **I, II& III**

CORRUPTED BY A GANGSTA I, II III, IV

BLINDED BY HIS LOVE

THE PRICE YOU PAY FOR LOVE I II

DOPE GIRL MAGIC I II III

By **Destiny Skai**

WHEN A GOOD GIRL GOES BAD

By **Adrienne**

THE COST OF LOYALTY I II III

By Kweli

A GANGSTER'S REVENGE **I II III & IV**

THE BOSS MAN'S DAUGHTERS I II III IV V

A SAVAGE LOVE **I & II**

BAE BELONGS TO ME I II

A HUSTLER'S DECEIT I, II, III

WHAT BAD BITCHES DO I, II, III

SOUL OF A MONSTER I II III

KILL ZONE

A DOPE BOY'S QUEEN I II

By **Aryanna**

A KINGPIN'S AMBITON

A KINGPIN'S AMBITION **II**

I MURDER FOR THE DOUGH

By **Ambitious**

TRUE SAVAGE I II III IV V VI VII

DOPE BOY MAGIC I, II, III

MIDNIGHT CARTEL I II III

CITY OF KINGZ

Askari

By **Chris Green**
A DOPEBOY'S PRAYER
By **Eddie "Wolf" Lee**
THE KING CARTEL **I, II & III**
By **Frank Gresham**
THESE NIGGAS AIN'T LOYAL **I, II & III**
By **Nikki Tee**
GANGSTA SHYT **I II &III**
By **CATO**
THE ULTIMATE BETRAYAL
By **Phoenix**
BOSS'N UP **I , II & III**
By **Royal Nicole**
I LOVE YOU TO DEATH
By Destiny J
I RIDE FOR MY HITTA
I STILL RIDE FOR MY HITTA
By **Misty Holt**
LOVE & CHASIN' PAPER
By **Qay Crockett**
TO DIE IN VAIN
SINS OF A HUSTLA
By **ASAD**
BROOKLYN HUSTLAZ
By **Boogsy Morina**
BROOKLYN ON LOCK I & II
By **Sonovia**
GANGSTA CITY
By **Teddy Duke**
A DRUG KING AND HIS DIAMOND I & II III

Trap Bastard

A DOPEMAN'S RICHES

HER MAN, MINE'S TOO I, II

CASH MONEY HO'S

THE WIFEY I USED TO BE

By Nicole Goosby

TRAPHOUSE KING **I II & III**

KINGPIN KILLAZ I II III

STREET KINGS I II

PAID IN BLOOD **I II**

CARTEL KILLAZ I II III

DOPE GODS I II

By **Hood Rich**

LIPSTICK KILLAH **I, II, III**

CRIME OF PASSION I II & III

FRIEND OR FOE I II

By **Mimi**

STEADY MOBBN' **I, II, III**

THE STREETS STAINED MY SOUL

By **Marcellus Allen**

WHO SHOT YA **I, II, III**

SON OF A DOPE FIEND I II

Renta

GORILLAZ IN THE BAY **I II III IV**

TEARS OF A GANGSTA I II

3X KRAZY I II

DE'KARI

TRIGGADALE I II III

Elijah R. Freeman

GOD BLESS THE TRAPPERS I, II, III

THESE SCANDALOUS STREETS I, II, III

227

FEAR MY GANGSTA I, II, III IV, V
THESE STREETS DON'T LOVE NOBODY I, II
BURY ME A G I, II, III, IV, V
A GANGSTA'S EMPIRE I, II, III, IV
THE DOPEMAN'S BODYGAURD I II
THE REALEST KILLAZ I II III
Tranay Adams
THE STREETS ARE CALLING
Duquie Wilson
MARRIED TO A BOSS... I II III
By Destiny Skai & Chris Green
KINGZ OF THE GAME I II III IV V
Playa Ray
SLAUGHTER GANG I II III
RUTHLESS HEART I II III
By Willie Slaughter
FUK SHYT
By Blakk Diamond
DON'T F#CK WITH MY HEART I II
By Linnea
ADDICTED TO THE DRAMA I II III
IN THE ARM OF HIS BOSS II
By Jamila
YAYO I II III IV
A SHOOTER'S AMBITION I II
By S. Allen
TRAP GOD I II III
By Troublesome
FOREVER GANGSTA
GLOCKS ON SATIN SHEETS I II

Trap Bastard

By Adrian Dulan

TOE TAGZ I II III

LEVELS TO THIS SHYT

By Ah'Million

KINGPIN DREAMS I II

By Paper Boi Rari

CONFESSIONS OF A GANGSTA I II III

By Nicholas Lock

I'M NOTHING WITHOUT HIS LOVE

SINS OF A THUG

By Monet Dragun

CAUGHT UP IN THE LIFE I II III

By Robert Baptiste

NEW TO MONEY, MURDER & MEMORIES

THE GAME I II III

By **Malik D. Rice**

LIFE OF A SAVAGE I II III

A GANGSTA'S QUR'AN I II III

MURDA SEASON I II III

GANGLAND CARTEL I II III

CHI'RAQ GANGSTAS I II

By **Romell Tukes**

LOYALTY AIN'T PROMISED I II

By Keith Williams

QUIET MONEY I II III

THUG LIFE I II

EXTENDED CLIP

By **Trai'Quan**

THE STREETS MADE ME I II

By **Larry D. Wright**

THE ULTIMATE SACRIFICE I, II, III, IV, V, VI

KHADIFI

IF YOU CROSS ME ONCE

ANGEL I II

By **Anthony Fields**

THE LIFE OF A HOOD STAR

By **Ca$h & Rashia Wilson**

THE STREETS WILL NEVER CLOSE

By **K'ajji**

CREAM

By **Yolanda Moore**

NIGHTMARES OF A HUSTLA I II

By **King Dream**

CONCRETE KILLAZ

By **Kingpen**

HARD AND RUTHLESS

By **Von Wiley Hall**

GHOST MOB II

Stilloan Robinson

MOB TIES

By **SayNoMore**

BODYMORE MURDERLAND

By **Delmont Player**

BOOKS BY LDP'S CEO, CA$H

TRUST IN NO MAN

TRUST IN NO MAN 2

TRUST IN NO MAN 3

BONDED BY BLOOD

SHORTY GOT A THUG

THUGS CRY

THUGS CRY 2

THUGS CRY 3

TRUST NO BITCH

TRUST NO BITCH 2

TRUST NO BITCH 3

TIL MY CASKET DROPS

RESTRAINING ORDER

RESTRAINING ORDER 2

IN LOVE WITH A CONVICT

LIFE OF A HOOD STAR

CPSIA information can be obtained
at www.ICGtesting.com
Printed in the USA
LVHW050358140422
716185LV00008B/323